THE PRISONER
OF AL-HAKIM

Published by Blue Dome Press
335 Clifton Avenue, Clifton, NJ 07011

www.bluedomepress.com

Library of Congress Cataloging-in-Publication Data Available

ISBN: 978-168206-016-2

Printed in Canada by Marquis Book Printing.

THE PRISONER
OF AL-HAKIM

Bradley Steffens

New Jersey

To Eva

Chapter One

Alhasan lifted a large, leather-bound manuscript into the sunlight that streamed through the small window high on the south wall of his study. He tilted the page in the light to make sure the ink was dry and gently blew the blotting powder from the inscription he had just completed. "In the name of Allah, the most Gracious and the most Merciful...." He admired his calligraphy one last time and closed the book.

At last his annual labor was done. He could deliver this copy of Euclid's *Elements*, along with his copies of Ptolemy's *Almagest* and *The Intermediate Books*, to Rashid Al-Bariqi, the amateur mathematician and astronomer who lived six blocks away, near the center of Basra. In return he would receive one hundred fifty silver dinars, his non-negotiable price for copying the texts. It was just enough money to live comfortably for a year. He would return to his studies for the next nine months, reading, thinking, and writing until the day would arrive when he once again would take up his pen to earn his livelihood.

Alhasan slipped the manuscripts into his leather bag and stepped into the street. The sun was bright and the air was warm. It was the end of the month of Shaʻbān, the time of year when the ancient Arab tribes "scattered" to find water. Alhasan smiled. You didn't have to search for water in Basra; it was everywhere. A system of canals connected all parts of the city to Shatt al-Arab, the waterway formed by the confluence of the Tigris and Euphrates rivers.

Incongruous as the name of the month might be in Basra, it reminded Alhasan of his ancestors, the desert people who had swept out of Arabia nearly four hundred years earlier, bringing their language, customs, and—most importantly—the revealed Word of God to the people of Basra and all of what was now the Abbasid Caliphate, a vast empire centered in Baghdad that stretched from India in the east to Egypt in the west.

Alhasan nearly skipped across the cobblestones as he made his way toward the corner. "Lighthearted" was the last word most people would associate with him. "Serious," "dour," and even "grim" were the words he heard most often. Many people said he seemed to have no feelings at all. Somehow the fire that burned in his heart never seemed to warm his face or light his eyes. But whether his face showed it or not, Alhasan felt lighthearted, even giddy, as he made his way toward Al-Bariqi's home. The manuscripts completed, he at last would be able to begin work on the commentary he had been thinking about every day for the last three months. He felt like a child racing home from school.

As he turned the corner, he bumped into a man who was leaning against the wall. "Pardon me," Alhasan said. "Many apologies for my clumsiness." The phrases sounded wooden and hollow, but the man seemed to accept his apology.

"Of course," said the stranger, who spoke with a strange accent and wore unusual clothing.

"If you are a visitor to Basra, I hope you will not judge all of our citizens by the awkwardness of one," said Alhasan.

"Surely not," said the stranger, smiling. His teeth gleamed like a strand of pearls—straight, white, and evenly spaced.

"Enjoy your stay," said Alhasan with a slight bow before turning again toward Al-Bariqi's street. He glanced at the sun. If he hurried, there might be time to get to the marketplace after delivering the books. He could stock up on the paper, ink, and pounce he would need to write his next commentary.

Alhasan thought again about the accent and clothing of the man on the corner. His consonants rattled like a dagger in a sheath. Instead of a robe, he wore a tunic and trousers; instead of a turban, a felt hat. And on his feet he wore ankle-high boots, similar to the Roman *caligae*, but covered with squares of colorful carpeting.

It was not unusual to see people from distant lands in Basra. The city was a cosmopolitan port, the gateway to the Persian Sea. Indeed, the Arabic word "Basra" was derived from a Persian word that meant "where many paths meet." Arabs, Persians, Chaldeans, Greeks, Indians—all of these populated sections of Basra. Upon occasion Alhasan had even seen colorfully dressed Malays sail into the harbor. But he had never seen clothing like that of the man on the corner. Perhaps he should have asked him where he was from. Would that have been rude? Alhasan was unsure. When it came to people, he rarely knew what to say or do.

He crossed four more streets and then turned left. Al-Bariqi's home was halfway down the block on the right. He knew it by the ornately carved door. How many times had he visited the older man's home to borrow books from his library? Now he was about to add several more beautifully copied manuscripts to his friend's collection.

As Alhasan knocked, he noticed the man in odd clothing crossing the street at the end of the block. When the foreigner had bumped into him, Alhasan had thought the man was walking toward his street, but now he was walking in the other direction. Maybe his assumption was wrong. Perhaps the stranger had been walking in this direction all along and simply had leaned against the wall to rest. Or perhaps he was lost. Alhasan called out to the man, but he already had passed out of view. Alhasan started out after him just as Al-Bariqi opened the door.

"Ah, it is you, Alhasan," said Al-Bariqi, calling the younger man by his given name. Al-Bariqi had been friends with Alhasan's late father, who also was named Alhasan, "the handsome." Al-Bariqi always said that Alhasan was even more handsome than his father had been in his younger days and it was fitting that they shared the same name.

"Peace be upon you," said Alhasan.

"And upon you be peace," replied Al-Bariqi. "Where are you going, my friend? I know I am slow getting to the door these days, but I wasn't that slow, was I?"

"No, of course not," said Alhasan. "It was just that I saw a man who seemed to be lost, and I was going to help him."

"I see," said Al-Bariqi. "Well, if you wish to go after him...."

"No," said Alhasan, looking down the street. "There is no way of knowing for certain if he is lost." He turned up the corners of his mouth in an awkward smile. "The truths are immersed in uncertainties," he said, quoting from one of his own treatises.

Al-Bariqi smiled at his friend's attempt at humor. "Yes, they are," he said, clasping Alhasan's hands and giving him a kiss on each cheek. "Come in, my friend."

Alhasan removed his sandals and stepped into the cool, dark entryway. Al-Bariqi called to his servant. "Khalid! Bring bread, cheese, and dates. We have a guest." He motioned toward a phalanx of embroidered cushions arranged on the carpet in the great room ahead. "Please make yourself comfortable."

Alhasan sat on the edge of a cushion.

"What brings you here, my friend?" asked Al-Bariqi.

"I have great news," said Alhasan. "I have completed your copies of *Elements*, *Almagest*, and *The Intermediate Books*."

"Wonderful. Praise Allah."

"By the grace of God, they came out well, I think."

"When can I see them?"

Alhasan patted his bag. "I have them here," he said. One by one he removed the manuscripts and handed them to Al-Bariqi.

"Beautiful, beautiful," said Al-Bariqi, handling the books reverentially.

"They are my finest copies yet," said Alhasan. "I used the best materials, especially for you."

"Exquisite. I am grateful indeed."

Al-Bariqi closed the book and looked toward the kitchen. "Khalid! Dates and bread for our guest!"

Khalid, a boy of twelve or thirteen, appeared at the door with a tray holding two cups of water, a plate of dates, a bowl of soft cheese, and a small bowl of honey. He set the tray before the men. "The bread is not ready," said Khalid. "I will bring it when it is."

"Thank you," said Alhasan, nodding at the boy. Thanking a servant was not necessary, but Alhasan was in such a pleasant mood that he couldn't restrain himself.

"Have one of these dates," said Al-Bariqi, proffering the plate.

Alhasan plucked a dark fruit from the plate and bit into it. The skin was firm, but the flesh was soft and moist, melting on his tongue, without the graininess he expected. "Delicious," he said.

Al-Bariqi leaned forward and whispered conspiratorially: "Here we sit, surrounded by the largest date palm groves in the caliphate, but these dates are not from here. They come all the way from the Fatimid Caliphate in Africa."

Alhasan flinched inwardly at the mention of the Fatimid Caliphate. He was not a political person, but he held a vague tribal grudge against the Shi'a Ismailis who had broken away from the Abbasid Caliphate one hundred years earlier and established a separate caliphate centered in Cairo. Before then, the Abbasid Caliphate had stretched not only to Egypt, but across most of North Africa. It had been one of the largest empires the world had ever seen.

"But how?" asked Alhasan, marveling at his friend's claim.

"I know someone who knows someone who is a traveling merchant," said Al-Bariqi. "He gave me a basket of these dates as a gift several years ago. I told him if his friend ever returned I would gladly pay whatever price was necessary for a sack of my own. My friend remembered, and here they are."

Alhasan finished his date and took three sips of water.

"Have another," said Al-Bariqi.

Alhasan took another date and bit into it. It was as good as the first. "Perfectly smooth," he said. "Not grainy or sugary."

Khalid returned, carrying a large plate. "Here is the bread," he said, setting the plate on the tray.

Alhasan took a piece of the hot flatbread from the plate, tore off a corner, formed it into a shovel, and dipped it into the cheese. He realized he was hungry. In his haste to finish copying the books, he had forgotten to eat. The cheese, made with camel milk, tasted wonderful.

Al-Bariqi followed Alhasan's lead and dipped his bread into the cheese. "Tell me, Alhasan, how much do I owe you for these books?"

"One hundred fifty silver dinars," replied Alhasan before taking another bite of bread and cheese.

"One hundred fifty silver dinars?" said Al-Bariqi. "You must be joking."

Alhasan swallowed. "One hundred fifty silver dinars. That is my price."

"My dear boy, you must know these copies are worth much more than one hundred fifty dinars. Be serious. How much do I owe you?"

"I have worked out the price carefully, Rashid," said Alhasan. "All I need is my daily food, a servant, and a maid to look after me. If I amass more than the barest minimum I need, I shall turn into your slave, and if I spend what I save, I shall be held liable for wasting your wealth."

Al-Bariqi laughed. "Alhasan, you may look like your father, but you do not reason like him. I tell you, your father would have asked at least six hundred dinars for such fine copies, and I gladly would have paid four. But I can see there is no negotiating with you. If you want one hundred fifty silver dinars, I will pay you one hundred fifty silver dinars and keep the rest to buy dates from Africa."

The price settled, Alhasan relaxed. He dipped his bread into the cheese and took another bite.

"Everything is delicious," said Alhasan. "I was so anxious to finish copying your books that I am afraid I didn't eat."

"And now that your work is done, Alhasan, what will you study next?"

"Oh. Well, I would rather not say." He took another bite of flatbread and cheese.

Al-Bariqi leaned forward. "Is it a secret?" he whispered, grinning.

Alhasan chewed on and on. Seeing Al-Bariqi would not let him dodge the question, he swallowed and sipped his water. "No, it's not a secret," he said at last. "It's just that, well, I don't think you will approve."

"Not approve?" exclaimed Al-Bariqi. "Ah, let me guess. Ptolemy again, is it?"

"Yes," admitted Alhasan.

Al-Bariqi shook his head. "My dear Alhasan, I do not understand you. You are a great mathematician—the greatest since Al-Khwarizmi. Some would say greater. You refined Al-Khwarizmi's method of calculation by completion and balancing, and you used it to solve geometrical problems of Euclid that had gone unsolved for more than a thousand years. You completed the *Conics* of Apollonius of Perga as if he himself had sat at your elbow. No one—least of all I, who loved your father and loves you as a son—doubts your genius. But the calculations of Claudius Ptolemy have stood the test of time. You cannot deny it. His astronomical predictions have been confirmed over and over. I can't understand why you keep questioning his findings."

"It's not his findings that I question," said Alhasan. "It's his failure to explain what in nature he is predicting."

Al-Bariqi looked at him uncertainly.

"Ptolemy predicts the motions of the celestial bodies with the utmost precision," Alhasan continued, "but he never explains what the celestial bodies are or how they move through the heavens. His calculations are based upon the motions of imaginary points on the circumferences of imaginary circles resting on an imaginary plane. But the stars and planets are not imaginary. They are real. What are they? What causes them to move? Ptolemy says nothing."

Alhasan stood and looked out the window high on the wall. "Take the movement of Mars," he said, tracing a diagram in the air with his hand. "It travels eastward across the constellations, but then it pauses and reverses itself. It travels westward for a short time; then it pauses, reverses itself again, and continues traveling eastward across the stars. Yes, Ptolemy predicts these movements exactly. He calls them oscillations. Oscillations!"

Alhasan threw up his hands. "This is utter nonsense and contradicts his previous doctrine that the heavenly motions are equal, continuous, and unceasing."

Alhasan sat back down. "Real bodies must have sensible motions," he said.

"But Alhasan, you forget: Allah made the universe and all that is in it. If He wishes for the celestial bodies to reverse direction, then they will reverse direction. The Creator can make the heavenly bodies dance, if He likes."

"Of course He can," agreed Alhasan. "But that is my point. He does not make the stars dance, or anything else in nature. Does a raindrop reverse itself, fly upwards, then change course again and fall to the earth? Does water flow uphill? Does the half moon return to the crescent? No. The crescent moves inexorably toward the half; and the half, inexorably toward the full. Allah made manifest laws for nature as surely as He made them for humankind, but, having no free will, Nature obeys continuously, unceasingly. The Greeks called the planets 'wanderers.' I tell you they neither wander nor oscillate. They appear to, but that is only from our perspective. They are moving sensibly, obeying some great law, one we have not yet discovered."

The two men sat quietly, sipping their water and contemplating the enormity of the heavens.

At last Alhasan spoke. "There must be some way to reveal the truth about real objects with the same precision that geometry permits with imaginary points, lines, planes, and solids. If I am vouchsafed a longer life by the grace of God, I shall write a commentary that unravels these mysteries." He looked Al-Bariqi in the eyes. "There is no better way to gain closeness to God than to search for truth and knowledge."

"God willing, you will accomplish these things," Al-Bariqi said softly.

"God willing," repeated Alhasan, staring at a few, bright beads of water stretched out like stars across the bottom of his cup.

Chapter Two

High in a minaret near the center of Basra, a muezzin called the faithful to their midday prayers. Sometimes Alhasan set out his prayer rug and prayed at home, but it was better to pray at the mosque. He had planned to go to the market after prayers, but Al-Bariqi had not yet paid him. He realized he would have to accompany his friend to the mosque and then back to his home. It was selfish to think only of his schedule and his work. He would pray and spend time with his friend, who had been the friend of his father as well.

They arrived at the mosque as the muezzin sounded the call to line up. Alhasan looked around to see if the man in odd clothing had come to prayer. Alhasan scanned the lines of worshippers, but he didn't see the stranger.

After prayers, Alhasan and Al-Bariqi strolled around the center of Basra. They passed by the government offices where both Alhasan and Al-Bariqi had once worked and where Alhasan's brother, a tax accountant, still did. Their talk returned to the subject of Ptolemy and the motions of the planets.

When they returned to Al-Bariqi's home, Alhasan helped his friend carry the newly completed manuscripts into the library. "I will examine these carefully before shelving them," said Al-Bariqi, setting his books on a table at the side of the room. "Khalid," called Al-Bariqi, "bring khawa!" The older man winked at Alhasan. "Wait until you taste this beverage. It is his own brew."

Alhasan sat while Al-Bariqi went to another room. The older man soon returned with an ornately carved box. He set it on the floor, opened the lid, and began to remove silver coins.

As Al-Bariqi counted out Alhasan's pay, Khalid walked into the room with a ceramic pot in his left hand and two small cups in his right. Alhasan watched the boy pour a small amount of yellowish liquid into the cup on top. He offered it to Alhasan, who regarded it with the same doubts he had expressed about Ptolemy.

"Try it, my friend," urged Al-Bariqi.

Alhasan took the small cup with his right hand and held it to his nose. "It smells wonderful."

"It's made with a bean, ground and mixed with spice," said Al-Bariqi, taking the other cup. "Can you tell what spice it is?"

Alhasan sipped the steaming drink. "No, I can't."

"It's cardamom."

"It's good," said Alhasan. "Where did he learn to make it?"

"From the crew of a ship," said Al-Bariqi. "He himself is from a small peninsula on the eastern Arabian coast. He said the tribes in his village are either Desert People or Sea People. He is one of the Sea People. His brothers are pearl divers, but the poor boy was born with weak lungs and couldn't work underwater. He got tired of shucking oysters and joined the crew of a ship from al-Habasha, bound for Basra. The crew drank this beverage and taught him how to make it. I found him in the marketplace, asking for work. My manservant had just left, so I hired him. One day he returned from the market with cardamom and mixed it with the beans the crew had given him. He made this brew, and now I drink it every afternoon."

Khalid smiled at his master's retelling of his story. "More *khawa*, Sir?" he asked Alhasan.

"Yes, please," said Alhasan, holding out the cup. Khalid took the cup and poured a small amount of the beverage into it.

"Don't drink too much," said Al-Bariqi. "It's stimulating."

"'Eat and drink, but be not excessive,'" said Alhasan, quoting a verse from the Qur'an. "My father used to say that."

Al-Bariqi smiled. He finished counting out the payment, and Alhasan put the coins in his bag. As the light outside waned, the two friends sipped their *khawa* and talked awhile more. As Alhasan feared, it was too late to buy writing supplies. If he hurried home, however, he might be able to catch his maid, Nada, before she left. He had not yet paid her for the month of Sha'bān. It would be a nice surprise for her if he could pay her today. He picked up his bag and bade Al-Bariqi farewell.

As Alhasan hurried home, he caught a glimpse of the oddly dressed foreigner disappearing into a doorway up ahead, on the other side of the street. As Alhasan neared the entryway, he glanced across the street. The stranger stood before the door, waiting for it to be opened. *At last, he has found the house he was looking for,* thought Alhasan. After he walked past the man, Alhasan looked back. No one had yet answered the door.

Alhasan walked on. When he turned the corner of his street, he had a strange idea. He stopped and crept back to the corner. He put his face against the wall and slowly turned his head until he could see around the corner with one eye. The stranger was no longer standing in front of the door. He was crossing the street, walking directly toward the spot where Alhasan stood watching.

Alhasan withdrew from the corner and began to walk toward his home. He had a strange feeling in the pit of his stomach. It seemed improbable that the foreigner would be following him, yet that is how it felt. He walked briskly and tried to think. Why would the man be following him? The stranger couldn't possibly know he had just been paid.

It made no sense, but as Alhasan crossed the street toward his door he decided to keep going. He walked past his home without slowing or looking back. He pretended to look at a mockingbird that whistled, shrilled, and chortled high in a date palm in a neighbor's courtyard across the street. The whole thing was absurd, but Alhasan's heart pounded with fear.

When he reached the next corner, he turned left. As soon as he was around the corner, he stopped again and edged back. Instead of looking around the corner at eye level, he crouched down and peered back. The stranger was coming down his street.

Alhasan tried to think. Nothing like this had ever happened to him before. He cleared his mind and looked around. He had tutored a boy who lived down the block, on the left. He ran down the street and knocked at the student's door. His heart pounded, partly from running and partly from alarm.

He strained to hear if anyone was inside. As he listened, he saw a movement out of the corner of his eye. He couldn't help turning his head. The foreign stranger had come around the corner and was walking toward him. Their eyes met. Alhasan turned back toward the door, but he knew the stranger would not pass by. He was coming for him.

"Peace be upon you."

The voice came from inside the door, which was open a crack.

"And upon you be peace," said Alhasan. "Is Ihab here?"

The stranger was just a few steps away.

"Yes, please come in," said Ihab's mother, opening the door.

Alhasan slipped off his sandals and stepped inside. The stranger walked past the door just as it clicked shut.

"Ihab!" called the student's mother. "Ibn Al-Haytham is here to see you!"

Alhasan looked around the room. Ihab's sisters, who had been play-ing on the floor, looked up at him. On the wall hung a sword that Ihab said had belonged to his grandfather. Everything was normal, in its place. Alhasan felt embarrassed. Standing here, the whole scene on the street seemed unreal. Alhasan wondered if he was losing his mind.

Ihab, Alhasan's best student, greeted his old teacher. "Peace be upon you."

"And upon you be peace," said Alhasan.

"Why are you here?" asked Ihab.

Alhasan looked at him blankly. "I am here, Ihab, because I seek your help with a problem."

"A problem?"

"Yes, you see—" Alhasan looked toward the courtyard. "I was won-dering, could we go up to your rooftop, where we used to observe the stars and the planets."

"Of course, Teacher, but the sun has not yet set."

Alhasan felt ridiculous. "That is true, of course, but I do not want to observe the heavenly bodies. I have a different problem, yet it requires such a vantage point."

"Oh. I see. Well, follow me." Ihab led Alhasan into the courtyard and up the staircase. "It is wonderful to see you."

"How are your studies going?" asked Alhasan.

"Fine. I am progressing well, my teacher says."

When they reached the roof, Alhasan looked down on the street. The foreigner was nowhere to be seen.

"What is the problem?" asked Ihab.

"Excuse me?" said Alhasan.

"The problem you want me to help you with?"

"Ah, yes. Well, Ihab—" Alhasan looked into the young man's eyes. "Do you remember when I taught you how to determine of the height of a pole with the greatest precision?"

"Of course. The altitudes of poles, the altitudes of mountains—all the principles of measurement."

"Yes, well, I have been working on a new way of calculating the lengths of things."

"I see."

"And remember that I told you to verify your calculations with measurements, whenever possible?"

"Yes, Teacher."

"Yes. Well, I have calculated the length of the street outside my house. And I want to verify that distance by walking down the wall that divides the houses on my side of the block from the houses on the other side of the block."

"You want to walk on the wall? Couldn't you just walk on the street?"

"Of course I could. I mean, I have. I have done that. But the most curious thing: I have measured all four sides of this block, and it appears that the block is not square. Do you see?"

Ihab looked doubtful.

"I could be wrong," said Alhasan. "But my calculations suggest the block is not at all square. So, by measuring the wall, that is, the diameter,

I will have a better idea of the true shape of the city block, and therefore I will know if my new method of calculation is correct."

"And how can I help?" asked Ihab.

"Well, if you will fetch my sandals for me and allow me access to the wall, that is all I need."

"That's all?"

"Yes, Ihab. I know it is a ridiculous request, but if you would be so kind as to get my sandals, I would be most grateful."

"Yes, Teacher."

The student descended the stairs and entered his home. When he was out of sight, Alhasan crept toward the low wall on the perimeter of the roof and peered down on the street. He looked at every doorway up and down the block. It appeared the stranger was gone. However, he might be around the corner, waiting for him to return.

Alhasan looked down the wall that divided the block. He could see the olive tree in his own courtyard. If he could manage to negotiate the wall, he could drop into his own courtyard and avoid the stranger altogether.

Ihab returned with his sandals. Alhasan held one in each hand and stepped onto the wall. "That is all, Ihab," he said. "Thank you. You may go."

Ihab looked disappointed, but he went down the stairs and watched from the courtyard. Alhasan first looked down at his feet, but then focused on the wall ahead. "One, two, three, four," he said counting his paces.

He continued counting even after he left Ihab's house behind. He had to steady himself a couple of times, but he made good progress. He nearly lost his balance when he stepped onto a loose block, but he managed to stay upright. A small boy watched from the courtyard below. "Peace be upon you," said Alhasan. The boy said nothing but continued to stare wide-eyed at the strange man towering above him.

Alhasan could smell Nada's cooking even before he reached his home. She had learned to cook with spices from India, and the aroma of curry drifted up from the underground kitchen, through the ventilation grate in the floor of the courtyard.

As he neared the olive tree, Alhasan reached out and grabbed a branch. One hundred eighty paces. For a moment he thought about continuing on, just to see how many paces it was to the end of the block, but this was no time to amuse himself. Besides, the stranger might be able to see him from the street. Instead, he noted where he stopped and told himself he could finish the measurement another time.

He looked past the olive tree toward the house. How would he explain to Nada why he had come in from the courtyard? How could he enter through the back door without frightening her? He took a deep breath and looked for a way down. Perhaps Nada had left the stew simmering on coals and had already gone home. All he would have to worry about was surprising Kareem, his boy servant. If he was lucky, Kareem would be in his quarters.

Alhasan saw a place to put his foot on one limb of the olive tree and another foothold on a limb below that. From there he could drop to the courtyard.

It was a long step to the limb. Alhasan tossed his sandals into the courtyard. He slipped the bag from his shoulder, lowered it along the wall as far as he could reach, and dropped it. The silver coins jingled when the bag hit the ground.

Alhasan took hold of a branch and swung his right leg toward the foothold. He missed the spot on the limb and began to fall. The branch in his hands bent with his weight, but it didn't break. Fortunately, his foot came to rest on a lower limb. His balance restored, Alhasan stepped onto a second foothold and then dropped into the courtyard. He brushed leaves, stems, and bits of bark from the front of his robe, put on his sandals, picked up his bag, and stepped toward the back door.

He stopped by the door and listened. It was quiet inside. He opened the door a crack and looked around. Nada had folded his laundry and left it on the table. That was out of place, but she was not in the room. Neither was Kareem.

He took off his sandals, pushed the door open, and stepped inside. As he turned to close the door, he saw a flash of silver coming toward his eyes and felt a dull thud on the side of his head. The room spun, and then it went dark.

Chapter Three

The first thing Alhasan felt when he awoke was something smooth and cool pressing against face. He opened his eyes a little and realized he was lying on the floor, his left cheek resting on the tile.

The second thing he felt—bursting on top of the first—was a painful throbbing behind his eyes. He closed his eyes to see if the pain would go away. It did not. It got worse.

The third thing he felt was a damp cloth on his forehead. He opened his eyes and saw Nada's slender fingers, tattooed with henna, daubing his brow. Only then did he remember how he came to be lying on the floor.

"Why...did...you...hit...me?" Alhasan asked.

"I am so sorry," said Nada. "I should have warned you."

"Warned me? Warned me of what?"

The question hung in the air.

"So, the great scholar has rejoined us," boomed a voice with an unmistakable accent.

Alhasan rolled onto his side and looked up. The foreigner he had bumped into was standing over him. In one hand he held a curved dagger with a silver handle.

"We meet again," said the man. "You ran into me, and now I have run into you." The stranger laughed at his own joke.

Alhasan glared at the stranger.

"What's wrong? You don't think that's funny?" asked the foreigner. "Well, I didn't think your game of hide-and-seek was funny, either."

Alhasan propped himself up on one elbow. "Get out," he said.

"I don't care for the tone of your voice," said the stranger. "After all, I have allowed the beautiful Nada to tend to you. You don't seem to appreciate the gesture."

"Get out of my house before I call for help."

"That would not wise, Ibn Al-Haytham," said the stranger. "I would hate to have to silence you again."

"Who are you? And what business do you have with me?" asked Alhasan, sitting all the way up. His head continued to throb.

"Now we are getting somewhere," said the stranger. "I will tell you my business, but first I think you need some water."

At the mention of water, Alhasan struggled to his feet and stepped toward the door.

"Stop!" commanded the stranger. "What are you doing?"

"I am going to the latrine," said Alhasan.

"I will come with you."

"That's ridiculous!" said Alhasan.

"Is it? Perhaps you have a weapon stashed in your courtyard. Or you are going to climb your olive tree to escape, the way you came in."

"I have no weapons. I'm not trying to escape. Please. Allow me some privacy."

Alhasan felt dizzy. "I'm going to be sick," he said, bolting out the door and toward the small tent that surrounded the latrine. The stranger followed him outside.

"You are a brilliant man, Ibn Al-Haytham. I hope you are learning not to play games with me."

Alhasan straightened up. "Privacy. Please."

"As you wish. It doesn't look like you have a weapon out here. But if you do, think carefully about using it. My dagger has two ends. You have felt the convincing end. Next you will feel the killing end."

The intruder returned to the house; Alhasan soon followed.

"I must wash my full body," he told the foreigner. "I lost consciousness."

He went to the washing room and performed the ritual ablution, reciting the Shahada when he was done. As he put on a clean robe, he tried to form some kind of plan to deal with the intruder, but he realized there was nothing he could do until he had more information about him. *Why is he here?* He thought about his bag. *Does the stranger have it? If so, why didn't he leave?* He had an idea.

He called Kareem. The boy must have been in the great room, because he knocked at the door almost immediately. "Come in," said Alhasan. "Empty the washbasin in the garden," he said loudly enough for the stranger to hear in the next room. As Kareem came nearer, Alhasan bent down and whispered. "Then climb the olive tree and walk down the wall to Ihab's house. Tell him we are in trouble. Have him bring his father and brothers."

"What are you doing, Ibn Al-Haytham?" called the stranger from the other room.

"I am getting dressed," replied Alhasan as Kareem carried the washbasin out of the room.

"And where are you going?" the stranger asked Kareem.

"To empty the washbasin," said Kareem.

"Stop right there."

Alhasan listened as he put his vest on over his robe.

"Ibn Al-Haytham!" called the stranger.

Alhasan went out to the great room. The stranger studied Alhasan's face and then turned toward Kareem.

"Do you remember how you felt when you saw your master lying on the floor?" the stranger asked Kareem.

The boy nodded.

"You were upset—so upset you attacked me. Yet he awoke after a few minutes. Now imagine if you were to find him on the floor again, but this time with his guts in a bloody heap next to him. That is exactly what you will find if you play any more tricks. Do you understand?"

Kareem glanced at Alhasan. Alhasan tried to look away, but it was too late.

"So, you did have a plan!" The stranger's eyes flashed with anger. "Do you think I am so easily fooled? Do you think I have come all this way without being prepared?"

Alhasan gave the stranger a blank look.

"You must think I'm stupid. Did you really believe when you ran away that I didn't already know where you lived? Did you think I would let this boy get help? You are supposed to be a genius, but you are acting like a fool."

He turned back to Kareem. "You are going to empty that washbasin and then come right back. Your master's life depends on it. Understood?"

Kareem nodded.

"Then go."

Kareem hurried into the courtyard and emptied the washbasin beside the olive tree.

"Your little servant put up quite a fight when he saw you on the floor," said the stranger. "He would make a good soldier."

Alhasan felt guilty. Somehow, he not only had put himself in danger, but he had put Kareem and Nada in danger as well. *What did I do to bring this man into my home?* Alhasan wondered. *Did I say something wrong when I ran into him this morning? Did I insult him at a local discussion, or perhaps at the House of Wisdom?* Too often he gave blunt answers to ridiculous questions asked by other scholars, only to learn later he had offended them. This man was no scholar, but perhaps he had a relative who was.

Kareem returned the basin to the washing room just as the sun set over Basra and the muezzin sounded the call to prayer. "Shall we go to the mosque?" asked Alhasan.

"No," said the stranger. "We will pray here."

One by one, Kareem, the stranger, and Nada performed their ablutions. Alhasan unrolled his prayer rug on the floor of the great room with its niche toward the Qibla. He then turned the rug sideways so he,

Kareem, and the stranger could share it. Nada took up a place behind them.

After the *takbir*, the stranger stood with his arms at his sides rather than folding them across his body as Alhasan, Kareem, and Nada did. Alhasan recognized the difference as that of the Shi'a.

The devotions concluded, the stranger turned to Nada. "Let's have some of that food I smell."

"I am sorry, but I must go," said Nada. "My family will wonder where I am."

"No," said the stranger. "No one leaves. Besides, I doubt if this will be the first time you will be late. I suspect your master has kept you late before, losing track of time, making last-minute requests."

Nada said nothing.

"Someone might come looking for you, but not yet. Now, let's eat. I haven't eaten since morning."

Nada descended the stairs to the kitchen, and Kareem followed. Alhasan glanced around the room. He did not see his bag.

"You seem to have taken a great deal of care to find out about me," said Alhasan. "I would like to know why. Who are you, and why are you here?"

"Of course. Sit down."

Alhasan just looked at him.

"Sit down, now!" the stranger commanded, his hand on his dagger.

Alhasan sat. Kareem came up the stairs with a tray full of flat bread. Nada followed with a pot of stew and four bowls. She ladled the curried chicken into the bowls and handed them around."

"Eat," the stranger said to Alhasan. "We have a long journey ahead of us."

"Journey?" said Alhasan. "What are you talking about?"

"Let me start at the beginning," said the stranger. "My name is Mourad Al-Ghazi. I am a captain of the guard of Al-Hakim Bi-amr Allah, the sixth ruler of the Fatimid dynasty. I, myself, am not Arab. I come from the mountains to the south and west of Egypt. I have served Al-Hakim since I was old enough to carry a sword."

Al-Ghazi took a sip of the stew. "This is good," he said.

"Thank you," said Nada.

"I am here," Al-Ghazi continued, "as a representative of Caliph Al-Hakim," he said. "I have come to invite you to Cairo. The caliph seeks an audience with you."

Alhasan took sip of Nada's stew. The hot broth made him forget about the throbbing in his head for a moment. He had heard of the Ismaili caliph, the one whose name meant "Ruler by God's Command." The Sunni Muslims had another name for him. They called him "The Mad Caliph" for ordering attacks on them and other religious minorities in the Fatimid Caliphate.

"This is ridiculous," Alhasan said. "Are you trying to tell me you have traveled for what—a month or more?—from Cairo to Basra, to invite me to the court of Al-Hakim?"

Al-Ghazi nodded and finished the last of his stew. He handed his bowl to Kareem. "More."

"But why? What could the caliph possibly want with me?"

"I will tell you," said Al-Ghazi, dipping his bread into the fresh bowl of stew. "He has read your treatise on civil engineering. You have some interesting ideas. How did you put it? 'Had I been in Egypt, I could have done something to regulate the Nile so that the people could derive benefit from its ebb and flow.' These are your words, are they not?"

"Yes, but—"

"Yes. The caliph is anxious to meet you and to have you put your ideas into action." He turned toward the kitchen. "Boy, bring milk, water, dates, and honey!"

Alhasan tried to think of a way to get rid of the caliph's emissary. "I am sorry," said Alhasan. "Please extend my apologies to Caliph Al-Hakim. I am afraid I am engaged here in Basra on an important project. Tell him I will come to Egypt when I am done."

"Ha, ha, ha," bellowed Al-Ghazi. "What are you doing? Building another water clock for the governor?"

"No, I—"

"No, you are not! You have not worked for the government for five years."

It was true. At one time—after he had written a commentary on Euclid's *Elements*—the governor of Basra had put him in charge of the city's civil engineering. He wrote several treatises on measurement, hydrodynamics, and the construction of a water clock. But the job was too much for him. Not the engineering. The people. He had to oversee the work of two dozen engineers, none of whom were particularly bright. They pestered him with questions, interrupting his work. If he pointed out their errors, they got angry. If he told them they knew best and to leave him alone, they became even angrier. He never could explain himself properly. Finally he stopped talking to them altogether. Eventually he was relieved of his duties. Someone had started the rumor that he had feigned madness to escape his responsibilities, but it wasn't true. That would have entailed deception—a sin against man and a sin against God. It would have meant making a fool of the governor, and that was something he would never do. But the rumor stuck. He had once been a popular teacher of mathematics, but not after leaving his post. Only Ihab's parents had sought him out as a tutor. That was when he turned to copying. He could always find a buyer for his copies of *Elements*, *Almagest*, and *The Intermediate Books*. Best of all, he worked alone. And when he finished, he could concentrate on his own work. It was the perfect life, and he had to think of a way to preserve it.

Kareem came into the great room carrying a tray with the jug of water, a pitcher of goat milk, four cups, a plate of dates, and a small bowl of honey. Alhasan hoped he wouldn't try anything stupid. He watched as Kareem set the tray on the ground in front of Al-Ghazi. The boy poured a cup of the goat milk and handed it to the stranger. No more heroics. Wise boy.

Al-Ghazi tore off a corner of bread, dipped it in honey, and shoved it into his mouth. "What is there to keep you here?" he asked between bites. "A student or two? The copying of books? Believe me, if you tame the Nile, Al-Hakim will pay you more than you could earn in a hundred lifetimes." Al-Ghazi picked up a date and took a bite. "You should thank me for tracking you down, Ibn Al-Haytham," he said. "I am going to make you a rich man."

Alhasan decided to try a different approach. "It is a long journey to Egypt," he said. "I need time to prepare."

"You have one hour. We leave tonight."

"That is ridiculous," Alhasan blurted out. "I can't settle my affairs in one hour."

"We leave in one hour," said Al-Ghazi, "before anyone comes looking for your Nada."

"Let me ask you this: If I am so valuable to Caliph Al-Hakim, why didn't he send an emissary to obtain my services from the governor of Basra, or even from Caliph Al-Qadir? Why did he send a thug like you to threaten me and force me against my will?"

"Unfortunately Caliph Al-Qadir is not on good terms with Al-Hakim. I am sure you are aware of the Baghdad Manifesto. He would never have consented to let you go."

"Why didn't you just explain all this to me? Why did you think you had to attack me in my own home?"

"Listen to you, asking why I used force, even as you sit there, planning your next escape. I could see in your eyes that you feared me. You would never agree to come along. I knew I had to convince you that I am serious."

"But why? What is so important? Can't you just tell the caliph I refused to go?"

"Come now, Ibn Al-Haytham. You know the stories about Al-Hakim. I assure you they are true. If I fail to bring you to Cairo, it's not just my life that will be at risk. I have a wife, three daughters, and a son. I must protect them. I have two brothers in Egypt as well, and they have families. I cannot fail. Too much is at stake."

"What if I tell Al-Hakim that you attacked me, that you knocked me out?"

"Ha, ha, ha—go ahead and try. First you are a Sunni Muslim from the Abbasid Caliphate. Do you think he is going to take your word over mine? Second, even if he believed you, he likely would commend me for it. He expects me to get things done. He doesn't care how."

Alhasan realized this probably was true.

"Third," said Al-Ghazi, his voice hardening, "if you do anything to cost me my position or my livelihood, I will have no choice but to take revenge. I know where Nada lives, and Kareem. I know where the old man you visited lives, and the family that helped you escape this afternoon. If you cross me, I will come back to Basra and slit their throats. Don't think I wouldn't do it. I have killed many men. You get used to it. God forgive me, but you even learn to like it."

Al-Ghazi sipped his water and then set down his cup. "Now, go and pack, but lightly. No more than one bag or a trunk."

Alhasan stood and motioned toward the table where his laundry was stacked. "Please bring my things," he said to Nada.

He went to his bedroom and knelt in front of a small, cedar trunk his father had made for him when he went away to study at the House of Wisdom in Baghdad. He removed some linens from the chest and placed them on his bed. Nada came into the room carrying four white robes and some undergarments. Alhasan forced a smile. "I am lucky that today was laundry day," he said, taking the fresh, scented garments. He motioned for Nada to come close. "Does the stranger have my bag?" he asked.

"No. He searched it, but then he gave it to me. I took it to your study."

"Please bring it."

Alhasan placed the clean garments on the bed and gathered his toiletries. Nada returned with the bag and offered it to Alhasan. "You keep it," he said. "It contains one hundred fifty silver dinars. After I have left, take it to your home. Take out thirty dinars for yourself. That is your pay for the next year. Continue coming to my home as usual. Keep it clean and keep my books in order. Give ten dinars to Kareem. That should make him the richest servant boy in Basra! And take fifteen dinars to the mosque for Zakat.

"If I am not back by second Eid, give five more dinars to the mosque for sadaqat. I expect to be back within the year, but if I am not, repeat the process next year: thirty dinars for you, ten for Kareem, and five for sadaqat. If I am not back in two years, repeat the process one more time. That will be the last of the money. If I am not back after three years, assume I am dead."

"Don't say that!" said Nada.

"Nada, listen. This might be my last chance to get my affairs in order. After three years, give my books and papers to Ihab, my former student. You know where he lives. He will know what to do with them.

"You will have married your fiancé by then. God willing, you will have a family. If I have not returned, move your family into this house. It will be yours."

"But no one will believe me!"

"If anyone questions you, go to Rashid Al-Bariqi. Tell him what I have told you. Say that the house is my non-negotiable payment for your loyal service. He will understand."

"You are too generous."

"Don't worry," said Alhasan. He smiled in his awkward fashion. "Remember what our visitor said: I will return to Basra a wealthy man."

Nada smiled.

"I will buy a large house overlooking Shatt al-Arab, and you can work for me again."

Nada laughed. "Thank you."

Nada left with the bag, and Alhasan went his study. He looked around his beloved room, wondering how long it would be until he saw it again. He picked up his astrolabe, a copy of Ptolemy's *Almagest*, which he would need to write the commentary he had been planning, and his Qur'an. He debated for a moment and then picked up *Elements* and *The Intermediate Books*, including Theodosius's *Spherics* and Autolycus's *Rising and Setting of Fixed Stars*, and his calligrapher's pens, just in case he needed to earn money along the way.

He returned to his bedroom and set the books in the bottom of the trunk. He placed his pens, made of dried reeds, between the books so they would not get broken. He laid his robes over the books, his prayer rug over the robes, and his astrolabe on top of everything. He opened a small compartment in the lid of the trunk and placed ink, pounce, and a few toiletries inside. His father had thought of everything.

"Now we go," called Al-Ghazi.

Alhasan closed the trunk and latched it. "Kareem, help me with this," called Alhasan. The boy grabbed one handle, Alhasan grabbed the other, and they lifted. The trunk was more awkward than heavy. They carried it into the entryway where the stranger and Nada stood, waiting.

"Goodbye, Master," said Nada.

"Goodbye, Nada."

"Follow me," said Al-Ghazi.

The two men and the boy wound their way through the streets of Basra, crossing several canals. Alhasan thought of his father. The elder Alhasan never would have imagined that the trunk he had made for his son someday would be used for a journey to Egypt—especially under circumstances such as these. As they neared the outskirts of Basra, Alhasan's arms were getting tired. His head was throbbing as well. He glanced at Kareem. The little fellow was holding up well.

Al-Ghazi stopped outside an inn. "Wait here," he said.

Alhasan and Kareem set down the trunk as Al-Ghazi went inside.

"Kareem, I want you to go to my house as usual tomorrow," said Alhasan. "Nada will be there. She will pay you for this month and for the rest of the year. I expect to return in a few months, but if I am not back in one year, visit her again. She will pay you for the next year, and so on, for three years."

"But I want to come with you," said Kareem.

"No, Kareem, you must stay here. I have some important business for you. I want you to go to the mosque and enroll in the school. Study diligently. When I return, we will resume our studies."

Kareem smiled.

"And Kareem, this is important. If I do not return—"

"No!"

"Listen. If I do not return in three years, go to Ihab. You know where he lives? Go to him and ask him to be your tutor. Say I sent you. He will not refuse."

Al-Ghazi opened a gate beside the inn. "In here," he said.

Alhasan and Kareem picked up the trunk and followed Al-Ghazi through the gate and into a stable behind the inn.

"I don't want you to go," Kareem said.

"I don't want to go, either," said Alhasan. "But knowing you will do these things will make it easier for me."

Al-Ghazi stopped beside two horses—a black one and a gray one. "Let him come along," said Al-Ghazi. "I will teach him how to really fight."

Alhasan ignored the soldier's remark. He set down his end of the trunk, put his hands on Kareem's shoulders, and looked the boy in the eyes. "Promise me that you will do what I ask."

"I promise."

"Remember the words of The Prophet, peace be upon him: 'He who travels in search of knowledge, travels along Allah's path to paradise.'"

Kareem smiled again.

Al-Ghazi ran a rope through the handles of Alhasan's trunk and secured the loop with a knot. "Lift this so I can fasten it on the back of the gray."

Alhasan and Kareem lifted the trunk onto the horse's back and held it steady while Al-Ghazi looped the remaining length of the rope under the horse's belly and back to the top. The soldier cinched the rope tight and turned to Alhasan. "Do you know how to ride?" he asked.

"No," Alhasan admitted.

"Then I will teach you," said Al-Ghazi. "Don't worry," he added, patting the neck of the gray, "this one is tame. It will follow mine."

Small of stature, Alhasan needed a boost from Al-Ghazi to climb into the saddle. Al-Ghazi showed him how to use the reins to turn and stop the horse. He then led the horses out of the stable and into the street.

"Wait here," the soldier said. He returned to the gate, closed it from the inside, and reemerged from the front of the inn. He slipped his horse's reins over its ears and onto its neck, climbed into his saddle, and urged the black stallion forward.

"Goodbye, Master," said Kareem.

"Goodbye, Kareem," said Alhasan. "Remember: Go to the mosque. Study well."

The boy nodded.

Alhasan's gray horse followed the black one down the street, walking calmly and evenly. The leather reins lay slack in Alhasan's hands as he left Basra behind.

The moon was nearly full, lighting the road before them. Mars, a real object, not an imaginary point, glowed like an ember overhead. Nearby, Momsek Al-A'aennah, the Reins-holder, drove his wagon across the sky. The Greeks called the constellation Auriga, The Charioteer. No legend survived to say where Auriga was from, where he was headed, or whether the goats he held were for market, consumption, or sacrifice—and, if sacrifice, to whom. Alhasan felt a kinship with the celestial traveler. He knew where he was from, but not what lay ahead.

Chapter Four

The most traveled route from Basra to Cairo followed the Tigris River northwest toward Baghdad. The road between Basra and Baghdad was well worn, wide, and mostly straight, but it also was long. Alhasan had traveled it many times since he first left Basra to study at the House of Wisdom, when he was just sixteen. The journey took fourteen days if you walked at a brisk, steady, military pace. Alhasan usually took longer—sixteen to twenty days, since he traveled with a donkey carrying water, provisions, and his chest. Riding a horse was much faster. Late in the afternoon of the seventh day, Alhasan could see the domes and minarets of the Round City on the horizon. High above the dome of the Basra Gate, the great silver weathervane depicting Abu al-Abbas's victory over the Umayyads glinted in the shifting wind.

The armies of Nebuchadnezzar, Cyrus, Alexander, Trajan, and Umar Al-Farooq had all marched along this road to conquer Mesopotamia. As a young man, Alhasan had dreamed of becoming a warrior like the great generals of history, including his own grandfather, nicknamed Al-Haytham, "The Lion," for his courage in battle against the Buwayhids.

Alhasan's father had counseled him against becoming a soldier. "There are many ways to serve God and your people," the elder Alhasan had said. "Taking up the sword is one way. Taking up the pen is another. Give your people knowledge, and you will make them great."

In the end, Alhasan had taken his father's advice. He had given his people knowledge, but now he found himself at the mercy of a brute with a sword.

"We will go into the city for supplies," said Al-Ghazi. "Mind you, any attempt to draw attention to yourself or to run away will cost you not only your life, but also the lives of your friends and servants."

"You do not have to keep threatening me," said Alhasan. "I understand you now."

"I thought I should remind you," Al-Ghazi said. "The lump on your head has disappeared. Perhaps your memory has disappeared with it—ha, ha, ha!"

Al-Ghazi turned his horse down one of the side roads that led into the city. Alhasan's gray followed. Al-Ghazi seemed to know the way to the marketplace, or else had a good sense of how to find things. As they neared the marketplace, Alhasan caught the aroma of roasting fish. He recognized it as *shabbout*, the popular carp from the Tigris, grilled in open air.

"Have you had our *masgouf*—roasted carp from the Tigris?" asked Alhasan.

"No," said Al-Ghazi. "Is that what I smell?"

"Yes," said Alhasan. "We should have some. It is the most popular dish in Baghdad."

"Then we will have it," said Al-Ghazi, "but I will pick the vendor, and you will not say a word. Don't even ask if the fish is fresh."

"It is always fresh."

"Not a word. Understood?"

Alhasan nodded.

Al-Ghazi stopped at the edge of the market, and the travelers dismounted. Alhasan followed his captor to a palm, where they tied the animals.

"Speak to no one," warned Al-Ghazi once more.

Alhasan enjoyed the sights and smells of the marketplace after so many days in the saddle. He couldn't help lingering at the stall of a stationer and bookseller, but a glance from Al-Ghazi ended his reveries.

His captor seemed to have an endless supply of money in the purse on his waist. He bought food, oil for a lamp, and a few pieces of jewelry. "My daughters will like these," Al-Ghazi said, holding up brass bracelets decorated with crystalline stones.

Alhasan said nothing. Perhaps he should have brought some of the dinars Al-Bariqi had paid him instead of the few he had in his purse. He could have bought a scarf for his mother or bracelets for his nieces.

He thought about the bag he left behind. He wondered what his brother, the accountant, would say about the arrangements he had made with Nada. Actually, he knew what his brother would say: "If you pay a servant in advance, you will never see him again. He will keep what you gave him and think himself all the wiser for it, even if it means forfeiting a job that could last for years." But Nada and Kareem were not that way. They enjoyed the work he gave them, and if he were to make it home alive, they would return to work for him, he was sure of it.

The supplies secured, Alhasan and Al-Ghazi returned to their horses. The Fatimid soldier was stowing the provisions when a voice rang out.

"Alhasan! It is you!"

Alhasan turned and saw Abdelali Haddaoui, a teacher at the House of Wisdom. Something of a polymath, Haddaoui taught theology, astronomy, and mathematics. He was the first person to introduce Alhasan to Al-Khwarizmi's method of calculation by completion and balancing.

"Peace be upon you," said Alhasan, extending his hands to his former teacher.

"And upon you be peace," said Haddaoui. "What brings you to Baghdad? I didn't know you were coming."

"The mathematician is on his way to Cairo," Al-Ghazi broke in. "Peace be upon you."

"And upon you be peace," replied a surprised Haddaoui.

"My name is Mourad Al-Ghazi. I am an envoy from Caliph Al-Hakim Bi-amr Allah, ruler of the Fatimid Caliphate. Ibn Al-Haytham has been kind enough to lend Caliph Al-Hakim his services."

Haddaoui looked at Alhasan with amazement. "Is this true? You are going to Egypt?"

"Yes," said Alhasan. "It seems the caliph is eager to hear my thoughts about how one might go about holding back the floodwaters of the Nile and releasing them when they are needed."

"Ah, yes. I remember that suggestion you made at the end of your treatise on civil engineering," said Haddaoui. "This is exciting news."

"Exciting, and urgent," said Al-Ghazi. "We were just leaving Baghdad. We have far to go."

"But you must stay the night with me," said Haddaoui, "and give a lecture at the House of Wisdom tomorrow."

"I'm afraid that's not possible," said Al-Ghazi. "Caliph Al-Hakim eagerly awaits the distinguished scholar's arrival."

"But I insist," said Haddaoui. "You cannot visit Baghdad without sharing your thoughts about this exciting venture, or whatever it is that you have been studying recently."

"I am afraid Al-Ghazi is right," said Alhasan.

"I won't hear of it," said Haddaoui. "It's already late in the afternoon. You won't get anywhere tonight. You will come to my home, have a proper dinner, bathe, and sleep in a comfortable bed."

Before Al-Ghazi could object, Haddaoui called to his servant. "Essam, take these animals. Water them and groom them."

The servant untied the reins of the horses and led them away.

"You are too kind," said Al-Ghazi. He gave Alhasan a severe look. "We would be most honored to break bread with you."

Alhasan, Al-Ghazi, and Haddaoui walked toward the Baghdad scholar's home, talking about the trip to Egypt and the latest findings at the House of Wisdom. Alhasan felt a strange calm. It might only last an evening, but he felt at home in the world of ideas. He was grateful for the respite his old friend provided.

At Haddaoui's home, Al-Ghazi ate with his usual gusto and filled the opulent rooms with his great guffaws. Alhasan answered Haddaoui's questions with precision, even though he was tired. It was a pleasure to have someone to talk to.

As they settled in for the night, Alhasan pushed all thoughts of escape out of his mind. He had come to respect Al-Ghazi's cunning and determination. His situation was hopeless, and he resigned himself to the prospect of meeting Caliph Al-Hakim in Cairo. In the mean time, he at least would have the chance to lecture again at the House of Wisdom the next day. That was a gift he had not expected, and he drifted off to sleep, thinking about what he might discuss before the eager students and scholars in the great hall where he had first learned the art of calculation by completion and balancing.

He was awakened the next morning by the call to morning prayer. He joined the household in prayer, ate breakfast with Haddaoui and his family, and then made his way to the House of Wisdom with his host and Al-Ghazi.

When they reached the House of Wisdom, Alhasan asked Haddaoui if he might have a student to assist him with his presentation. He was introduced to several students and chose one who reminded him of himself at that age. He told the student he would need his help when he gave a demonstration in front of the great window at the back of the amphitheater where the lecture would be held. The student positioned himself as instructed.

Alhasan stood by a pillar at the bottom of the amphitheater. According to tradition, the pillar was inscribed with the names of great scholars who had taught there. Alhasan glanced up and saw the name of none other than Muhammad ibn Musa Al-Khwarizmi, the mathematician and astronomer who not only had developed the method of calculation by completion and balancing, but had also introduced the world to the Hindu numbering system with its nine numerals and placeholder, the *punta*, or point, that some were beginning to call the zero. Beneath Al-Khwarizmi's name was the name of Abu Yusuf Yaʿqūb ibn Isḥāq Al-Sabbah Al-Kindī, who also had lectured on the use of Indian numerals, but who had made his greatest contributions in the area of philosophy. Haddaoui's name appeared on the list as well. Alhasan dreamed that someday, God willing, his name would be inscribed on the pillar, though it likely would not be for the lecture he was about to give.

"Today I would like to discuss the mystery of vision," Alhasan began. "We have all read Aristotle and his followers, the physicists, who state that vision occurs when a physical form arises from the visible object and travels through the air and into the eye."

The members of the audience nodded.

"Alternatively, Euclid, Ptolemy, and their followers, the mathematicians, state that vision is effected by a ray that comes out of the eye and travels through the air in a straight line to the visible object and perceives it. These two notions appear to diverge and contradict one another if taken at face value."

Everyone in the audience looked interested, except for Al-Ghazi, who watched impassively.

"Now, for any two different doctrines, it is either the case that one of them is true and the other, false; or they are both false, the truth being other than either of them; or they both lead to one thing, which is the truth. That being the case, and because the manner of vision has not been ascertained, I think it is appropriate that we direct our attention to this subject as much as we can, and seriously apply ourselves to it, and examine it, and diligently inquire into its nature."

The audience murmured its approval for this line of inquiry.

Alhasan continued, "Let me begin by first discussing the eye itself. The Greeks taught that vision occurs in the eye, but I do not believe that is the case. We know that the eye is tethered to the brain by a thin but strong cord. The existence of this cord is a clue that vision actually occurs in the brain, not in the eye. Why do I say this? First, this cord must have a function, and it occurs in animals as well as human beings.

"But the evidence that vision occurs in the brain can be gleaned by the existence of what we might call visual illusions. Two people can look at the same thing, yet not agree on what they are looking at. For example, a child with little experience in the world might never have seen a man riding on a horse. However, the child might have seen a camel. Now, if this child happens to observe a horse and rider in the distance, he might believe he is seeing a camel, with four legs and a hump rising from the back. An adult, seeing the same thing, but with the knowledge that men ride horses, would not make this mistake. Experience informs what is being seen, and experience resides in the brain."

The audience remained attentive with the exception of the man who no doubt wanted to be riding a horse at that very moment.

"Similarly," Alhasan continued, "an adult, can be enslaved by experience and assume that what he is seeing is something he has seen before. But it might not be what he has seen before. However, a child, with no preconceived ideas, might see the thing for what it really is and not fall into error.

"Allow me to demonstrate. Everyone remain seated, but please keep your eyes on me," said Alhasan as he walked toward the stairs that led to the back of the amphitheater. "Watch me and, if possible, do not even blink."

He began to climb the stairs along the far wall. As he neared the back of the amphitheater, his shape was backlit by the large window at the top of the stairs.

"That's right, everyone watch carefully," Alhasan continued.

When he reached the top step, Alhasan stumbled to his knees. "Not to worry," he called out. "I'm all alright. Keep watching."

Backlit by the window, the figure at the top of the stairs appeared completely black.

Now, what color is my turban?" asked Alhasan.

A voice shouted out, "Yellow."

"I ask you," said Alhasan, "do you truly see that it is yellow, or are you merely remembering that it is yellow? Look carefully."

The group below murmured.

"I see yellow," said one student, "I think."

"Now, watch," called Alhasan.

The figure in front of the window raised his arms and began to unwind his turban. He pulled at the fabric slowly, painstakingly. Al-Ghazi stifled a yawn.

Around and around went the hands of the demonstrator until the entire turban was a length of fabric. He then raised the fabric up with two hands, higher and higher. No one could tell for sure what color the fabric was.

"Now what, Ibn Al-Haytham?" one student called.

"Yes, what are we supposed to see?" called another.

The figure at the top of the stairs said nothing. A long minute passed in silence as he lowered his arms with the length of cloth draped across them. Then he stood still.

"Please, Alhasan," called Haddaoui. "Explain yourself."

"Yes," said one of the students. "Please continue."

The room was silent.

Suddenly Al-Ghazi shifted in his seat. "Ibn Al-Haytham, answer!" he shouted.

Nothing.

The soldier was on his feet in an instant. "Ibn Al-Haytham!" he bellowed, stepping over members of the audience. "Ibn Al-Haytham, answer me!"

Al-Ghazi ran up the stairs, taking two at a time. When he got to top, he nearly knocked the man holding the cloth through the great window.

"Where is Ibn Al-Haytham?" Al-Ghazi roared.

"I don't know," said Alhasan's assistant. "He's gone."

Chapter Five

"Wait, I will get a doctor," Sadeem bint Mourad told the man lying on the ground.

"No," the stranger said. "There is no time. Come here."

Blood darkened the sand around the man's body. Sadeem knew there was nothing she could do to save his life. She climbed down from her mount and approached the stranger, making sure to keep more than an arm's length away.

"What do you want?" she asked.

"Do you know the home of Mourad Al-Ghazi?" he asked.

"Yes. Mourad Al-Ghazi is my father."

The man's eyes widened as he looked at Sadeem.

"Yes, I see it," he said. "That's good."

He forced a smile.

"I have some papers that must be delivered to Caliph Al-Hakim. Your father...." The man took a deep breath and coughed. Blood dribbled over his lip and into his beard. "Your father will know what to do with them."

He reached inside his robe. Sadeem stepped back until she saw that all the man had in his hand was a leather pouch.

"My father is not here," said Sadeem. "He has traveled to the Abbasid Caliphate."

The man wheezed. Blood trickled from the corner of his mouth.

"Then you must do it. No one else. These letters are for the Caliph only. Your father is the only man I trusted...."

He stopped abruptly and coughed again.

"Take them."

Sadeem took the pouch from the man's outstretched hand. It was light.

The stranger looked at Sadeem with the satisfaction of someone who had completed an important task.

"The Kaaba? Which direction?" he asked.

Sadeem nodded to the southeast. The man tried to turn but was too weak to move. Sadeem stepped behind him, put one arm under his arm and across his chest, and lifted, the way her mother had shown her to turn a patient. She rolled the man over so he was facing Mecca.

"The Kaaba is there," she told him.

He fixed his eyes on the distance. "Verily my return is to Thee; I rely upon Thee and turn unto Thee," he said, reciting a verse from the Qur'an.

The man closed his eyes and let his head sink to the sand.

Sadeem prayed for his soul. She had prayed for the dead many times, but never as fervently as she did for the lifeless stranger at her feet.

Her prayer completed, Sadeem looked around. They were alone on the road. Or, rather, she was alone. She picked up the pouch and unfastened the flap. Three letters, folded and sealed with wax, stood like crisp, paper soldiers in the soft leather bag. The pouch was meant for her father. She tried to think what he would do.

She rode back to her house, left the pouch in her horse's stall, and ran inside to get her mother.

"I'm sure he is dead," Sadeem told her mother, explaining the situation. "He turned toward Mecca and recited a verse from the Qur'an."

"You never know, Sadeem," said her mother. "The body can appear lifeless, but the spirit might be trying to survive."

Within a few minutes Sadeem's mother confirmed what her daughter already knew. For the second time that afternoon, Sadeem prayed for the stranger's soul.

"Someone needs to notify the authorities," said Sadeem's mother.

"I can do it," said Sadeem.

Mourad Al-Ghazi's wife looked at her twelve-year-old daughter.

"I suppose you can," said her mother. "To be honest, I trust you more than your sisters with something like this. Go straight to the chief of police. Tell him you are Mourad Al-Ghazi's daughter. He will listen to you."

"Shall I ride?" asked Sadeem.

"Yes. Go quickly," said her mother.

Sadeem had visited her father's headquarters often enough to know that the office of the chief of police was just down the hall in the caliph's palace. She saddled her bay horse, grabbed the dead man's pouch, and rode as fast as she could to the palace of Al-Hakim.

"I must see the chief of police," Sadeem told the officer who greeted her inside.

"You will need an appointment," said the officer.

"I am the daughter of Mourad Al-Ghazi," said Sadeem. "This is important business, and I must see the chief at once."

An officer on the other side of the room raised an eyebrow.

"I thought Mourad Al-Ghazi said his daughter was marrying age," said the officer. He and the other officer chuckled.

"That's my sister, Rania," said Sadeem. "She is seventeen."

"And you are sixteen?" asked the officer, laughing.

"I am old enough to tell my father you are being rude."

The officer across the room spoke up: "I am Ali bin Ahmad Jarjarai, the secretary to the chief. Perhaps I can help you."

"I want to see the chief of police."

"The chief is not here, but I am his secretary and his closest assistant. I can help you. Please come inside my office and tell me what this is all about."

The man motioned to a small room off to the side. Sadeem went inside.

"Please be seated," said Al-Jarjarai, gesturing toward a wooden bench beside a table.

Sadeem sat. Al-Jarjarai sat on a bench across from her.

"Please tell me why you are here," said Al-Jarjarai.

"A man is dead on the road near our home," said Sadeem.

"Are you sure he is dead?"

"Yes, my mother is a doctor. Her name is Khadija bint Muhammad. Perhaps you have heard of her."

"Yes, I am aware that Mourad Al-Ghazi's wife, your mother, is a doctor."

"She examined him and confirmed that he was dead."

"Confirmed?" asked Al-Jarjarai.

"Yes."

"Who thought he was dead?"

"I did."

"You found him?"

"Yes."

"By the road?"

"Yes."

"And he was bleeding?"

"Yes. How did you know?"

"Please allow me to ask the questions," said Al-Jarjarai. "Was that his bag?"

"This? No. This is my bag," said Sadeem.

"Your bag has blood on it."

Sadeem said nothing. She wanted to glance at the bag, but she kept her eyes on Al-Jarjarai.

"It doesn't look like a young woman's bag," said Al-Jarjarai, smiling. "It's plain. It's leather. To me—I am not an authority on these matters—but, to me it looks like a courier's pouch."

"I have made my report," said Sadeem, getting up from the bench. "I will go now."

"Sit down. We're not finished," said Al-Jarjarai.

Sadeem headed for the door.

"Tariq!" shouted Al-Jarjarai.

The other police officer filled the doorway. Sadeem glanced at him and then at Al-Jarjarai. She returned to her seat on the bench.

"Tariq, have the boy bring us water and dates, please," said Al-Jarjarai. He smiled at Sadeem. "You like dates, I imagine."

Sadeem said nothing.

"Your father likes dates. He always asks for them."

"My father will hear about this interview," said Sadeem.

"A threat? That is rather unbecoming," laughed Al-Jarjarai. "You won't find a husband that way."

Sadeem glared at the man.

"May I see the pouch?" asked Al-Jarjarai, as if he were asking to admire a beautiful ring or bracelet.

"It *was* a threat, Al-Jarjarai," said Sadeem. "Stop now, or else I will tell my father everything that has transpired here."

"I have nothing to fear from your father. You came to my office to report a death. I asked you questions. You are in possession of stolen property. It appears he has more to worry about than I do. Unless, of course, you have come to turn in the dead man's articles."

"Your dates, Sir," said the boy at the door.

"Yes," said Al-Jarjarai.

The boy, about the same age as Sadeem, set a tray with a plate of dates, a jug of water, and two ceramic cups on the table. He carefully poured the water into the cups."

"Thank you," said Al-Jarjarai.

The boy left. Al-Jarjarai picked up a date and bit into it.

"Please join me," he said.

"Alright," said Sadeem.

"Good," said Al-Jarjarai, pushing the plate of dates toward his guest.

"No, I mean I will give you the pouch."

"Even better."

"But you must give me your word that you will take these messages directly to Caliph Al-Hakim yourself."

"Of course," said Al-Jarjarai.

"Not 'of course.' Say you will do it."

"I will do it, Daughter of Mourad Al-Ghazi. I give you my word as an officer of the court of the Fatimid Caliphate."

He paused to sip his water.

"Is that sufficient?"

Sadeem didn't trust the man, but knew she had no choice.

"Yes, that will do," she said.

She raised the pouch's shoulder strap over her head and slipped it off her arm. Handing the pouch across the table, she saw the bloodstain for the first time.

Al-Jarjarai opened the pouch and peered in.

"Yes, these look important," he said. "I will take them to Al-Hakim immediately."

He looked at Sadeem a long time.

"I would guess you are fourteen. Is that correct?"

"No," said Sadeem.

"Have you been promised in marriage?"

"No."

"Ah, then I still have a chance," said Al-Jarjarai, smiling.

"Yes, you have a chance," said Sadeem, standing. "As much of a chance as the dead man on the road."

This time Al-Jarjarai did not stop her from leaving.

Chapter Six

Alhasan already was in the street outside the House of Wisdom when he heard Al-Ghazi shout his name. His student accomplice had played his part well. When Alhasan had pretended to trip and fall, the student had crawled into place at the top of the stairs. He then had risen to his feet, drawing the audience's attention, just as Alhasan had slipped around the corner. The young man had waved his hand as Alhasan reassured the audience he was not hurt. The student then had proceeded to unwrap his turban at the right time. That was the last thing Alhasan had seen before he had dashed down the hallway to the stairs that led to the building's exit. The student must not have broken his silence during the demonstration, just as he had promised. His diligence had given Alhasan at least a small head start on Al-Ghazi. Alhasan only hoped that the Fatimid soldier had not taken out his anger on the young man.

How much more of a head start Alhasan would get depended on what Al-Ghazi did next. As Alhasan hurried past ox-drawn carts and around slow-moving camels, he tried to calculate Al-Ghazi's next move. If the soldier searched the House of Wisdom even cursorily, Alhasan would gain valuable minutes. It seemed like the smart thing for Al-Ghazi to do: After all, when Alhasan first considered trying to escape, he had imagined hiding within the great library's labyrinth of bookshelves. He had entertained this idea for at least two days as they rode toward

Baghdad, but eventually had discarded it as impractical. He wasn't certain Al-Ghazi would return to Basra to harm Kareem, Nada, or Al-Bariqi, but he couldn't bear the idea that he might.

The next thing Al-Ghazi might do is head for Haddaoui's house to see if Alhasan had taken the gray horse or even the black one. This was an option Alhasan had considered as well, but he had discarded it almost immediately. No matter what kind of lead he had on Al-Ghazi, he knew the more experienced horseman would have overtaken him long before he could reach Basra. It seemed logical that Al-Ghazi would take this course of action anyway, because he would want to retrieve his horse before looking for Alhasan. This would give Alhasan at least half an hour's head start. That should be enough time for him to execute the plan that had appeared in his mind, fully formed, when he had awoken that morning.

Alhasan labored for breath as he turned a corner and shouldered past a group of teenage boys walking side by side without a care in the world. Up ahead was the palace of Caliph Al-Qadir, the building he had envisioned upon waking. Alhasan's sides ached as he panted for breath. This was his only hope, the only plan that might succeed. He would know in a moment, because it would all depend whether or not he could get inside for an audience with the Caliph Al-Qadir's vizier, Shafqat Ali Farooqi.

Alhasan slowed his pace as he climbed the steps outside the palace. He had to catch his breath so he could speak intelligibly. When he reached the guard outside the great door, he stated his business. "I am here to see Vizier Shafqat Ali Farooqi."

"Do you have an appointment?" asked the guard.

"Of course," said Alhasan, trying think of some way to rationalize the lie.

The guard let him in, but it was the vizier's secretary who would be the person he had to convince. Alhasan had had an audience with the vizier shortly after assuming his position in the government of Basra, so he knew the protocol. He entered the anteroom outside the vizier's office and greeted the secretary.

"Peace be upon you," said Alhasan.

"And upon you be peace," replied the secretary. "How can I help you on this fine day?"

"I would like to speak with Vizier Ali Farooqi."

"The vizier is in a meeting. I don't recall that he had any other appointments this morning."

"I am afraid I don't have an appointment," said Alhasan. "But I am an old friend, or acquaintance, and I am sure he would be happy to see me."

The secretary eyed Alhasan, sweaty from his dash through the streets, with suspicion.

"Who shall I say is calling?" asked the secretary.

"My name is Alhasan Ibn Alhasan Ibn Al-Haytham. I am a mathematician from Basra. The vizier and I met here three, maybe four years ago. I am sure he will remember me."

"The vizier is a busy man," said the secretary.

"Of course," said Alhasan.

"He is not in the habit of seeing people without an appointment."

"Of course not," said Alhasan. "However, I am sure he will make an exception in this case."

The secretary looked at a log book on the desk in front of him.

"Why don't you come back at this time tomorrow? I will put your appointment in the calendar, and I am sure the vizier will be happy to meet with you."

"No."

The secretary looked up from the log book. "Excuse me?" he said sharply.

"I'm sorry. I mean I must see him today. Right now. It is of the utmost importance. Lives are at stake."

"Lives?" repeated the secretary, arching his brows. "You mean, this is a matter of life and death?"

"Yes, exactly," said Alhasan.

The secretary laughed.

"I know it sounds crazy," admitted Alhasan, "but it's true. You must believe me. My life is in danger, and so are the lives of several people in

Basra. I can explain it all to the vizier. You must believe me. Just tell him my name, and tell him it is urgent. I am sure he will see me."

"This is most unusual," said the secretary.

"Please," said Alhasan. "Time is running out."

"Wait here," said the secretary. "I am going to speak to the vizier. If he does not recognize your name, I will have you thrown into the street like the mad dog you seem to be."

"Fine, fine," said Alhasan. He tried to smile. "I am most grateful to you."

The secretary gathered up his robe and disappeared through an opening in a curtain behind his desk. Alhasan heard a door open and close, then silence. He grabbed the cuff of his robe and daubed the perspiration from his brow. He took a few deep breaths, trying to slow his racing heart. *This is taking too long,* he thought. *Where is Al-Ghazi now? He must be nearing Haddaoui's house; perhaps even inside it. Would he threaten Haddaoui's family? They know nothing about my plan. Have I put them in jeopardy, too?*

Alhasan's mind raced.

The door behind the curtain opened and closed, and the secretary parted the curtain with his hand. "The vizier will see you," he said, holding open the curtain. "Come this way."

Alhasan walked around the desk and into the opening. "Many thanks," he whispered to the secretary.

"State your business, listen carefully to what the vizier says, and then leave," said the secretary as he opened the heavy door. "Don't waste his time."

"Of course not," said Alhasan as he stepped past the secretary and into the large room.

On the floor was a huge carpet of deep indigo, decorated with a gold-and-white geometric design. The walls were paneled with ornately carved wood. Incense burned in the corner. Blue smoke drifted up toward the window high on the wall. The vizier sat behind a large table covered with ledger books and assorted manuscripts.

"Peace be upon you," said Alhasan.

"And upon you be peace," said the vizier, taking Alhasan's hands in his own and giving him three kisses on his cheeks. "Ibn Al-Haytham, the Mad Mathematician," said the vizier, smiling. "How are you doing?"

"I am well, Your Excellency," said Alhasan. "Thank you for seeing me on such short notice."

"Short notice?" said the vizier. "You mean no notice at all! Tell me, Ibn Al-Haytham, what is so urgent that it could not wait even one day?"

"Your Excellency, this will not be easy to explain in just a minute or two."

"Take your time. I am not nearly as busy as my secretary wants everyone to believe," said Ali Farooqi. "Please sit down and tell me."

The two men arranged themselves on embroidered cushions that matched the indigo carpet. A servant entered with a silver tray and two tall cups.

"Please have some water," said Ali Farooqi.

Thirsty from his run through the streets, Alhasan drank the water in three quick sips.

"What is this business about lives at stake?" laughed Ali Farooqi. "Honestly, Ibn Al-Haytham, such histrionics are not required."

"I'm afraid these are not exaggerations, Your Excellency," said Alhasan. "I have come to you because my life is in danger, and you are the only person who can help me."

The smile disappeared from the vizier's face. "If this is some kind of joke, Ibn Al-Haytham, I will not be amused."

"I am serious, Your Excellency. I have never been more serious in my life. Let me explain. A week ago, a stranger appeared at my door—well, actually, he broke into my home—claiming to be an emissary of Caliph Al-Hakim Bi-amr Allah of Egypt. He told me a story about how the Caliph wanted to meet me and discuss my plans for taming the waters of the Nile. Naturally I didn't believe a word of it, and I refused the invitation. He abducted me at knifepoint, threatening to kill me, my friends, my servants, and my family members if I disobeyed him or tried to escape. We arrived in Baghdad yesterday. By the grace of God, Abdelali Haddaoui— you know the scholar from the House of Wisdom?"

Ali Farooqi nodded.

"By the grace of God, Abdelali Haddaoui noticed me and invited us to his home for the night. He asked me to give a lecture at the House of Wisdom this morning, and of course we couldn't refuse. I was giving my talk when I endeavored to make my escape. I came straight here to ask for your help."

"I see," said the vizier.

"You must give me a detachment of soldiers to ride to Basra," said Alhasan. "If we cannot overtake him on the road, we at least can stop him, or capture him in Basra. Perhaps we could send a messenger ahead to tell the governor of Basra what is happening, so he could dispatch some guards to the people whose lives are in danger."

The vizier looked unperturbed, as if he heard about murder plots every day. "Tell me, Ibn Al-Haytham, why did you think this man's story about Caliph Al-Hakim was untrue?"

"It's absurd, that's why," blurted out Alhasan.

The vizier shot him a reproachful glance.

"I mean, it's quite improbable, you must agree," said Alhasan. "If he actually were an emissary of Caliph Al-Hakim, he would have had papers or something."

"Yes. That is why I fail to understand your story."

"What don't you understand?" asked Alhasan, certain he had told his everything clearly and unambiguously.

"This man, this Captain Al-Ghazi, I believe was his name, came here two weeks ago. In fact, he was sitting where you sit now when he presented me with a letter from Caliph Al-Hakim, asking for your services."

Alhasan stared at the vizier in disbelief.

"I have the letter here, somewhere," said the vizier, standing. He rummaged through the papers on his table. "Yes, here it is."

He removed a vellum scroll from the table.

"You are a calligrapher, I believe. Take a look. It seemed genuine to me."

Alhasan stared at the ornate writing, the fine inks and colored decorations, and the seal at the bottom of the page. "Yes, it appears genuine," he admitted.

"You can see for yourself that the Caliph is offering a fine price for your services. Twenty thousand silver dinars, payable to our emissaries when you reach Cairo safely. Then, upon your safe return to Baghdad, we will remit five thousand dinars back to the Caliph. That is our insurance that no harm will come to you. It's all there."

"Excuse me, Your Excellency," said Ali Farooqi's secretary from the doorway. "You have another visitor."

Alhasan glanced up from the scroll. At the secretary's side, smiling a broad, toothy smile, stood Mourad Al-Ghazi.

Chapter Seven

"Peace be upon you," said Al-Ghazi, bowing to the vizier. "And upon you be peace," replied Ali Farooqi. "We were just speaking about you, Captain Al-Ghazi."

"Peace be upon you," Al-Ghazi said to Alhasan.

"And upon you be peace," said Alhasan. His mind was reeling. Clearly the vizier knew Al-Ghazi, but of course he did not know everything about him. Would the vizier believe his version of events? It was the truth, and the truth had always served him well.

"It is the most amazing thing, Captain Al-Ghazi," said Ali Farooqi. "Ibn Al-Haytham was just telling me that you have kidnapped him."

"Ha, ha, ha," bellowed Al-Ghazi with his customary laugh. "I'm sure he was joking."

"Was it a joke, Ibn Al-Haytham?" asked the vizier, narrowing his eyes.

"No, Your Excellency," said Alhasan. "This man broke into my home and forced me—upon threat of death—to come with him."

"But this is absurd," said Ali Farooqi. "This man sought you out with my full knowledge and cooperation. Why would he threaten you?"

"I don't know," said Alhasan. "I can only tell you the facts of what happened."

"I am afraid there has been a misunderstanding, Your Excellency," said Al-Ghazi.

"Go on," said the vizier.

"Ibn Al-Haytham is confused, that's all. I thought we had cleared things up, but apparently he harbors dark thoughts about me."

"That is a lie," said Alhasan.

"Is it?" said Al-Ghazi. "Let me ask you this: You say I broke into your home. You state this as a fact. But were you at home when I came to your door?"

The vizier looked at Alhasan.

"Well, were you?" asked Ali Farooqi.

"No, I was not," said Alhasan.

"Certainly, you were not," said Al-Ghazi. "I knocked at your door and I politely inquired if you were home. I explained my business, and your servant—Kareem, I believe was his name—let me in. Do you deny this?"

"I, I don't know. I wasn't there," said Alhasan, "but you attacked me and you threatened me."

"Another misunderstanding, Your Excellency," said Al-Ghazi. "I was waiting inside Alhasan's house when he unexpectedly jumped down into his own courtyard from atop the wall outside and came in through the back door. Do you deny this, Alhasan?"

The vizier gave Alhasan a perplexed look.

"I don't deny it," said Alhasan, "but he was following me."

"Ha, ha, ha," guffawed Al-Ghazi. "Another misunderstanding, Your Excellency. The fact is Alhasan was not expecting to see me when he crept through his back door and he lunged at me. Under the circumstances, it was quite understandable. Naturally, I defended myself, but it was all over in an instant. I then introduced myself and stated my business. Isn't that right, Ibn Al-Haytham?"

Alhasan said nothing.

"Upon hearing about the Caliph's interest in his work, Ibn Al-Haytham packed his things—books, papers, clothing. I can bring you his trunk if you like. It's just outside."

"Is this true, Ibn Al-Haytham?" asked the vizier. "You packed your things for a trip to Egypt?"

"It is true."

"My dear boy, I can understand your confusion," said the vizier. "As Captain Al-Ghazi says, you no doubt were startled by his presence in your home. But you were right to come with him. All the arrangements have been made. This is a great opportunity for our blessed caliphate and for the Fatimid Caliphate to take the first steps toward reconciling after so many years of mistrust and misunderstanding."

Alhasan looked at Al-Ghazi. His face was beaming.

"You are doing the caliph and your people a great service," continued the vizier. "You should be honored that the caliph to the west seeks your counsel. Am I right, Ibn Al-Haytham?"

"I suppose you are."

"And if I might say so, considering how your service for the governor of Basra turned out, it would be fair to say you owe it to the caliphate to perform this service to your utmost ability."

"Yes, Your Excellency," said Alhasan.

"Good, good," said Ali Farooqi. "Then it's settled." He called to his secretary. "Prasanna! See to it that guards are dispatched with these men." He turned to Al-Ghazi. "I would say a party of twelve would be sufficient."

Al-Ghazi nodded.

"Send twelve men to accompany them to Egypt, as we discussed. Arrange for a wagon to carry the treasure back from Cairo. Have the men come here and load the wagon with gifts for Caliph Al-Hakim."

The vizier turned back to Alhasan. "I am proud of you, Ibn Al-Haytham. I have informed Caliph Al-Qadir of this extraordinary offer and opportunity. He is most pleased."

Ali Farooqi put his arm around Alhasan and led him aside. "I would expect—now, this is not a promise—but I would expect that if all goes well, God willing, Caliph Al-Qadir will create a special position here in Baghdad for you."

"I would be most grateful, of course," said Alhasan.

"Very good," said the vizier. "May God keep you safe upon your journey."

"Thank you, Vizier," said Alhasan.

Al-Ghazi stood by the door, waiting for Alhasan. "Shall we go?" he asked.

Alhasan nodded. He and his captor or guardian—he couldn't decide which—went through the door, the opening in the curtain, and down the hallway toward the entrance.

"You have cost me a great deal of money," said Al-Ghazi under his breath.

"What are you talking about?" asked Alhasan, skeptically.

"This money that Caliph Al-Hakim must pay for your services: He would have paid part of it to me, if I could have brought you to him on my own."

"So that is why you bullied me and beat me."

"Ha, ha, ha," laughed Al-Ghazi as they went through the great doorway and started down the steps of the palace. "I hit you in self-defense, didn't you hear?"

"You put on quite a show," said Alhasan.

"You can't blame me for trying, can you? Do you know what five thousand silver dinars would have meant to me and my family?"

Alhasan shook his head.

"That's fifty times my annual salary. I wouldn't have had to work another day in my life! And my son would have had a large enough dowry to marry any woman he chooses. You have cost me a great deal, Ibn Al-Haytham."

"You didn't tell me any of this," said Alhasan. "I didn't mean to deprive you or your family of anything, but you didn't trust me enough to be honest with me."

Al-Ghazi said nothing.

"Where are the horses?" asked Alhasan when they reached the street.

"They're where we left them," said Al-Ghazi.

"But you said my trunk was right outside."

"Ha, ha, ha," laughed Al-Ghazi. "As you said, I put on quite a show."

"So everything is still at Haddaoui's house?"

"That is where we left it. Of course, you will have some explaining to do."

"What do you mean?"

"Your friend was not happy with your sudden departure, leaving his class in an uproar."

"Is that what he said? How would you know?"

"Do you think I rushed after you? Ha, ha, ha! Only a fool thinks as he runs. I apologized to Haddaoui for my outburst and then paused to consider what to do."

"How did you know I would go to the vizier?"

"Know? I knew nothing. I had no idea you were there."

"You went there to get the vizier's help in finding me," said Alhasan, thinking aloud.

"Indeed. And I got it—ha, ha, ha!"

"And if I had tried to run, he would have helped you find me. Apparently I am a valuable asset—to be traded like a camel."

"Yes, and I am the camel herder," laughed Al-Ghazi. "Come along my beauty. You have a new master to serve."

The two men crossed through the Round City and made their way to Abdelali's house, near the Tigris River. Essam answered the door and let them in. Abdelali kept them waiting a few minutes. When he swept into the room, he looked angry.

"Peace be upon you," said Alhasan and Al-Ghazi, together.

"And upon you be peace," answered Haddaoui.

"I have come to apologize for my behavior this morning," said Alhasan. "I am sorry for the disruption I caused."

"You might try putting a little feeling into your words, Alhasan, if you want them to be believed."

"I am sorry that you cannot sense my sincere regret," said Alhasan.

"You are as mechanical as your water clock," said Haddaoui with a shake of his head. "But in that, you have never changed. I know you mean what you say, but I still am angry. You embarrassed me in front of my students and my colleagues."

"I know. I am sorry," Alhasan said.

Haddaoui glanced at Al-Ghazi.

"I, too, regret disturbing your class," said Al-Ghazi.

"Yes, yes, apologies accepted all around," said Haddaoui. "What is done is done. But I still do not know what you hoped to accomplish with your histrionics, Alhasan. I was quite fascinated in your line of reasoning, then, before we could explore it further, you were gone."

"It was foolish of me, Abdelali," said Alhasan.

"Foolish indeed," added Al-Ghazi.

Alhasan glared at his nemesis.

"Come, let us have refreshments," said Abdelali. He led the two men into his sitting room and called for his house boy. "Essam, bring water and the dates with sesame seeds on the outside." He then turned to Alhasan. "I want to hear more of your thoughts about the mystery of vision."

"Yes," said Al-Ghazi, "what point were you making when you disappeared?"

Alhasan sensed the sarcasm in Al-Ghazi's question, but he ignored it. "Only that these errors of vision, these illusions, contradict the Greek notion that the eyes send out rays to sense things. If the eyes sent out rays toward me when I was at the top of the stairs, why wasn't I seen clearly?"

"Because it wasn't you at the top of the stairs," said Al-Ghazi, his mockery barely concealed.

"That is true," said Alhasan. "But why couldn't you tell it wasn't me, if the rays originate in the viewers' eyes and move in straight lines toward the object of vision?"

No one said anything.

"The fact that the figure appeared as a silhouette against the window suggests that the alternate explanation—the one that says that objects of vision give off forms or particles—more accurately describes what happens when there are errors of vision," said Alhasan. "Somehow the form of the window overpowers the form of the person in front of it, and the eye cannot separate them."

Haddaoui nodded. "So you believe in the intromission theory of vision."

"Yes, but I am not certain. The geometry behind Euclid's extromission theory is impressive, but so many questions linger about the rays themselves, such as their failure to illume. Intromission makes more sense to me, but there is much more to be learned about it. What are these forms or particles? How do they travel through the air and even through water? Do they compress and 'stamp' the air between the object and the eye, as Democritus said, or do they act on another medium, as Aristotle suggests?"

"I never thought of the forms traveling through water, but of course you are right. We can see the bottom of a pool quite clearly," said Abdelali.

"More clearly," Alhasan said. "The water magnifies the forms at the bottom of a pool."

"That is true," said Abdelali.

"We also can see objects reflected in the surface of a pool or even a puddle," added Al-Ghazi.

"That is an interesting point," said Alhasan. "It is easy to imagine how a three-dimensional object can leave an impression in the air, as a signet ring leaves an impression on wax, to paraphrase Aristotle, but the surface of a pool or puddle is flat. How does an image from a flat surface compress the air in the form of the three-dimensional object?" Alhasan had to admit this was a valuable observation. Simple, but valuable. "And here is another mystery," he continued. "Let us say, as Lucretius does, that a mountain has a form that it gives off like the skin of a snake or the shell of a cicada."

"Yes," said Abdelali.

"The form of the mountain must be enormous," said Alhasan. "And when you are near the mountain, it fills your sight. But when you are far from the mountain, it can appear as nothing more than a ripple on the horizon. The form is in your vision, but it is small. So the form given off by the mountain—or any visible object—must shrink as it travels through the air. But why would it do that? It makes no sense at all."

"I see," said Abdelali.

"I see also," said Al-Ghazi, "and that's all I care about—I don't care how I do it."

Essam brought the water and dates.

"One more mystery," said Alhasan, watching the house boy pour the water. Lights and colors danced through the clear liquid as it streamed into the cups. "Al-Ghazi, you have built many fires."

"Of course. You and I had a fire every night."

"Yes, and we sat and stared at the fire, did we not?"

"I suppose we did. I like to watch fire."

"Have you ever looked away suddenly—perhaps because you heard a noise?"

"Of course I have."

"What did you see?"

"What did I see? Which time?"

"Any time."

"I don't know. It's hard to see in the dark."

"Is it? Or are you seeing something that makes it hard to see into the dark?"

"I know what you mean," said Al-Ghazi. "There is a bright shape— like the ghost of the fire—in your sight, obscuring what is hidden in the dark."

"Exactly. But why? You have looked away from the fire, but the ghostly image is still there."

"I have seen this, too," said Haddaoui.

"The form from the fire is entering the eye, according to the physicists. When you look away, it ceases to enter the eye. But it has left a kind of impression. I think of it as a small pain, like the heat from the fire on your face. When you turn away, your face is still warm. This also happens in the eye, but only at night or in a dark place."

"Yes, yes," said Al-Ghazi.

"If God grants me a longer life, I would like to investigate matters of vision thoroughly," said Alhasan.

"God willing, you will do so," said Haddaoui.

"God willing, you will," Al-Ghazi added, "but only after you have tamed the Nile for Caliph Al-Hakim."

Chapter Eight

Sadeem rode her horse away from the palace and then turned right, stopping beside the outdoor market. Justice was swift and severe under Al-Hakim, so she had little to fear from leaving her horse unattended. Still, she asked a spice merchant she knew to watch the bay. She walked back toward the main street, stopping at various stalls as if she were shopping. When she reached the corner, she saw the police officer named Tariq and two others riding at a full gallop toward her house and the dead man who never reached it.

She turned up the street and headed for the palace. When she could see the entrance to the police headquarters, she stopped at a vegetable stand. She examined eggplant, squash, and beans carefully, glancing from time to time at the headquarters' door. She noticed a boy in ragged clothing playing on the other side of the street.

"You, there," she called to the boy. "I have an errand for you."

The boy crossed the street to Sadeem.

"Peace be upon you," she said.

"And upon you be peace," said the boy.

"Do you want to earn five dirham?" asked Sadeem.

"Yes," said the boy, smiling.

"Can you run fast?" asked Sadeem.

"As fast as anybody on this street," said the boy.

"And if someone is chasing you, can you lose them?"

"For ten dirham I can disappear like a djinni."

"Good," said Sadeem. "Here's what to do: Run over to the police station and tell the officer inside that there is a fight—two men with daggers, and one is bleeding. When the police officer comes out, tell him to follow you, and then run down the street that way, away from here. Understand?"

"Yes."

"Keep running as long as he follows you. If he comes too close, return to the Djinnestan."

"I will," laughed the boy.

"Don't let him catch you," Sadeem told the boy.

"I won't."

"And don't tell anyone about this errand."

"Don't worry, I won't say a word."

Sadeem gave the urchin ten dirham and watched him from the vegetable stand.

"Are you going to buy anything?" asked the vegetable merchant just as the boy ran out of the police station followed by Al-Jarjarai.

"I'll take these," said Sadeem, handing the merchant a pile of eggplant. "I'll be back in a moment."

She hurried down the street to the police headquarters and glanced inside. It was empty. She crossed the main room to Al-Jarjarai's office. The leather pouch, unclean from blood, lay on the floor. The table was bare. Sadeem opened a cabinet that stood against the wall. She searched the shelves, but found only log books, writing materials, and a few personal effects.

She returned to the main office and glanced outside the door. No one was coming. She quickly crossed the room and tried the door to the police chief's office. It was unlocked.

At the side of the room stood a table with a bench beside it. On the table were a lamp, a log book, and some papers. Sadeem approached the table. The paper soldiers were resting on their sides. Coming closer,

Sadeem saw that their wax seals had been broken. Whatever secrets they held now belonged to Al-Jarjarai.

Sadeem heard a voice outside.

"Yes, I can run like a race horse," Al-Jarjarai called out to someone. "That kid better hope I don't see him again."

Sadeem knew there were only two places Al-Jarjarai could be heading: to his office or to the one she was in. *He will check the papers,* she thought.

She crossed the police chief's office, closed the door, and slipped into Al-Jarjarai's office. Standing against the wall next to the door, she heard Al-Jarjarai walk past and enter the police chief's office. She looked around the corner. The door to the police chief's office was ajar. She crept through the main room and out the front door. *That boy isn't the only djinni on this street,* she joked to herself, walking toward the vegetable stand.

Glancing from time to time at the police headquarters, Sadeem casually examined the garlic and onions before paying for the eggplant. Al-Jarjarai did not come out. She took the eggplant, walked to the open air market, untied the bay, and climbed into the saddle.

"Thank you," she called to the spice merchant.

"Fresh peppercorns today," he called. "Are you sure you don't need any?"

"Maybe tomorrow," said Sadeem.

All the way home, Sadeem tried to think of an alternative to the plan that had formed—unbidden, unwanted, and unforeseen—in her imagination. *If Father were here, he would take care of it,* she thought. But he would not be back for weeks. There wasn't time.

"Where have you been?" Sadeem's mother asked when she got home.

"Al-Jarjarai, that secretary to the police chief, had a lot of questions for me."

"But I saw the police tending to the body almost an hour ago."

"I know. He kept asking questions. I think he thought I killed the man," Sadeem laughed. "Besides, I stopped at the vegetable stand."

"We already have eggplant," said her mother.

"I know, but I like it," said Sadeem.

She went to her room and listened. Her sisters were in the great room, discussing nonsense. Her brother was either reading or outside. She crept to his room and peered inside. It was empty. She took a tunic, a pair of trousers, a pair of riding boots, and a hat from his wardrobe and returned to her room. The djinni had succeeded a second time that day, but it was the third time that would count.

Nightfall came. Every time Sadeem thought of her plan, her heart thumped in her chest. She kept trying to think of an alternative, but nothing came to mind. Her sisters went to bed, then her brother, and finally her mother. Sadeem lay awake, staring at the ceiling and listening. Certain that everyone was asleep, she got out of bed and put on her brother's clothing. There was no other way. She had to do it.

She walked down the hall past her parents' room, across the dining room, and outside to the kitchen. She crossed the yard to the stable and saddled the bay. None of the horses made a sound. Before she could stop herself, she was riding toward the Al-Muqattam hills on the outskirts of Cairo.

Obscured by clouds, the moon barely illuminated the desert. Sadeem had ridden this trail many times, but never at night and never alone. Her horse was alert, but not on edge. Sadeem urged him up the first hill, and he went willingly. When they got to the top, Sadeem pulled the reins gently. Though far from the city, Sadeem was afraid even to say "stop." The bay pulled up without the command and stood still, breathing heavily from the climb. Sadeem patted his neck.

The light was dim, but from high on the hill, Sadeem could see the trail that led to Cairo. She waited. It was out of her hands now. She had done her part.

She stroked the bay's neck and played with his mane, winding and unwinding the coarse hairs around her fingers. The moon climbed higher in the eastern sky. It was almost overhead when Sadeem saw a ghostly light on the trail below. From a distance, the shimmering luminescence could be taken for a djinni, a demon, or an angel, but Sadeem knew it was something else: the solid silver tack of the donkey ridden by the "Ruler by God's Command," Caliph Al-Hakim.

Sadeem leaned forward in the saddle. "Easy now," she whispered, lifting the reins off the bay's neck. The horse took a step forward, then another. "Easy, Big Boy," said Sadeem, urging the horse down the trail.

Dressed in dark clothing and riding a dark horse, Sadeem assumed she would be difficult to see from a distance. She thought about what she would say when she got within calling distance. The plan was vivid in her mind, and she would carry it out just as it presented itself.

If Al-Hakim saw her, he was unmoved; his donkey continued up the trail at a steady pace. When Sadeem got within calling distance, she took a deep breath.

"Peace be upon you," she shouted in the deepest voice she could manage.

The caliph did not answer but continued toward her. She decided not to call again. When she was close enough to make out the Caliph's face, she drew the bay to a stop, got down from its back, and knelt on the trail.

"Your Highness," she said, again affecting a deep voice.

The caliph said nothing but rode up to her. She saw the donkey's hooves, but she did not look up.

"And upon you be peace," said the caliph.

Sadeem remained kneeling, staring at the ground. The plates of the donkey's harness threw patches of silver light on the sand before her.

"Rise, My Son," said Al-Hakim.

When the caliph saw Sadeem's face, he looked surprised.

"You are just a child," he said.

"Your Highness, I have a message," said Sadeem.

"A message? Out here? In the middle of the night?"

"Yes, Your Highness. I am sorry to disturb your meditations, but it was the only way."

"Proceed, then."

"Your Highness, soon you will receive three letters. The letters are sealed. Before you break the seals, examine them carefully."

"Why?"

"To be certain they have not been broken and made to appear like they were not."

"These letters are to me?"

"Yes, Your Highness."

"And someone believes the seals have been broken?"

"Yes."

"Do you know this yourself, or are you only the messenger?"

"Your Highness, I am the messenger." She paused. "And the witness. I am telling the truth, but do not take my word for it. Examine the seals. They will tell you everything."

"Who broke them?"

"Not the courier. He was attacked and died this afternoon. The seals were intact when the letters were delivered to the palace. Watch the one who brings the letters to you. Make sure he is present when you examine the seals. If he is innocent, it will show in his eyes. If he is guilty, you will know."

"I will watch him."

"Your Highness, you were right when you said I am young. I cannot defend myself against a member of your court who seeks revenge. Please do not mention this meeting. Let it appear that your own curiosity led you to examine the seals."

"I will."

"Please do so. You will see. I have come here only to warn you that those letters have been read by someone in your court. I don't know what the letters say or if they need to be secret, but I believe I have a duty to tell you what I know."

"Yes, you do. And if it is as you say, I will reward you amply."

"No, Your Highness, that is not necessary. Serving you and serving the truth is reward enough," said Sadeem.

"Serving truth for its own sake? I wish more of my subjects—and especially more of my courtiers—were like you."

"Thank you, Your Highness."

"Thank you, My Son. May the blessings of Allah be upon you."

With that, the caliph urged his donkey forward and continued up the hill. Once the Fatimid ruler had passed by Sadeem's mount, she returned to it, climbed into the saddle, and rode down the hill toward Cairo. When she reached the outskirts of the city, she circled around toward her home. The moon broke through the clouds and lit the road. As she neared her house, she noticed a dark patch in the sand by the side of the road where the courier had fallen.

Sadeem stopped. "I did my best," she said to the messenger, wherever he was. "I hope it was enough."

Chapter Nine

It took three days for the twelve-man squad to be outfitted for the journey to Egypt. Ali Farooqi sent several gifts to be delivered to Caliph Al-Hakim: a large carpet woven in the Persian style; a scimitar inlaid with gold and jewels; and a Qur'an copied by Ibn Al-Bawwāb, "the son of the doorkeeper," whose elegant cursive style was admired throughout the Abbasid Caliphate.

While Al-Ghazi prepared the caravan, Alhasan returned to the House of Wisdom each morning to give a lecture—a token of his regret for having embarrassed Haddaoui. In the first lecture, he explored the mysteries of vision he had discussed at Haddaoui's house. The next morning, he described the most accurate methods of measuring heights at distances. On the final day, he gave a talk on theology, examining the differences between the various sects of Islam. "I am now convinced," he said at the conclusion of his lecture, "that whatever differences exist between various sects are based not on the basic tenets of faith, or the Ultimate Reality, but on societal content." This statement caused quite a stir. A long and sometimes heated debate ensued.

"You have given our theologians something to chew on," said Haddaoui. "Thank you for visiting and for stirring things up. You are an original thinker and a first-rate scholar. I wish you would make your home in Baghdad and become a permanent member of the faculty here. I could nominate you for a position."

"Perhaps when I return from Egypt."

Bidding Haddaoui farewell, Alhasan made his way to the Round City's Damascus Gate, where Al-Ghazi and the Abbasid guards were making final preparations for the journey. "You are a horseman, now," Al-Ghazi said as Alhasan approached the caravan. "Prepare your mount."

Alhasan made his way to the horse he had ridden from Basra. He stroked its soft, gray muzzle with its flesh-pink snip. "Peace be upon you, Old Friend," he said, patting the horse's jaw. "Are you ready to go home?" He picked up the blanket and saddle and fastened them to his mount the way Al-Ghazi had shown him. "At least you don't have to carry my chest anymore. They loaded it on the wagon."

The saddle secured, Alhasan got a leg up from one of the guards and climbed atop the gray.

As the caravan was about to leave, a messenger ran up to Alhasan. "This is a letter for Caliph Al-Hakim," said the messenger. "You are to deliver it to him personally."

"God willing, I will do so," replied Alhasan.

"God willing," said the messenger.

Alhasan placed the letter in the purse he wore at his waist, took the reins in hand, and rode up to Al-Ghazi.

"Follow me," said the soldier. "That is where your horse will be most comfortable."

The caravan of twelve mounted horsemen, including Al-Ghazi and Alhasan, a wagon with two teamsters, and six camels bearing supplies started on the road toward Damascus, the next city on the way to Egypt. As he rode, Alhasan reflected on the events of the last few days and on the ideas he had discussed at the House of Wisdom. He tried to work through his concepts as a way to pass the time, but the heat and his inability to jot down his thoughts caused a never-ending circuit of incomplete ideas to race through his mind. Alhasan sank into despair as he realized how long it would be before he could resume his studies.

"I know the answer to this question before I ask," said Al-Ghazi, dropping back to Alhasan's side, "but have you ever received training in swordsmanship?"

"No," said Alhasan, happy to abandon his useless thoughts. "Why do you ask?"

"It probably never occurred to you, but now that I have no incentive to bring you to Cairo alive, I am not going to go out of my way to defend you, if we are attacked by bandits."

It was a sobering thought.

"On the other hand, I don't wish for any man to be defenseless," Al-Ghazi continued. "I was thinking of outfitting you with a sword and dagger, but it occurred to me that you probably haven't had any training in their use."

"No, I haven't."

"I can teach you the basics before we break camp in the mornings. At least it would give you a fighting chance."

"Are you expecting bandits to attack us?"

"I saw several groups along the way when I came to Baghdad. I avoided them, because I was alone. Obviously, we won't be able to do that with this wagon."

"If you think it's best, I will take your lessons."

The next morning, after prayers and before breakfast, Al-Ghazi led Alhasan to a clearing. "We will start with the sword," he said. He handed the mathematician a scimitar with a modest bronze hilt and leather grip. "Now hold it up in front of you, like this," said Al-Ghazi, holding his sword in front of his body. Alhasan copied the soldier's stance. "The first rule of swordsmanship is to hold onto your sword. Do you understand?"

Alhasan nodded.

With that, Al-Ghazi swung the blade of his sword against Alhasan's with such force that the weapon flew out of the scholar's hand.

"If you don't hold onto your sword, you are dead," said Al-Ghazi with a slight smile, stepping toward him.

Alhasan felt the tip of Al-Ghazi's scimitar under his chin. "I see," he said, unable to nod.

"Pick it up and hang onto to it," said Al-Ghazi.

Alhasan took a firmer grasp of the sword and returned to the ready position. Al-Ghazi smashed his sword against Alhasan's. This time, the mathematician held fast.

"Better," said Al-Ghazi. "Now, the second rule of swordsmanship is that the sword is your protector before it is your weapon. It is the only thing standing between you and certain death."

"I understand," said Alhasan.

"Good. Now, to protect you, the sword must block the other sword crossways, like this." Al-Ghazi brought the blade of his sword against the blade of Alhasan's, forming a right angle.

"The blades must be perpendicular to each other," said Alhasan.

"If you like, yes, perpendicular. If you meet an attacking blade less than crossways, see what happens." He tilted his sword so it was at almost the same angle as Alhasan's, then pushed. His blade slid down the side of Alhasan's sword all the way to the hilt. "It's a matter of lever-age," said Al-Ghazi. "What did the mathematician, Archimedes, say?"

"Give me a lever long enough and a place to stand, and I will move the earth."

Al-Ghazi pressed his blade downward against the hilt of Alhasan's sword. Alhasan was powerless to resist. Once the hilt was below Al-Ghazi's blade, he gently slid his sword against Alhasan's wrist.

"If I cut you here, you will release the sword...."

"And I will be dead."

"Exactly. So meet my sword crossways."

The two men practiced clashing their swords together so that Alhasan could feel the strength of the proper defense. Al-Ghazi then showed him how to meet the blade at a right angle, no matter which direction it came from, proceeding in a circle from top to bottom and from bottom to top.

"That's enough for today," said Al-Ghazi when camp cook shouted that breakfast was ready.

"But what about attacking?" asked Alhasan.

"Save your life first. If you survive, you can attack."

The lessons continued every morning for the next three days. On the fourth day, Al-Ghazi canceled the lesson so he could secure a barge to ferry the caravan cross the Euphrates River. The crossing completed, Alhasan resumed his morning training and exercise on the fifth day.

"Here," said Al-Ghazi, handing Alhasan a curved dagger with a blade about the length of a hand. "Put it in your belt. I will teach you about fighting in close quarters."

Al-Ghazi showed Alhasan where to place the dagger in his belt and then continued, "The most dangerous fighting is in close. Here it is kill or be killed. You might not have time to get to your sword, so you must know how to protect yourself in tight quarters." He paused. "And also how to kill."

Alhasan's face showed no change, but inwardly he felt sick. The matter-of-fact way that Al-Ghazi discussed taking another life was repulsive.

"The key is to move toward the attacker, not away from him. You want to crowd his movements and pin his arms to limit the amount of damage he can do. Watch. Pretend you have the dagger in your hand and grab me from behind."

Alhasan did as he was told.

"If I pull away, like this, what happens?"

"I have room to stab you," said Alhasan without emotion.

"Right. But what if I do this?"

Al-Ghazi pushed himself up against Alhasan.

"It is harder to stab you."

"Yes. And if I turn toward you like this."

He spun his shoulder against Alhasan's chest. It was impossible to stop him.

"All you can do is stab at my back."

Alhasan was uncomfortable with his teacher's body pressed against his own, his breath in his face.

"Now, I can pin your fighting arm with one arm and reach for my dagger with the other. If I can't reach my dagger, then I must find another way to kill you."

Another wave of nausea swept through Alhasan. At last Al-Ghazi released him and moved away.

"I once killed a man like that," said Al-Ghazi.

"Like what?"

"Face to face, without a weapon."

"What do you mean?"

"We had just put down an uprising in a village outside Cairo. Well, Al-Hakim called it an uprising. I didn't see any fighters, to be honest. We were ordered to put down the rebellion by killing all the adult males. It was a massacre, I'm afraid. It didn't last long. After it was over, I was told to secure one of the streets while the bodies were removed by the women. As I was walking along the street, a weight hit my shoulders. A villager had jumped onto my back from a rooftop. We fell to the ground, and he stabbed me with a knife. I had no time to reach my sword or my dagger. I just spun into him and pinned his arms to his sides. He rolled around, but I would not let go. He worked his hand free and stabbed my back, right above my belt. I could feel the blade slicing into my flesh. My face was below his, my eyes at his neck. I realized one of us was about to die, and I prayed to Allah that it would not be me."

"What happened?" asked Alhasan.

"Allah opened my eyes," said Al-Ghazi. "I saw a small movement; it was his windpipe, moving as he breathed. I turned my head to the side, placed my teeth on his throat, and bit down with all my strength."

Alhasan stared at Al-Ghazi in disbelief.

"Without air, he panicked," Al-Ghazi said. "He stopped stabbing me and struggled to get away, but I kept his arms pinned to his sides. We rolled over once, twice. Suddenly, his body went limp."

Alhasan said nothing as waves of nausea swept through his body.

Al-Ghazi seemed to read his thoughts. "It was brutal, but necessary. I did what I had to do to survive. I tell you this because I want you realize that when it's a matter of life or death, you must choose life. It does not matter how you do it. Live."

Alhasan nodded, but inwardly he doubted if he could do something like that. His grandfather had once told him that in battle you survive not for yourself, but to protect others in your fighting unit. That is the bargain: Everyone fights for the survival of the group. That made sense to Alhasan. He could see doing anything—even giving his own life—for the sake of protecting others. But to take another life solely to protect your own implied that your life was more valuable than the one you would take. How could you make that judgment? Al-Ghazi had done it, but he had a wife and four children depending on his survival. Alhasan had no one.

"Many people are depending on you," Al-Ghazi said, seemingly able to read his thoughts. "If you tame the Nile, you will save thousands from starvation."

Alhasan nodded again.

"It is your duty to survive. That is why I am teaching you these things. And tomorrow I will teach you more. Tomorrow we start fighting on horseback."

Throughout the day's ride through the rolling plains of Syria, Alhasan's mind returned again and again to the scene of Al-Ghazi and his assailant, Al-Ghazi's prayer that his life be spared, and the brutal solution that had presented itself. Each time Alhasan pictured the barbaric act, he pushed the image from his mind and thought of the next day's lesson. He patted his gray horse on the neck. "Finally, we will learn to attack," he whispered.

Alhasan awoke the next morning before the early call to prayer. The iridescence of dawn flecked the night sky with yellow, like the iris of a deep blue eye. Alhasan marveled at how the sky brightened even before the sun was visible. He wondered why. When the shining pupil of the Eastern eye looked over the horizon, the muezzin began to sing the *fajr*. Alhasan spread out his prayer rug and waited for the others to gather around for morning prayers.

The devotions completed, Alhasan saddled the gray and waited for Al-Ghazi to join him. The North African rode up and handed Alhasan the scimitar he had practiced with before. "You know how to defend yourself with this," said Al-Ghazi. "Now you will learn to attack with it."

They walked their horses up a small ridge and down the other side to a clearing, away from curious eyes. Al-Ghazi wheeled his horse

around so the two riders faced each other. "Again, you must not try to
do too much with the sword," said Al-Ghazi. "It is designed for slashing
from horseback. Let the design do the work."

Alhasan nodded.

"Hold the tip up, like this," said Al-Ghazi, extending the blade ver-
tically, "just as when you defended yourself on foot. You might have to
defend yourself on horseback, so be ready. The same principles apply."

"I see."

"Now, when it comes to the attack, do not whirl the sword about or
do anything that changes the angle before you."

"Keep it perpendicular to the ground?"

"Exactly, just as before. When you attack, simply allow the blade to
fall on the target. Believe me, the curve of the blade and its keenness will
do the rest."

"Let it fall in a straight line?"

"A straight line to your target," Al-Ghazi repeated. "Show me."

Alhasan allowed the blade to fall toward the earth in a quick but
smooth arc.

"Good," said Al-Ghazi. "Now, picking your target is crucial. I
recommend you forget about people for awhile and think of carving a
roasted sheep or goat. When you are cutting off a leg, you place the tip
of the knife in the joint, correct?"

Alhasan nodded.

"You can slice right through the joint?"

"Yes."

"The joints are the weak points. In combat, the weakest point must
be your target. Fighting is hard work. You want to achieve the maximum
amount of damage with the least amount of effort."

"Target the weakness."

"Yes. For example, if you ride up to someone, you might be tempted
to aim for the neck, but that requires tilting the blade of your sword."

"And tilting the blade is bad," Alhasan interjected.

"Yes. Keep the blade upright. Also, unless the blow to the neck is struck perfectly, which it rarely is, part of the blade will strike the back or the shoulder, keeping it from slicing all the way through."

Alhasan hoped his face did not betray the queasiness that touched his stomach as he realized Al-Ghazi was not talking about a sheep or a goat.

"An errant attack might cause pain, but pain is not enough. You must dismember the enemy to stop him. Dismemberment causes a sudden loss of blood and confusion in the mind of the combatant. I have never seen anyone lose a limb without becoming dazed, seeing a part of themselves gone."

Alhasan nodded, wondering what horrors the man before him had seen. And had inflicted.

"When you ride up, fix your eyes here," Al-Ghazi said, tapping the top of his shoulder. "Raise your sword, and let it fall in a straight line toward the joint where the arm meets the shoulder. Aim for the arm that is not holding a weapon, as it will be moving less. If the shoulder is not an option, aim for the elbow. Use the same technique; drop the blade on it. If the elbow is not available, the wrist will do."

Alhasan kept nodding without knowing in his heart if he could do any of it to a fellow human being.

"One last thing: You have heard of battle cries, and you might have the urge to scream at your enemy. Don't do it. Stealth is your ally. Ride up as quietly as possible and drop the blade in silence. You don't want the target to move even the width of your blade."

As Alhasan nodded once more, he heard a distant shout followed by yelling. As he turned to look in the direction of the sounds, Al-Ghazi had already kicked his horse in the sides and started off in a gallop toward the ridge. "Stay here!" the North African commanded.

Alhasan watched his teacher in the art of combat disappear behind the earthen mound that lay between him and camp. He lifted the reins from his horse's neck and urged the gray toward the ridge. Halfway up, Alhasan could see the camp through a cloud of dust. Al-Ghazi was riding straight into a fray. Bandits had attacked the camp and appeared to have commandeered the wagon. Two horsemen saw Al-Ghazi approaching and rode out to attack him. Alhasan watched as Al-Ghazi's horse veered toward one of the attackers' mounts. Al-Ghazi dropped his scimitar toward the rider's shoulder, but the bandit blocked the blow with his own sword. At just that moment, the other bandit leapt from his horse and collided with Al-Ghazi. The two men toppled to the ground, landing hard. They rolled in the sand for a moment until Al-Ghazi broke away and stood up.

Alhasan chirped into the gray's ear, kicked him in the sides, and rode straight toward the melee. The man fighting for his life might be Alhasan's captor, but he also was the father of four children—and a member of the squad to which Alhasan was attached.

The mathematician gripped his reins with his left hand and held his scimitar upright with his right. He fixed his eyes on the left shoulder of a bandit who had circled his horse between him and Al-Ghazi. The bandit urged his mount closer to the North African and raised his sword overhead. Alhasan wanted to cry out a warning, but he didn't. Instead, he stood up in his saddle, raised his scimitar, and let the blade fall toward his target.

Chapter Ten

Alhasan's scimitar worked exactly as Al-Ghazi had said it would. The bandit's limb fell to the ground, leaving a red streak across Alhasan's robe as he rode by.

Alhasan felt blood on his cheek, but he took no notice. His eyes were fixed on Al-Ghazi's adversary on the ground, who was looking at him in surprise. Alhasan already had raised his sword and identified the fighter's weakest point. As his horse raced past, Alhasan dropped the blade toward the man's right elbow. He missed. The blade bit hard into bone. The bandit dropped his sword, but Alhasan lost his grip on his sword as well. He pulled the gray up short, but by the time he wheeled around, Al-Ghazi had killed the bandit.

That was the last clear thing Alhasan saw for several seconds. Something hit him from behind, knocking him over the gray's neck. He saw a bit of sky and then a mass of brown. He put out his arms to break his fall, but he saw nothing but black dots and orange flecks as a great weight landed on his back, knocking the wind out of him.

He tried to roll over to try to get some air, but he couldn't move. The man who had knocked him off his mount was on the ground beside him, blocking the way. Alhasan tried to roll away, but the other man locked his arms around him. Alhasan looked down and saw a curved dagger in the man's fist.

Alhasan remembered how it felt when Al-Ghazi had turned toward him in training. He duplicated the move, grinding his shoulder into the bandit's chest and turning to face him. Their faces touched, beards entangled. Alhasan's left arm was locked against his side by the bandit's grip and his right arm was pinned against his chest. He felt his assailant twist the dagger into his flesh.

Alhasan tried to free his right arm. His elbow was bent upward and his palm was flat against his own chest. He turned his wrist so his palm was against his assailant's chest, but he could not move it to the side. All he could do is slide it upward. An image flashed into his mind—the dried skull of a camel he had come across in the desert. He looked his assailant in the eyes.

"Forgive me, Brother," Alhasan said.

"No mercy for you," whispered the bandit, twisting his dagger deeper into Alhasan's back.

"No, Brother," said Alhasan. "Forgive me for this."

In one motion, Alhasan shoved his hand along the bandit's neck, across his bearded cheek, and toward his ear. His thumb covered the man's bare eyeball for an instant. Alhasan pushed upwards until the man convulsed and the dagger slipped from his hand.

Once Alhasan was certain the man was dead, he pushed himself up, onto his knees. His lower back burned with pain. He looked up and saw the remaining bandits retreating down the trail toward Damascus.

"You are wounded, Mathematician."

Al-Ghazi was standing next to him.

"I killed him," said Alhasan, staring at the dead body before him.

"You survived," said Al-Ghazi. "And you saved my life. You dismembered my attacker in a single stroke, like a butcher in the marketplace."

Alhasan heard pride and approval in Al-Ghazi's voice.

"I will call you the Butcher of Basra," boomed Al-Ghazi, laughing.

As the reality of what he had done sank in, Alhasan felt sick. He vomited into the sand beside his victim.

"Don't move," said Al-Ghazi. "I will get something to treat your wound."

"Bring water and a clean robe," said Alhasan.

Two of the guards in Alhasan's party were dead. Four of the bandits were dead as well, including the two Alhasan had killed and the one he had wounded and Al-Ghazi had finished. Everyone had sustained injuries in the attack, but Alhasan's wound was the most serious. A gash the length of a dagger ran from his spine toward his side. His kidney was untouched, but he was bleeding.

Al-Ghazi returned with water and strips of cloth he had cut from one of the robes in Alhasan's chest. "Your Nada washed this well," said Al-Ghazi, pressing the clean fabric onto the wound. "I don't have anything this clean."

"Help me with my robe," said Alhasan. "It is unclean."

The Fatimid soldier helped Alhasan out of his despoiled garment. He then dampened a strip of cloth and handed it to Alhasan so he could clean himself. Alhasan thoroughly washed himself, making sure to wash each area where blood touched three times, as commanded by Islamic law. Al-Ghazi brought a blanket from the supply wagon and spread it on the ground.

"Lie here," ordered the North African. Alhasan lay face down so Al-Ghazi could tend to his wound.

Al-Ghazi sprinkled water on the wound to wash away the blood. He then daubed the wound with a clean strip of cloth. "It's deep," he said. "I will sew it closed."

Al-Ghazi left for a few minutes and then returned with an iron needle and a length of catgut he carried to repair damaged reins, belts, sandals, bags, tents, and other goods. Al-Ghazi gave Alhasan a piece of cloth and told him to bite down on it.

"This will hurt," he said.

The blade of his dagger searing hot from the fire, Al-Ghazi cauterized the wound. Alhasan flinched, but he did not cry out. The North African took the needle and catgut and began to close the wound. The next minutes were excruciating, but Alhasan lay still. Grateful to be alive, he whispered verses from the Qur'an into the cloth to take his mind off the pain.

As Al-Ghazi tended to Alhasan, the other members of the party prepared to bury the dead. One of the guards approached Al-Ghazi.

"Can I take that water?" said the guard, pointing to the water skin Al-Ghazi had used to clean the wound. "We need to wash the bodies."

"Which bodies?" asked Al-Ghazi.

"All of them."

"Not the attackers. Only our men."

Alhasan opened his eyes. "Al-Ghazi."

"What?"

"They are our brothers. They must be presentable to the angels."

"They are swine!"

"Allah shall judge."

Al-Ghazi picked up the water skin, doused his hands, and washed off Alhasan's blood. He did it a second time, and then a third. When he was done, he handed the skin to the guard. "Wash them, but once only. Our men you can wash three times. We don't have enough water for all. Once is enough, according to the law."

"Do you have shrouds?" Alhasan asked the guard.

"No."

"Bury them in their clothes," said Al-Ghazi, "as they did after the battle of Uhud. This is a battlefield."

"Al-Ghazi," Alhasan whispered. "They must be presentable. The Qur'an says so."

"We have no shrouds. You heard him."

"I have robes," said Alhasan. "Use them for our men. Cut off one sleeve and use it to wrap the head. Cut off the other sleeve and use it for the feet. Use the rest of the robe for the body."

"Fine. You can give your clean robes to the dead and you can wear the one that is unclean."

Too weak to answer, Alhasan closed his eyes.

"Don't fall asleep in the sun," said Al-Ghazi. "We will move you to your tent."

"I can walk," said Alhasan.

"And spoil my handiwork?" said Al-Ghazi. "Stay where you are. I will have the soldiers move you."

Al-Ghazi called a few of the guards over and had them grab the edges of Alhasan's blanket. On Al-Ghazi's command, they lifted the scholar, carried him to his tent, and placed him on the carpet inside.

"Rest. Move as little as possible. I will check on you," said Al-Ghazi.

"I am famished and thirsty," said Alhasan.

"Yes, our little skirmish delayed our breakfast. I will send one of the guards with something for you."

A little while later, the cook brought Alhasan water and hot flatbread. After the meal, the scholar slept. He awoke at the muezzin's call to noon prayer, but heeded Al-Ghazi's advice and did not get up. Later that afternoon, Al-Ghazi looked in on him.

"There is a little blood, but not much," said the North African.

"Can I stand and kneel to pray?"

"Yes, but be careful. Don't stretch out your back."

The tent was hot, and Alhasan dozed on and off throughout the day.

He was awakened by the sound of picks clanging against stones. He looked out of the tent and saw that it was dusk. The sun had set and a few stars dotted the sky. He had slept through evening prayer. He watched two men digging a grave.

"Wait," said Alhasan. "Stop."

The soldiers halted work and turned toward him.

"What is it?" said one of the men.

Alhasan came out of his tent. "The grave must be perpendicular to the Qibla, so the head can be turned to the right to face the Kaaba."

"Isn't Mecca over there?" asked one of the guards, pointing toward the southern horizon.

"Where?" asked Alhasan.

"There. To the south."

"What's going on?" asked Al-Ghazi.

"The graves must be perpendicular to the Qibla," Alhasan repeated.

"And?"

"And they are not."

"We prayed toward the south this morning."

"Yes, but this is a burial. It must be precise; it will last until Judgment Day."

"Listen, Mathematician, the dead will be fine."

"Al-Ghazi, it is our duty."

"But we are in the middle of the desert. What are we supposed to do?"

"Bring me the astrolabe out of my chest."

"Why?"

"I thought you knew all about me, Al-Ghazi. Did you forget that I wrote a treatise entitled *On Finding the Azimuth of the Qibla by Calculation?*

"I never heard of it," Al-Ghazi said.

"I can calculate the Qibla from anywhere in the world. Make them wait until I do."

"Stop," Al-Ghazi said to the guards. "Apparently our honored guest is an expert on digging graves as well as canals."

Al-Ghazi returned with the astronomical device. Alhasan pointed it at Sirius, the Dog Star, low in the southeast sky. He noted the altitude of the star and the spot on the horizon directly below it. He then used spherical trigonometry to calculate the azimuth, or angle, between true north and the spot on the horizon. Once he had this number, finding the Qibla was easy. A few more calculations, and he had the direction. He traced a perpendicular line upward from the horizon until he found a bright a star in its path.

"That star, there, he said, pointing toward Rigel. Make sure the grave is perpendicular to that direction."

The gravediggers did as they were told, adjusting the angle of the grave they were digging and aligning the new ones perpendicular to the Qibla.

"Now, when the angel comes, the dead can face him properly," said Alhasan.

"Very well," said Al-Ghazi, "but when the angels escort the bandits back to their graves, they will not give them spacious quarters to await Judgment Day. Their faces might be turned toward Mecca, but their mouths will be filled with worms."

"Allah will judge," said Alhasan.

"Let me see your wound," said Al-Ghazi. They returned to Alhasan's tent and lit a lamp. Al-Ghazi removed the dressing and examined the seam he had sewn in Alhasan's flesh.

"How is it?" asked Alhasan.

"Still oozing. I wish my wife were here."

"Your wife?"

"She is accomplished in the art of medicine."

"How can that be?"

"How can it be? Women can read, you know."

"Your wife can read?" Alhasan blurted out.

"Yes, she can read," said Al-Ghazi, replacing the dressing. He sat before Alhasan. "Don't look so surprised, Mathematician."

"I'm sorry, it's just that...."

"It's just that what? That I seem to have contempt for all books but the Qur'an?"

"Well, yes."

"Ha, ha, ha. So I am not the only one who can be fooled by appearances!"

Alhasan gave him a wry smile.

"Do not confuse a soldier's tactics with his beliefs. They might not be the same."

"Of course," admitted Alhasan. "But tell me, how did your wife come to study medicine?"

"Her father was an imam at the Azhar mosque in Cairo—a learned man. He taught her to read so she could study the Qur'an, but he let her roam through his library. She became interested in the works of Al-Razi and read *The Comprehensive Book of Medicine*, all twenty-three volumes. When she was older, she helped a local midwife, and later she became one herself. Her reputation grew throughout Cairo until she was summoned to help the Caliph's wife deliver a son, Ali az-Zahir. She saved the queen's life, and was appointed to be a general physician in the court of Al-Hakim. When I was wounded in battle, she looked after me. It wasn't just my body she cared for; it was my spirit as well."

Alhasan nodded. "The 'science of physic' Al-Razi called it, separating the physical from the spiritual, but believing a good physician must master both to heal the body."

"Yes. My wife mastered both. I wouldn't be here if she hadn't. The memory of killing that man...." Al-Ghazi stopped himself.

"Go ahead," Alhasan said. "Say it."

"I had killed many men in battle, but not like that."

Alhasan looked into the distance.

"Perhaps she can see you when you get to Cairo," said Al-Ghazi. "She no longer serves in the court, but she still takes patients."

Alhasan looked at his hands, which had long held pens and books, but which had now killed a man.

"I remembered what you said, Al-Ghazi. I chose life. Allah will decide if it was right."

Chapter Eleven

Sadeem bint Mourad slammed down her pen.

"Words, words, words! I am tired of words."

Her mother and sisters looked up at her.

"If you break that pen, you will pay for the next one," said her mother.

"I am not talking about the pen; I am talking about philosophy," said Sadeem.

"'Words, words, words?' Is that Aristotle?" asked Rania, Sadeem's eldest sister.

"Funny," said Sadeem. "All I am saying is I am tired of all these words. Last week we copied the words of theologians who said the world was created at a certain time. Today we are copying the words of philosophers who say the world is pre-eternal."

"And?" asked Rania.

"And it can't be both!"

"You must understand both sides of the argument before you can draw a conclusion," said their mother.

"But Mother, the theologians understand the philosophers, and they disagree with them. And the philosophers understand the theologians, and they disagree with them. I understand them both, and I think they are both wrong."

"Perhaps they are, and you can write a book about it," said Hadil, Sadeem's older sister.

"And then my words will be added to their words, and my opinions to their opinions, and my errors to their errors."

"I don't understand this sudden frustration with your studies, Sadeem," said her mother. "You have never complained before."

"It's just that I am tired of arguments that can't be proven," said Sadeem. "It's like you always say: 'If the patient doesn't get better, throw away the book.'"

"That was an exaggeration."

"I know it was, Mother, but that is your belief. 'A book might pre-scribe a treatment, but if the body does not respond to it, that treatment must be discarded.'"

Sadeem lowered her voice, imitating her mother. "'It does not mat-ter how famous the physician is or how long his words have been fol-lowed. What matters is making the person well.'"

Rania and Hadil laughed. Even Sadeem's mother had to smile.

"You even said that you have discarded what was written by Al-Razi and replaced it with your own treatments," said Sadeem.

"That is true. I have."

"That is all I am saying. Study is just words, words, words."

"Sadeem, experience will teach you many things. Some of those things will contradict what you have been taught. In those cases, yes, trust your experience.

"But learning by experience is slow. Studying what has been written by the ancients and the modern scholars will help you gain knowledge more quickly, and knowledge will make your experiences more mean-ingful. These 'words, words, words' will help you understand what you experience. The experience will be deeper, richer, because it will have the context of knowledge."

"I suppose you are right," said Sadeem, getting up and sitting on the edge of the table. She pretended to have a horse's reins in her hands. "Someday I might be out in the middle of the desert, riding a horse and looking up at the stars and wondering, 'Did the universe have a beginning in time, or is it pre-eternal?'"

"That is correct," said her mother, approaching her daughter. "Or perhaps you will be at a festival, and a handsome young prince will come up to you and ask, 'What do you think, Young Lady? Was the world created in time, or is it pre-eternal?'"

Rania and Hadil laughed.

"That would depend, Your Highness," said Sadeem with exaggerated modesty.

"Depend on what?" said her mother in a deep voice.

"On whether Your Highness is a theologian or a philosopher."

Everyone laughed.

"All right, that is enough philosophy for one day," said Sadeem's mother. "If you want something with definite answers, let us turn to mathematics."

"Mother," said Sadeem, "can I study geometry with Rania and Hadil? I'm tired of arithmetic. It's too easy."

"Not today, Sadeem. I don't have time explain the basics to you."

"You don't have to!" said Sadeem. "I started reading *Elements* myself. I know I can keep up. Please!"

"I see," said her mother. "You gathered knowledge by reading 'words, words, words,' and now you think you are prepared for the real experience."

Sadeem smiled. "I suppose you could say that," she said. "What do you want me to say? You were right, Mother. You are always right."

"Your sisters were two years older than you are when they started with Euclid, but I suppose we can give it a try."

"Thank you, Mother! I promise I will work hard."

"Fine, but don't let this become an excuse for not studying philosophy."

"I won't, Mother. I promise I will study the philosophers' words, words, words until they are falling out of my ears, ears, ears."

Chapter Twelve

The murmurs of mourning doves and a shaft of light falling across his face stirred Alhasan into consciousness. He opened his eyes and gazed at a tessellated patch of light on the wall above him. Home at last, he thought for a moment. He closed his eyes and remembered his dream. Nada's slender hands, tattooed with henna, were folding his laundry. He watched, transfixed, and fell back asleep.

The mourning doves cooed on the ledge outside the window, rousing the mathematician from sleep. The air was humid, stifling. He opened his eyes and saw his cedar chest standing open with his Qur'an on top of the clothing. Where was he? Inebriated by his dreams, he closed his eyes and dozed again.

He was awakened by a shout; someone had called his name. He sat up and listened, his confusion dissipating like morning mist. This was not his home, but an inn; he was not in Basra, but in Al-Khandaq, a village on the outskirts of Cairo, where Al-Ghazi had left him the day before.

"Alhasan Ibn Alhasan Ibn Al-Haytham, come down!" a voice from the street commanded.

Alhasan stood and looked around the room. He picked up a chair, set it beneath the window, climbed on top of it, and peered through the latticework. The street below was filled with horses, each carrying a mounted soldier. In the midst of the horses stood a donkey festooned with a silver harness. On the donkey sat a man in a white robe with gold trim.

One of the soldiers called out his name again.

"Just a moment, please!" shouted Alhasan. "I am coming."

He removed a clean robe from his chest and slipped it on. He stepped to the water basin, splashed water on his face, and daubed it away with a towel before putting on his turban, a vest, and the belt that held his purse. He stepped out the door and rushed down the winding, stone staircase that led to a large room facing the street. He opened the door, stepped outside, and slipped on his sandals.

"Are you Ibn Al-Haytham?" asked a soldier.

"I am," said Alhasan.

"Come forward," said the soldier.

The soldier led Alhasan through the maze of horses. They reached an opening where the man in the white robe sat on his donkey. "Your Highness," said the soldier, pulling Alhasan down with him as he knelt. "This is Ibn Al-Haytham."

"So you are the great mathematician from Basra?" said the man on the donkey.

"I am a mathematician," said Alhasan, embarrassed. "Some call me great."

"Arise," commanded the man on the donkey.

Alhasan stood and looked at the man in the gold-trimmed robe. He had piercing blue eyes flecked with reddish gold. No one had introduced them, but Alhasan knew he was standing before none other than Al-Hakim Bi-amr Allah, ruler of the Fatimid Caliphate.

"You are the man who boasted that if you were in Egypt you would do something to regulate the Nile so that the people could derive benefit from its ebb and flow?"

"Yes, Your Highness. I wrote those words."

"And is it true? Can you do this thing?"

"I believe I can, Your Highness. I have not seen the Nile, but I have seen the Tigris and Euphrates, and I know their waters can be dammed and diverted."

"The Tigris and Euphrates? Do you dare to compare these to the Nile?"

"No, Your Highness. The Nile is in a category by itself. Yet every river is made of water, and water can be controlled."

"And how do you propose doing it?"

"I have drawn up plans," said Alhasan. "If it pleases Your Highness, I can get them from my room."

"Do it."

"Yes, Your Highness. But before I do, I wish to convey the sincere greetings from Caliph Al-Qadir, Ruler of the Abbasid Caliphate. I have a letter of introduction."

Alhasan reached toward his purse but stopped when he heard the sound of a sword being drawn.

"Don't move," commanded a voice behind him.

Alhasan froze in place.

"There is no need for a letter of introduction," said the Caliph. "Unless I am mistaken, there is only one man in the world who believes he can tame the Nile."

The Caliph laughed, and a few chuckles arose from his guards.

"Besides, Mourad Al-Ghazi delivered the gifts from Caliph Al-Qadir to my court in Cairo. We appreciate the gesture, and the payment for your services is on its way to Al-Qadir."

"I am honored that you have accepted these tokens of friendship," said Alhasan.

"Yes, yes. Now, the plans."

Alhasan slipped through the throng of soldiers, rushed into the inn, and ran up with winding staircase. He was not much of a diplomat, to be sure, but at least he had said the proper words. Now he could focus on things he understood well.

He removed his Qur'an and his clothing from his trunk and took out the large leather portfolio he had stored at the bottom. As he lifted it into the sunlight, the cover's gold leaf design shone. He thought of the young artisan in Damascus who had decorated the cover and of his beautiful sister, Hannah. He wished the artisan had told him that Hannah had three other brothers who would not look kindly on a suitor from Basra for their sister.

Alhasan put the portfolio under his arm and raced down the staircase for the second time. All the travel, all the danger, all the romantic diversions, and all the waiting was over. The moment he had been preparing for was here. As he made his way into the street and through the maze of soldiers, Alhasan asked God for wisdom, patience, and guidance.

"Your Highness," said Alhasan, kneeling again before the caliph.

"Arise. Now show me."

Alhasan started to hand the portfolio to the caliph, but Al-Hakim never moved.

"No, no, Mathematician," said a familiar voice. Alhasan turned and saw Al-Ghazi, seated his black stallion. "Hold it open for him."

Alhasan lowered the portfolio. "My apologies, Your Highness," he said, opening the portfolio. "You will see I have copied Claudius Ptolemy's map of the Nile."

"I cannot see anything," interrupted the caliph. "Get him something to stand on!"

The soldiers looked around. "Here, a bench," shouted one of the guards, dismounting. "Help me." Two others dismounted and followed the first. The crowd parted as the soldiers returned with the bench. They set it next to the caliph's donkey, and Alhasan stepped up onto it.

Alhasan carefully opened the portfolio. "You can see from this map that near the first cataracts, the river narrows as it passes through the rocky area. It's the rocky, uneven bottom that creates the rapids. There, the banks of the river are solid granite, forming a natural channel." He turned the page to show a drawing he had made. "If you were to block the channel with a dam made of stone, the water would not be able to flow around it. Held in by the granite banks, the water would rise behind the dam, forming a lake. At a certain height, we would allow water to run through a spillway." He turned another page to show the Caliph a schematic. "This will keep the water flowing, but at a reduced rate. As the level of the lake goes down in the summer, the spillway could be opened further, allowing more water to flow through it and preventing a drought."

"And how much stone will you need to block the river?"

"I have read that at this point the river is about seven times the width of the base of the Great Pyramid. A dam would have to be wider than that; say, eight times the width. To hold back a sufficient amount of water, the dam would have to rise at least 70 *dhirā' al-yad* above the level of the river, or about one quarter the height of the Great Pyramid. Of course, a dam would not have to be as thick as the Pyramid at its base; however, it would not be as tapered, either. Estimating the dam's average width at eighty *dhirā*, its volume would be almost exactly the same as that of the Great Pyramid—more than five million cubic *dhirā*. I would recommend using blocks no more than two *dhirā* cubed, or about two million five hundred thousand stone blocks."

"If the volume is the same as that of the Great Pyramid, why didn't the Ancients build such a dam? Surely they were capable."

"I agree, Your Highness. They had the knowledge and skill to do it. The problem, I imagine, was that the Ancients viewed things like rivers as living beings, deities. Remember how the Prophet Muhammad, peace be upon him, had to disabuse the people of Mecca of the notion that idols made of wood and stone could be divine. As Muslims, we know there is but one God, Allah, and that He made the world and all that is in it. We know a river is but a river, a body of water. It is not living. It is not holy. It is a gift from Allah, to be used by the people."

"I heard you were a theologian before you became a mathematician; now I believe it."

"I am not saying anything that is different than you would hear in any mosque. The Prophet, peace be upon him, freed mankind from all sorts of superstitions."

"How long do you believe this project will take?"

"That depends on the number of workers. My estimate is that ten thousand workers would need ten years to quarry the stone, transport it to the site, and put it in place."

"You want ten thousand workers for ten years?"

"Your Highness, I would need to see the site before I said anything definite, but that is my estimate."

"Let me ask you this: Have you calculated the cost of employing ten thousand workers for ten years?"

"No, Your Highness."

"The Ancients had slaves, you know."

"Of course."

"We pay men for their work, Alhasan. I abolished slavery."

"Yes, Your Highness."

"What are you paid?" Al-Hakim asked a soldier to his right.

"I receive one dinar a week," replied the soldier.

"Do you hear that, Alhasan? One dinar a week is fifty-two dinars a year—for each laborer. At that rate, a force of ten thousand laborers would cost five hundred twenty thousand dinars a year, isn't that right? You want me to pay more than five million dinars over ten years?"

"I am an engineer, not a financier, Your Highness. I studied the feasibility of the construction, not the cost."

"Cost is part of feasibility, isn't it? I had heard that you were mad, and now I believe it!"

The caliph turned to Al-Ghazi. "Take him back to Basra. And see if you can stop the emissaries with my payment to the Abbasids. I am not going to pay for this."

"Yes, Your Highness," said Al-Ghazi.

The caliph laid his reins against the neck of his mount and turned away from Alhasan. As the Fatimid ruler's donkey ambled away, Alhasan closed his portfolio and stepped down from the bench. Suddenly the caliph stopped and wheeled around. "And destroy the bench he was standing on!" he shouted.

Immediately two soldiers dropped from their mounts and kicked the bench apart.

Satisfied, the caliph turned and rode away, the soldiers closing ranks around him. Only one man was left in the street with Alhasan.

"So, we are together again, Mathematician," said Al-Ghazi. "I will return with the gray tomorrow morning. We will leave then."

"Wait," said Alhasan. "I have an idea."

Chapter Thirteen

"Take me to the Caliph."

"Ha, ha, ha. You are mad, after all."

"No, Al-Ghazi. Listen. I can explain it all to him—how to build a dam with fewer men and less expense."

"He already has made up his mind, Mathematician. Didn't you see what he did to your bench?"

"I know. I made a mistake. But I can rectify it. Believe me."

"Get some rest. I will be back tomorrow. You can finally go home."

"No, Al-Ghazi, I have come this far. I cannot go back a failure. Please, take me to him."

Al-Ghazi walked over to his mount, which was nibbling at a weed growing between the stones in the road. He took the reins in his hand and reached up toward the saddle. "We leave in the morning."

As Al-Ghazi put his foot in the stirrup, Alhasan came up from behind, grabbed the handle of the North African's sword, and pulled it from its scabbard.

"What are you doing?" said Al-Ghazi, turning around. He had a smile on his face, but it disappeared when he felt the tip of the sword against his throat.

"I have killed before," said Alhasan.

Al-Ghazi said nothing.

"Move away from your horse. I will ride to the caliph myself."

"No, Mathematician. I will take you."

"Get out the way. Don't try to stop me."

"Don't you realize what will happen to me and to my family if you ride up to the caliph, unaccompanied by me? You are my charge. If you leave me behind, he will have my head as well as yours."

Alhasan was unmoved.

"Please, Mathematician. If not for me, then for my wife and children. They need me."

"How do I know you won't push me from your mount once we are riding? You have no use for me now."

"First, I give you my word. But if that isn't enough, you can hold the sword to my neck. I think your plan is foolish, but it isn't worth dying over. If I accompany you, you have a chance of surviving."

Alhasan saw truth in Al-Ghazi's eyes. After all, he did owe his life to the man. When the brothers of the beautiful Hannah set upon him in Damascus, it was Al-Ghazi who had fought them off.

"Then let's go," said Alhasan, handing Al-Ghazi his sword.

Al-Ghazi slid the sword into its scabbard and climbed onto his mount. He then took his foot out of the stirrup. "Put your foot here and take my arm. The scholar grasped the North African's wrist with one hand and put the other on the horse's flank. He raised his foot to the stirrup and, with the soldier's help, clambered onto the horse's back. Al-Ghazi chirped into the black's ear, and they were off.

Caliph Al-Hakim and his entourage had not gotten far. Within minutes, Al-Ghazi caught up to them.

"Peace be upon you," said Al-Ghazi as he rode up to the last soldier in the train.

"And upon you be peace," said the soldier.

"I need to speak with the caliph."

"Of course," said the guard, recognizing Al-Ghazi. "Pass."

Al-Ghazi threaded his way through the mounted guards until he was directly behind the caliph. The donkey's silver harness clinked with every step the animal took.

"Your Highness," said the North African, "may I have a word with you?"

Without looking back, Al-Hakim motioned for Al-Ghazi to come forward.

Al-Ghazi rode up to the hindquarters of the caliph's donkey. "Your Highness, Ibn Al-Haytham wishes an audience with you."

The caliph stared straight ahead, saying nothing. The only sounds were the clip-clop of hooves on the cobblestone street and the tinkling of the donkey's silver harness.

"Your Highness, I was wrong to propose such an outlandish scheme," Alhasan said. "I sincerely apologize."

The caliph pulled on his reins, and his donkey came to a stop. Al-Ghazi and the caliph's entourage stopped as well.

Alhasan took this as a sign that he had been granted an audience. If nothing else, Al-Ghazi and his family appeared to have escaped the wrath of the caliph.

"Your Highness, what I said back there was ridiculous. I am sorry I wasted your valuable time. But your dismissal caused me to rethink the problem, and I believe I have a solution that would reduce the manpower needed—and of course the cost—by a factor of ten, and possibly more."

He paused. The caliph said nothing.

"My original plan called for the quarrying of symmetrical stone blocks to build a kind of wall across the river bed. The bulk of the manpower would have been used to quarry, shape, and transport these blocks to the building site. As you correctly pointed out, the Ancients used an army of slaves to perform these tasks when building the Pyramids."

A fly buzzed into the donkey's ear, and the caliph's mount shook its head. Its silver harness jingled like a set of chimes.

"Also, a great deal of time and labor would have been spent diverting the Nile so a foundation could be dug in the riverbed. My estimate for the work was likely correct, but I have realized that none of it is needed."

The caliph sat motionless in his saddle. His silence was encouragement enough.

"As I mentioned before, the cataracts are bounded by granite banks. What I propose is to use the granite already at the site to build the dam."

The fly buzzed into the caliph's face. He waved it away.

"Instead of symmetrical blocks, we would use rough-hewn ones. Instead of diverting the river and building a wall, we would use a crane to drop the granite blocks into the river, creating a solid but honeycombed base for the dam."

Alhasan paused momentarily.

"Continue," said Al-Hakim.

"I don't know if Your Highness has read accounts of the river animal in Al-Andulus that builds dams across small streams. These cunning creatures construct these dams with logs, branches, stones, and mud. The dams are not watertight, but they slow the water enough to create a small pool behind them—essential to the animal's survival. What I am proposing is similar. The dam will not be watertight, but it will slow the Nile enough to create a lake that can be tapped during times of drought. Water will flow through the honeycombed bottom—instead of through a spillway—to keep the river flowing throughout the year."

The caliph said nothing, so Alhasan continued. "By quarrying in place, by not diverting the river, and by creating a honeycombed base, the caliphate could build a dam across the Nile for less than half a million dinars in as little as five years."

Caliph Al-Hakim looked at Al-Ghazi. "Take him," said the caliph.

"Yes, Your Highness. I apologize for the intrusion."

"No," said Al-Hakim. "Take him to the cataracts. I want to know if this can be done."

"Your Highness?"

"Outfit him with whatever he needs—equipment, manpower, supplies."

"Yes, Your Highness."

"And Al-Ghazi, I recognize your part in this. It took courage to bring him before me a second time. I will reward you for your efforts in bringing him here from Basra."

"Thank you, Your Highness."

"I understand that you were attacked by bandits and that you saved Ibn Al-Haytham's life."

"Yes, Your Highness, but he saved my life first. You would be surprised at how well he handles a sword."

"I heard you had enough of your wife's medical knowledge to keep this man from dying in the desert. For this and for the courage you showed today, I will instruct my treasurer to pay you three thousand silver dinars for services rendered to the caliphate beyond the call of duty."

Al-Ghazi slid down from his mount and knelt in the street. "Your Highness, you are much too generous."

"You have earned it, Mourad Al-Ghazi. But I am not quite finished with you."

Al-Ghazi looked up. The silver plates on the donkey's harness cast a myriad of tiny reflections across the North African's face.

"I want you to accompany Alhasan to the cataracts and return him to me unharmed. Upon his safe return, you may remain in my service or, if you wish, you may retire."

"Yes, Your Highness. It is an honor to serve you."

The caliph turned to Alhasan. "Go to the cataracts. Survey the area. Do a precise analysis of the feasibility."

"I will, Your Highness."

"Don't forget—"

"The cost?"

The caliph smiled. He lifted the silver-plated reins and gave them a shake. His donkey ambled forward. "God willing, your plan will work."

"God willing," said Alhasan.

Chapter Fourteen

The next morning, Al-Ghazi brought the gray to the inn where Alhasan was staying. Alhasan was sitting outside when the North African rode up.

"I am almost packed," said Alhasan. He waited for the North African to dismount and then led him toward the door.

"I will carry your trunk," said Al-Ghazi. "I suspect the wound isn't fully healed."

"Thank you," said Alhasan. "As a matter of fact, it was a bit of a strain running up and down the stairs yesterday."

"Ha, ha! I hope you didn't ruin my handiwork!"

Alhasan touched the scar through his robe.

"I don't think so," said Alhasan. The truth was that he had felt something strange—like a tearing—inside the wound when had fetched the plans for the caliph.

The two men walked inside and greeted the innkeeper.

"Peace be upon you," they said.

"And upon you be peace," replied the innkeeper, a white-bearded man with deep lines in his forehead.

"You might have seen the commotion with the caliph yesterday," said Alhasan.

The innkeeper nodded.

"He has summoned me to the palace, so I will be leaving sooner than I expected. I would like to pay the bill."

"I wouldn't think of accepting your money for such a short stay," said the innkeeper.

"But we settled on a price," said Alhasan.

"Yes, we did, but I could never accept your payment now."

"Alright," said Alhasan.

"No, he insists," Al-Ghazi said to the innkeeper.

"Insists?" asked the old man.

"Yes. He insists on giving you something for his stay," said Al-Ghazi.

"Well, in that case, I will accept forty-five dirham for the three nights' stay."

Alhasan just stood there.

"Pay him, Mathematician," said Al-Ghazi.

Alhasan took his purse from his belt and removed a piece of silver.

"Never mind," said Al-Ghazi. "Your Abbasid coins will only confuse the matter."

The soldier reached into his own purse and produced Fatimid money.

"Here," he said, counting out five coins—four tens and a five.

"Thank you, Sir," said the innkeeper.

"We will get his things," said the Al-Ghazi, gesturing toward the stairs.

Inside the stairwell, Alhasan looked over his shoulder at his companion.

"That was stupid," said the Abbasid scholar. "That man wanted to give me the room for nothing."

"No, he didn't."

"Yes, you heard him—probably because the caliph himself has summoned me."

"Ha, ha, ha!"

Al-Ghazi's laughter echoed off the stone walls.

"You are new to Egypt, Mathematician. You didn't realize the inn-keeper was posturing. Every merchant here refuses payment at first. You have to insist on payment. Only then will he name a price."

"I see," said Alhasan. "So, you saved me from making a fool of myself."

"No, you made a fool of yourself. I saved you from debtors' prison."

Al-Ghazi laughed at his own joke.

Inside his room, Alhasan folded the robe he had worn and put it in his trunk. He picked up the papers he had been working on and slid them under his clothing. He placed his prayer rug on top of his belong-ings and the Holy Qur'an on top of that. He eased the lid closed and latched it.

"Let's go," he said.

Al-Ghazi hoisted the trunk onto his shoulder and followed Alhasan out of the room and down the stairs. As they passed by the innkeeper, the old man gave them a wave. "In my seven-three years, that was the first time I glimpsed a caliph," said the man, smiling. "I hope you will come again."

"Don't worry," said Al-Ghazi. "If he fails the caliph, he will be back soon enough."

Al-Ghazi hoisted the trunk onto the back of the gray. Alhasan steadied the cedar box as Al-Ghazi fastened it with rope.

The sound of horses' hooves on a cobblestone street pleased Alhasan. At last he was back in a city. As he and Al-Ghazi approached the center of Cairo, the walls and buildings got taller, and the decora-tions became more elaborate. They passed finely wrought palaces, mau-soleums, and pavilions. The marketplaces they passed were large and well kept. Tiled wells and pools beckoned along the way.

In the old capital of Fustat, they came upon a new mosque.

"What mosque is this?" asked Alhasan.

"It is called the Mosque of Rashida," answered Al-Ghazi. "Caliph Al-Hakim had it built two years ago. The site used to house a Christian church. That's why there are Christian graves around it."

Alhasan looked where Al-Ghazi was pointing and saw at least two dozen stone crosses laid out in rows.

Looking ahead, Alhasan saw six minarets in the distance, towering above the buildings. This puzzled Alhasan. He gestured toward the horizon. "I thought Cairo had four great mosques: Al-Azhar, Qarafa, Ibn Tulun, and Jami Al-Atiq. But I see six minarets."

"Al-Hakim has built another mosque as well. Its name is Bab Al-Futub, but everyone calls it the Mosque of Al-Hakim. It was begun by Caliph Al-Aziz, but Al-Hakim finished it."

"And what is the sixth mosque?"

"There is no sixth mosque."

"But I see six minarets," said Alhasan. "Count them."

"Yes, there are six minarets, but two of them belong to the mosque of Al-Hakim."

"Two minarets?" said Alhasan. "I've never heard of such a thing, except for the mosques in Mecca and Medina."

"And that, no doubt, is why Al-Hakim built it that way."

Alhasan waited for Al-Ghazi to explain what he meant, but the soldier fell silent. Perhaps he felt he had said too much already.

As they approached the walled inner city, known as the citadel, Alhasan could see that Al-Ghazi was right about the two minarets. The eastern wall of the citadel ended at the base of a square minaret; next to the minaret stood the mosque of Al-Hakim. On the other side of the mosque stood a cylindrical minaret. A wall extended westward from the base of the second minaret.

"One square minaret and one round one," said Alhasan. "How strange."

"It pleases the caliph," said Al-Ghazi.

As they passed through the eastern gate of the citadel, the call to midday prayer sounded throughout the city.

"Come," said Al-Ghazi. "We will pray at Al-Hakim's mosque."

They tied their horses to a tree outside the mosque and joined the line to go inside.

Looking up, Alhasan saw inscriptions carved into the pale, stone walls. He identified the inscriptions as Qur'anic verses. In the middle of the minaret was a clay medallion emblazoned with the words, "Your friend is only Allah, and His Messenger, and the believers who perform the prayer and pay the alms, and bow them down." Carved in the medallion's field were the words, "From the shadows into the light."

"From the shadows into the light," said Alhasan.

"What's that?" asked Al-Ghazi.

"The inscription," said the scholar of Basra.

"Ah, yes. The interior is covered with them as well," said Al-Ghazi. "Al-Hakim chose the verses himself."

Above the entrance to a staircase were the words, "My Lord, lead me in with a just ingoing, and lead me out with a just outgoing." Alhasan had seen this inscription on mosques before, but he had never seen the one engraved around a nearby window, known as the Parable of the Light:

> God is the Light of the heavens and the earth; the likeness of His Light is as a niche wherein is a lamp—the lamp in a glass, the glass as it were a glittering star—kindled from a Blessed Tree, an olive that is neither of the East nor of the West whose oil well nigh would shine, even if no fire touched it; Light upon Light. God guides to His Light whom he will. And God strikes similitudes for men, and God has knowledge of everything.

Alhasan loved these verses. They formed a perfect description of the God he loved. He thought about the man who ordered them carved into the edifice. Although Alhasan had spent only a few minutes with Al-Hakim, he felt a kinship with him.

His admiration for the caliph only grew when he entered the mosque. The interior was less ornate than other mosques he had visited. Its only decoration was a wide band of inscriptions running along the walls, just below the ceiling. Alhasan was impressed with the simplicity of the design.

As the faithful assembled for prayer, Alhasan scanned the verses. Each section of wall contained the beginning of a *sura* of the Qur'an.

Alhasan decided that the visible verses stood for the invisible ones as well, and that the entire Qur'an was represented on the walls. For a moment, the writer of books felt as if he were standing in the middle of one. He felt wonderfully small and insignificant, like a spider that had crawled through an opening of the binding. Perhaps this is what heaven is like, he thought as the prayers began. He delighted in the idea of spending eternity wandering through the pages of the Qur'an, surrounded by the Word of God.

Midday prayers completed, Alhasan and Al-Ghazi made their way toward the palace of Al-Hakim.

"First we must find quarters for you," said Al-Ghazi. "I will call upon the vizier. I assume he has been briefed on the matter."

"I thought I would stay with you," said Alhasan.

Al-Ghazi looked at Alhasan. "You're joking, right?"

"Not really," said Alhasan. "I welcomed you into my home. I thought you would return the favor."

Al-Ghazi let loose his customary belly laugh.

"Welcomed me, indeed!" Al-Ghazi said, placing his hand on the hilt of his dagger. "After I convinced you it was in your best interest."

"I understand that better now," said Alhasan, looking toward the palace of Al-Hakim. "Besides, I forgave you long ago, even before you came to my aid in Damascus. It's just that you have spoken of your wife and children so often, I would like to meet them."

"And meet them you shall, but not tonight. I have been away for four months."

As they climbed the steps of the palace, Alhasan watched his shadow moving up the stairs—a dark, oblong shape, rippling as it climbed the risers and crossed the corners of the treads. It looked like a dark fish, swimming up a stream.

The physics of the image baffled him. His body blocked the light from the sun, creating the shadow, but how, exactly, did the angles of the stairs alter the visible shape? How did the forms of the shaded stairs enter the eye so quickly? Or, if the eyes sent rays to the stairs, how did they transmit information about the shifting form back to the brain, which perceived it all as a fluid motion? He shook his head. How could something as simple as a shadow raise so many questions in his mind? What was wrong with him? Was he crazy, as the governor of Basra believed and as Al-Ghazi seemed to think?

"No," he said aloud.

"What did you say?" asked Al-Ghazi.

"Nothing," said Alhasan. "Nothing at all."

The vizier knew little about Alhasan—only that Al-Ghazi had been sent to retrieve him from the Abbasid Caliphate several months before.

"Four months to go to Basra and back?" asked the vizier.

"The Mathematician was easy to find, but hard to bring back," said Al-Ghazi. "It took a little convincing."

The vizier glanced at Alhasan. "You didn't want to come?" he asked.

Al-Ghazi broke in. "He was willing, once he understood the importance of the situation."

Alhasan saw a small grin cross Al-Ghazi's face.

"But the Abbasid Caliphate was a different matter. They were reluctant to part with their great scholar, even though they were not putting him to good use," Al-Ghazi added.

"But you persuaded them," said the vizier.

"The Caliph's silver persuaded them. I was but the courier."

"Still, four months."

"We were waylaid," said Alhasan. "Twice."

The vizier cocked an eyebrow.

"Bandits set upon us between Baghdad and Damascus," explained Al-Ghazi. "The Mathematician was severely injured."

"Al-Ghazi saved my life," said Alhasan. "He cauterized my wound and stitched me together like a sack of rice."

"Later, The Mathematician was imprisoned in Damascus," said Al-Ghazi.

"What was his crime?" the vizier asked.

"Attempted murder," said Al-Ghazi.

"I was defending myself," said Alhasan. "I fell into a fever when my wound became red. In my delirium, I said crazy things to the young woman who cared for me."

"Who happened to have four brothers," broke in Al-Ghazi.

"I thought she was an angel sent to bring me to heaven," said Alhasan, "and I greeted her as such."

"He was raving, and she called her brothers to restrain him," added Al-Ghazi.

"I thought they were the demons sent to torture me in my grave."

"He fought them off. A little too well," said Al-Ghazi. He gave Alhasan a look of pride. "He knocked one out. The man fell backward and hit his head on a stone bench. He lingered near death for a week. I convinced the authorities not to execute the scholar unless the man died. As it turned out, the man survived."

"The remaining brothers set upon me, but Al-Ghazi fought them off. When the injured man recovered, they let me go," said Alhasan.

"So it seems Al-Ghazi saved your life twice," said the vizier.

"Yes."

"You left out the best part," said Al-Ghazi.

Alhasan glared at Al-Ghazi but said nothing.

"It seems that the girl took the ravings seriously," Al-Ghazi continued. "She thought Alhasan had proposed marriage. Her brothers backed her up. They wouldn't let him leave town until he married her."

"You got married?" asked the vizier.

"No," said Alhasan. "We managed to escape."

"The Mathematician can disappear like a djinni when he has to," laughed Al-Ghazi.

"We slipped away in the middle of the night," said Alhasan.

"Don't leave out my diversion."

"Yes, Al-Ghazi hosted a feast on the other side of the city. He purchased a huge tent, carpets, and arranged for the food and entertainment."

"Everyone attended," added Al-Ghazi, "except, of course, for the guest of honor."

"By dawn, I was far away."

"Far? It took me two days to catch up to him!"

"That's quite an adventure," admitted the vizier.

"Yes, and I owe it all to Al-Ghazi," said Alhasan.

"No, you owe it all to Caliph Al-Hakim," said Al-Ghazi.

"Well, in any case, we are glad you are here," said the vizier. "God willing, you will help our people."

"God willing," agreed Alhasan.

Chapter Fifteen

"What is madness, Mother?" asked Sadeem in between bites she picked from the roasted lamb on the brass tray in the center of the carpet.

"Different physicians have described it differently. Indeed, no one seems to agree on what it is."

"A madman has no sense," said Al-Ghazi. "His body is in this world, but his mind is not."

"That would describe many men, Mourad—poets, dreamers, philosophers."

"What I mean is that a madman not only is unmindful of this world, but he is disconnected from it. Small things. Does he have the sense to survive? I have seen madmen who simply sit and stare, without the sense to eat or drink, and fools who rave, wallowing in filth."

"Is Ibn Al-Haytham mad, Father?" asked Sadeem.

Al-Ghazi chewed a large piece of the roasted lamb. "It is difficult to say. I have watched him for three months, and I still am not sure."

"You said he designed a water clock for the governor of Basra. A man who can do that cannot be mad, can he Father?"

"I never saw the clock, so I don't know if it's true of if it's one of the one thousand-and-one stories that Al-Jashyari told."

"He has the sense to eat and drink, does he not?" asked Khadija bint Muhammad.

"That he does, and to survive. I taught him how to protect himself with a sword and dagger, and he did it."

"Really, when?" asked Sadeem, leaning forward and plucking an olive from a small ceramic plate that lay near the lamb.

"Yes, when, Mourad? You never told me about any fighting." Khadija bint Muhammad gave her husband a withering look.

"There are always clashes when you cross the desert with treasure," said Al-Ghazi. "Some bandits set upon us in Syria, that's all. I had just been teaching The Mathematician how to fight on horseback, and he acquitted himself well."

"Really?" asked Sadeem. "What did he do?"

"Yes, Father," said Hadil. "Tell us about it."

"You girls think it is exciting, but it's not. It's just life. Some men would rather take the riches of others than to earn it for themselves. They think they can frighten and overpower. They must be met with brute force. There is no other way."

"But what happened?" asked Sadeem. "You said you had just taught Ibn Al-Haytham to fight. What did he do? Did he fight like a madman?"

Al-Ghazi looked at his wife.

"You're the one who brought it up," she said.

Al-Ghazi bent forward, placed the tip of a knife into the joint of the lamb's hip, twisted it, and pried free the leg. "We were in the rolling plains of Syria," he said, slicing a piece of meat from the bone. "I had taken Ibn Al-Haytham away from camp, behind a mound, and I was teaching him what to do—and what not to do—with a scimitar on horseback. I heard shouting, and I rode up to the top of the mound. A group of bandits, nearly twenty, had fallen on the guards at the camp. I told The Mathematician to stay where he was, and I rode into camp. Two bandits rode out to meet me. I attacked one, but the other leapt from his mount and knocked me to the ground. We fought with swords. I didn't realize the first one had circled back and was coming up behind me."

"What did you do?" asked Sadeem.

Al-Ghazi chewed the morsel of lamb. "This lamb is delicious," he said.

"Daddy!"

"What did I do? I didn't know he was there, so I didn't do anything. I was fighting the one who pulled me down when I heard a scream and saw Ibn Al-Haytham racing past on the gray. His robe was streaked with blood, so I knew something had happened. He attacked the one I was fighting, causing him to drop his sword. I finished him off. When I turned around, I saw the man on horseback without an arm—The Mathematician had cut it off at the shoulder, just as I had taught him. The bandit was trying to stop the bleeding with his hand, but he collapsed and fell from his mount. I knew he would die, if he wasn't dead already. I ran toward the wagon and attacked a bandit who was trying to lead it away. Then they all fled."

"Do you believe Ibn Al-Haytham saved your life?" asked Khadija bint Muhammad.

"Quite possibly," said Al-Ghazi, taking another piece of meat from the lamb's leg. "I mean, yes. I didn't see the one on horseback. If he had struck me, either he or the other one would have killed me."

"But you weren't hurt?" asked Khadija bint Muhammad.

"No."

"Was Ibn Al-Haytham hurt?" asked Sadeem.

"Oh, yes. I forgot. When the bandits fled, I turned and saw Ibn Al-Haytham on the ground, kneeling over a dead man. A bandit had knocked him off his horse, and they had fought hand-to-hand. The Mathematician was bleeding, but he had managed to kill his attacker with his bare hands."

"How, Daddy?"

"Yes, how?" asked Hadil.

Al-Ghazi leaned forward, placed his thumb on the eye of the lamb, and shoved it back into the skull. "Like that," he said.

"Oh, Mourad!" said Khadija bint Muhammad.

"Well, that's what he did. I thought it was skillful. I was proud of him."

"It sounds mad," said Sadeem.

"It's like I said, Sadeem: It's life. I taught him to do whatever was necessary to survive." He glanced at his wife, and she gave him a knowing look.

"The proper assessment of madness takes time and much observation," said Khadija bint Muhammad. "You cannot discern it from one or two actions."

"Did Al-Razi write about madness, Mother?"

"Yes. I will find the book, and we will discuss it at our lessons, if you and your sisters wish."

"I don't care about it," said Rania.

"Me, either," said Hadil.

"You two are just lazy," said Sadeem.

"How bad was Ibn Al-Haytham's injury?" Khadija bint Muhammad asked her husband.

"Pretty bad. You would have been proud of me: I stitched the wound closed the way you showed me."

"Did you cauterize it first?"

"Yes. It stopped the bleeding, and I was able to sew him closed with catgut."

"Will you show us how to do that, Mother?" asked Sadeem.

"Now, that is something I would like to know," said Rania.

"Me, too," said Hadil.

"I can show you if you want," said Al-Ghazi. "I'm an expert—ha, ha, ha."

"Yes, that will be part of your training," Khadija bint Muhammad told her daughters. "It's coming."

"The wound turned red," Al-Ghazi admitted.

"What did you do?"

"What could I do? We were in the desert. When we got to Damascus, I took him to a physician. He and his daughter tended to him. The herbs and compresses worked, but not before Ibn Al-Haytham suffered a delirium. But that's another story."

"I don't know why the wounds of some patients heal perfectly and the wounds of others turn red and swollen. I use the same materials and do the same thing every time."

"I don't know, either," said Al-Ghazi. "I am just glad my patient survived. Otherwise, Al-Hakim would not have blessed us with his generosity."

"What is another story?" asked Sadeem, plucking another olive from the plate.

"Oh, nothing," said Al-Ghazi, tearing a piece of flatbread into quarters and dipping a piece into a bowl of hummus. "Ibn Al-Haytham was delirious, and in his delirium he mistook his nurse for an angel and made her think he was in love with her."

"I hope she didn't take it seriously," said Khadija bint Muhammad. "A physician should know what is said in delirium is nonsense."

"She was quite young. I don't think she understood."

"Maybe she wanted to think it was true," said Sadeem. "Maybe she was like Rania, and she was afraid of becoming an old maid."

"If anyone is going to be an old maid, it's you," said Rania. "No one likes a know-it-all."

"I don't care if I am an old maid," said Sadeem. "I'm going to work with Mother and discover out why some wounds turn red and others do not."

"No one is going to be an old maid," said Al-Ghazi, "now that you are the daughters of the richest captain of the guard in the caliphate."

Chapter Sixteen

T hings happened quickly in Cairo. Less than a week after Alhasan had arrived, a caravan was ready to survey the Nile. The vizier had asked Alhasan to list the things he needed for the mission. Two days later, everything arrived: measuring sticks of various lengths, a plumb bob affixed to a tripod, and writing materials—paper, pens, ink, and pounce. He also asked for a team of experts to accompany him, including three engineers, a surveyor, a cartographer, a mathematician, and—mindful of the events of his trip from Basra—a medic. All reported for duty on the morning the expedition was to set out for the Nile.

Aware of the dangers of a journey through the desert, Al-Ghazi asked for a detachment of forty Mamluk guards. The Mamluks were fierce fighters who had been recruited as boys from far-flung corners of the Fatimid Caliphate. Like Al-Ghazi, the Mamluks were expert swordsmen, archers, and horsemen. Each followed the *furusiyya*, the Islamic code of military conduct that emphasized courage and sacrifice. Unlike local recruits, whose loyalties remained with their tribal leaders, the Mamluks could be trusted to fight to the death for Al-Hakim.

Twenty civilian servants were deployed to cook, set up tents, and tend a small herd of goats for eating. The caravan included three wagons pulled by oxen. The young secretary to the chief of police, Ali bin Ahmad Jarjarai, was assigned as Al-Ghazi's special assistant. When Al-

Ghazi introduced Al-Jarjarai to Alhasan, the scholar noticed that one of the young officer's wrists was bandaged and his hand was missing.

"What happened?" asked Alhasan, nodding toward the injury.

"Al-Hakim ordered my dismemberment. He believed I had opened some letters. He later apologized and had me reinstated, but not my hand, as you can see," said Al-Jarjarai, holding up the bandaged stump.

Alhasan understood the joke, but he did not laugh. "That is a shame," he said.

"I'm getting used to it. You do most things with one hand, anyway. At least I can ride a horse and serve on this mission."

"Yes," said Alhasan. "One's body need not be whole to serve Allah, as long as one's heart is."

Alhasan placed his cedar trunk in one of the wagons.

Al-Ghazi rode up. "Are you ready?"

"Yes. It appears all is in order," said Alhasan.

"I have your old friend, the gray," said Al-Ghazi, pointing to the horse. "Ride near the front, behind me."

Sitting high in his saddle, Al-Ghazi rode around the caravan, barking orders.

Alhasan patted the pink snip that ran down the gray's soft muzzle. "Ready for another adventure?" he asked the horse.

The gray bobbed his head and then shook it.

"That's an ambiguous answer," Alhasan joked to no one but the beast. He patted the gray's jaw. "I'm afraid I feel the same way." He stopped a passing Mamluk soldier to get a boost into the saddle and then joined the caravan, which had begun to move forward. He guided the gray past the carts and wagons and took his place behind Al-Ghazi and Al-Jarjarai.

Instead of leading the caravan south, Al-Ghazi abruptly turned right at the first street and headed west. Alhasan said nothing, since Al-Ghazi appeared as decisive as ever.

The ox-drawn wagons bumped along slowly. The horses walked, but, even at that, they often had to stop to wait for the wagons to catch up. The air was sweltering. Alhasan could not take his eyes off the Pyramids, which gleamed a bright white against the cerulean sky. He longed to examine them up close. *When I return from the cataracts, I will hire a boatman to ferry me across the river*, he thought, eyeing the slanting sails of the feluccas making their way up and down the Nile.

As they approached the great river, Alhasan saw a row of feluccas and several barges docked on its banks. As they crossed the last road leading south before the river, Alhasan rode up next to Al-Ghazi. "Where are we going?" he asked.

"We are going to cross the Nile," said the captain of the guard.

"Cross the Nile? Why?"

"Several reasons. For one thing, the road on the western side of the river is flatter and straighter than the road on the eastern side. As a result, you can see further on the western shore, so it's easier to spot trouble. There are hills and ravines on the east side that afford bandits the element of surprise. And, finally, the Pyramids are on the west side, as you can see."

"The Pyramids?" said Alhasan, astonished but pleased. "Are we stopping at the Pyramids?"

"Yes."

"But why?"

"Al-Hakim wants you to inspect them before making any decisions about the feasibility of building a dam."

"This is wonderful news," said Alhasan.

"Wonderful?" scoffed Al-Jarjarai. "What is wonderful about pagan tombs?"

"They are marvels of engineering," said Alhasan, "and monuments to human ingenuity, ambition, and vision."

"If I were the caliph, I would tear them down, stone by stone, and use them to build a mosque to the one true God," said Al-Jarjarai.

"Don't worry, Al-Jarjarai," said Al-Ghazi, "we are going to inspect them, not worship at them. However, we will make our camp some distance away. If you would prefer to stay behind, you are free to do so."

Al-Jarjarai glanced at the giant stone monoliths. "No, I will go with you," he said. "Al-Hakim told me to accompany you wherever you go, to observe and to learn."

The teamsters drove their wagons onto the barges; those on horse-back dismounted and led their animals onto the barges as well. Those traveling on foot boarded the feluccas. Alhasan stood next to the gray, stroking its neck. Panic shone in the horse's eyes every time the deck pitched. "Nothing to fear," Alhasan told his mount, not knowing for certain if it was true. He continued to soothe the horse. "Your forebears traversed the waters for months," he whispered, recalling the story of Nuh. "You can survive for less than an hour."

When they reached the far shore, the boatman maneuvered the barge so the horses could disembark down a ramp. The crossing com-pleted, the small party rode toward the giant, stone tombs. Alhasan couldn't take his eyes off the monoliths, so vast they hardly seemed manmade. They appeared as symmetrical as the books had said, but he couldn't wait to measure them himself.

They reached the Pyramids in late afternoon. The civilians set up camp while Al-Ghazi, Al-Jarjarai, and Alhasan examined the ancient structures. Al-Ghazi held the measuring rod and performed other tasks so Alhasan could take his measurements. The Abbasid scholar wrote everything in a small, leather-bound notebook he had ordered along with the other supplies. The three men returned to camp just before sunset. The tents were up, the fires had burned down to coals, and food was cooking. Alhasan calculated the Qibla, and at sunset everyone faced Mecca to pray.

After prayers and a meal of roasted goat, Al-Ghazi and Al-Jarjarai went to their tents. Alhasan was too excited to rest. As the moon rose, he returned to the ancient edifices he had read about all his life. Stand-ing near the center of the greatest monolith, Alhasan felt overwhelmed by its enormity. He felt small, insignificant, but not how he felt in the mosque of Al-Hakim. There, he felt surrounded by the love of God and the beauty of His Word. Here, he felt oppressed by a blank monument of death. True, the pharaoh was prepared for a journey to an afterlife, but the Great Pyramid seemed nothing more than a vast tomb of impon-derable weight.

The feelings of doom lasted only a few minutes. As Alhasan approached the structure, curiosity took over. The engineer shouldered

past the theologian, and the mathematician pushed aside the philosopher.

Alhasan marveled again at the mathematical precision of the structure before him. *These men were geniuses*, Alhasan thought. He walked up
to the monolith and touched its smooth surface. He knelt down, laid his
cheek against the limestone, and peered along the surface. There were
imperfections in the plane, but all within a narrow tolerance.

Kneeling in the sand, Alhasan saw a movement halfway down the
slanting wall. A dark figure, the size of a person, was moving toward
him. This surprised Alhasan. He was sure everyone in his party was in
the camp. He certainly would have noticed someone walking up to the
base of the pyramid, but he had not seen anyone approaching. Alhasan
was not a superstitious man, but logic told him this must be a spirit,
emerging from the tomb to walk abroad.

Hunched over and moving slowly, the figure came closer. Rather
than cower before the dark presence, Alhasan stood and greeted it.
"Peace be upon you," he said.

The figure stopped.

"Peace be upon you," Alhasan repeated.

The figure straightened up. In the moonlight, Alhasan could make
out a face within the hooded robe. It wasn't the mummified face of a
long-dead pharaoh; it was the smooth, angular face of a teenage boy.

"Don't you speak Arabic?" Alhasan inquired.

The boy bolted into the open desert. Alhasan heard the clinking of
metal on metal and saw something drop from boy's arms. The boy
looked back but kept running.

Alhasan ran to see what the boy had dropped. Something sparkled
in the moonlight. Alhasan bent down and saw a large gem lying in the
sand. He picked it up. The stone was attached to a small, gold ring.

"Young man!" Alhasan shouted. "You dropped a ring! Young man!
Come back!"

The figure disappeared into the darkness.

Alhasan held the ring up in the moonlight. A large stone—larger
than his thumbnail—was set in gold, with two smaller gems on each
side. He explored the inside of the ring with the tip of his index finger.

Too small. He tried it on his little finger. It stopped at the first knuckle. It was a woman's ring, perhaps a child's.

It is beautiful, thought Alhasan. *Probably worthless, but beautiful.*

As he slipped the ring into the purse on his belt, he saw something glittering in the sand ahead. Following the tracks of the boy, he came upon what appeared to be a dagger in a sheath. The sheath was inlaid with jewels. When he picked it up, he noticed its weight. *Heavier than my dagger*, he thought. When he pulled the dagger from the sheath, he knew why: It was made of gold. Either gold enameling covered a base metal, or it was solid gold. He hefted the dagger in his hand. *This is worth something*, he thought.

The dagger handle was in the shape of an Egyptian god. The fact that a gold dagger is too soft to do much cutting made Alhasan think of something Al-Mas'udi had written in *The Meadows of Gold and Mines of Gems*: The ancient Egyptians buried their pharaohs with ceremonial ornaments to be used in the afterlife. *No wonder the boy didn't stop*, thought Alhasan. *He's a grave robber.* Another thought immediately came to mind. "The tombs of the pharaohs are cursed," Al-Mas'udi had written.

Alhasan slid the dagger into its sheath. Normally, he dismissed such legends as nonsense, but the manner in which the grave robber materialized out of nowhere, the way the gems winked in the moonlight, and the sheer immensity of the stone tomb behind him made the hairs on the back of his neck stand up.

"There is no god but Allah," said Alhasan aloud, adding, "Muhammad is the messenger of Allah."

He looked at the dagger and tucked it into his belt. *There's no taking it back, now*, he thought to himself. *I will treat it as a gift from God.*

He looked around, but he did not see any more of the grave robber's booty.

He returned to his tent. He lit his lamp and took the ring out of his purse. In the moonlight, the ring did not have much color. Many times he had noticed how colors dissipate in darkness. That was another mystery of vision he would like to explore. He held the ring up in the lamplight. The large stone gleamed a deep green. He tapped it against his teeth. Emerald. Not so worthless after all. He slipped it onto his little finger, down to the first joint. *How delicate was the hand that wore this ring,* he thought. A hand once held in love, perhaps, but long since laid to rest.

He heard a noise outside his tent and slipped the ring back into his purse.

"Mathematician," boomed the voice of Al-Ghazi.

"Just a moment," said Alhasan.

He pulled the dagger from his belt and slipped it under the carpet. He walked across the tent, pulled back the flap, and stepped into the darkness outside.

"You disappeared earlier," said Al-Ghazi.

"Yes, I returned to the Great Pyramid."

"That's what I was afraid of," said the North African. "I meant to warn you. There are grave robbers around these tombs. You must not go near them at night."

Alhasan nodded.

"Remember, Mathematician, you are my charge. I cannot let anything happen to you. I want to live long enough to enjoy the windfall I received for delivering you to the caliph."

"I understand."

"Tomorrow, God willing, I will take you to see the Sphinx, but in the daylight."

"I am looking forward to it," said Alhasan.

"Stay in camp for now."

"I will."

Alhasan retired to his tent. For a long time he lay on his carpet, turning the dagger over in his hands. The gems sparkled in the lamplight. *Who made this beautiful object? And for whom? Was it for the same young woman who wore the emerald ring? Was she a princess? Or a female warrior who accompanied her queen into the afterlife?*

Alhasan blew out the lamp and closed his eyes. He had devoted his life to answering questions using logic and mathematics. *But some questions can only be answered with poetry,* he thought before he slept.

Chapter Seventeen

The Sphinx lay to the east of the Pyramids, on lower ground, facing the Nile. The approach was from behind. Sand mounds covered the great beast's haunches and back. From behind, the monument appeared to be nothing more than a dome atop a rough-hewn pillar of stone. Only as one came around the side did one glimpse The Terrifying One, The Father of Dread.

What appeared to be a dome turned out to be half of a dome, the front of which was made to look like a headdress at the sides, with a sculpted face at the center. The face was wide and smooth, with high cheekbones and eyes fixed on the eastern horizon. The slope fell away to the east, partially revealing the monster's front legs.

"Do you know the Riddle of the Sphinx," Alhasan asked Al-Ghazi and Al-Jarjarai.

"I have heard of it, but I don't know what it is," said Al-Ghazi.

"What creature walks on four legs in the morning, two legs at noon, and three legs at nightfall?" said Al-Jarjarai.

"Yes, that's it," said Alhasan.

"What's the answer?" asked Al-Ghazi.

"Don't you know?" asked Al-Jarjarai.

"No," said Al-Ghazi.

"For that, the Sphinx would have strangled you and devoured you," said Al-Jarjarai.

"Let him try!" laughed Al-Ghazi, putting his hand on his sword.

"It was a woman—but she had the body of a lion, the tail of a snake, and the wings of a bird. You might have met your match," said Al-Jarjarai.

"Perhaps, if she were this size," said Al-Ghazi, gesturing toward the sculpture before them. "What is the answer, Mathematician? I am sure you wouldn't have asked if you didn't know the answer."

"The answer is Man," said Alhasan. "He crawls on four legs as an infant, walks on two legs as an adult, and uses a third leg—a cane—in old age."

Al-Ghazi laughed. "That's pretty good," he said. "I'll have to remember that. And what about this Sphinx? What is its riddle?"

Alhasan thought.

"Well?" asked Al-Ghazi.

"What creature calls out two times in the morning, four times at noon, and three times at sunset?"

Alhasan looked at Al-Jarjarai. The police secretary just shrugged.

"I don't know that one, either," said Al-Ghazi.

"That's strange, since you are one of them."

"Man?" ventured Al-Ghazi.

"No. One who submits to God."

"Ha, ha, ha," laughed the North African. "The number of repetitions of the *rakat* at each prayer time, morning, noon, and sunset. That's pretty clever, Mathematician."

Alhasan looked up at the stony eyes, fixed eastward. *Perhaps it asks why only a bit of the sun is visible as it rises, if its form enters the eye. And if the eyes send out rays, why do grave robbers disappear into the darkness?*

"I wonder if its entire body lies under the sand," said Alhasan.

"Why?" asked Al-Jarjarai.

"I would like to see what it looks like," said Alhasan.

"If you manage to build your dam across the Nile, perhaps Al-Hakim will allow you to uncover this creature next," said Al-Ghazi.

As they left, Alhasan tried to estimate the length of the monument, counting his steps along what would be the creature's spine.

"What are you doing?" asked Al-Jarjarai.

"Estimating its length," said Alhasan. "The body must be seventy-five *dhirā' al-yad* long, so the overall length, including the front legs, must be more than one hundred *dhirā*."

He tried to imagine its depth in the sand. *If the body is proportional to the head, the entire sculpture must be at least thirty* dhirā *high. That would leave almost twenty* dhirā *under the sand.*

Alhasan did not know much about excavation, but he thought it would be interesting to calculate how long it would take to uncover the entire sculpture. *Perhaps Al-Ghazi is right. Perhaps the caliph would let me excavate the monument if I succeed with the Nile.* The prospect pleased him.

By the time they returned to camp, the civilians had taken down the tents, rolled them up, and packed them onto the wagons.

"Let's move," Al-Ghazi called to the wagoners. "We will try to make Saqqara by nightfall." He turned toward Alhasan. "If you like pyramids, you might like Saqqara. It has a dozen or more, but not like these. They are ruins."

The trip was long and dusty; the heat, as usual, oppressive. Alhasan tried to relieve the boredom by working out the excavation of the Sphinx.

He calculated the approximate size of the sculpture and estimated the amount of sand immediately surrounding it. He added a little extra space, to allow viewers of the monument sufficient room to walk around it. He rode over to one of the wagons, estimated its size, and calculated the volume of sand it could hold if its sides were, say, two *dhirā* high.

He imagined digging a channel next to the Sphinx until the base was revealed and the original ground level was reestablished. Wagoners could back the wagons into the channel, one after another. Workers standing above the wagons could shovel down the sand, filling the beds. The wagoners would take the sand to a dumping site, and other wagoners would take their place. Eventually the channel would encircle the statue, so the wagons could be driven around it, rather than being backed in and out. Knowing Caliph Al-Hakim would want to know the cost of the excavation, Alhasan kept a tally of how many workers, wagons, and draught animals would be used.

By mid-afternoon it was clear that the slow-moving caravan would not reach Saqqara as planned. Al-Ghazi ordered Al-Jarjarai to lead the wagons off the road and behind a large sand mound. From the back of the mound, Alhasan could see that it was a ruined pyramid. Lines of stone jutted into the stand, as if a staircase had been buried. With no casing to protect it, this tomb had been robbed, Alhasan was certain.

The next day the caravan passed through Saqqara. Al-Ghazi was right: Pyramids were everywhere, but not impressive. The North African was willing to stop, but Alhasan had little interest in examining the ruins. He suggested the caravan continue toward the Al-Fayoum Oasis, the next planned stop.

Alhasan's thoughts returned to the excavation of the Sphinx. He began by verifying his earlier calculations. He recognized that the optimum scenario depended on the number of wagons required to encircle the sculpture. The problem was that the draught teams took up space. *What if the wagons were connected to one another, with no draft animals between them?* he thought. *That way, no space would be wasted between the wagons.*

He pictured a large team of oxen pulling the connected wagons. But a train of wagons heavy with sand would be difficult to move. A solution presented itself. *If the wheels rested on something hard, such as stone, there would be less friction, and they would roll more easily.*

Again he pictured the team of oxen. They were in the sand, where they would have traction. But the wagons were on a limestone pavement, so they would roll. It might work.

The bed of each wagon was six *dhirā* long and four *dhirā* wide. Alhasan figured it could hold forty-eight cubic *dhirā*. He estimated that thirty wagons would encircle the Sphinx, meaning they could haul away one thousand four hundred forty cubic *dhirā* of sand at a time. If the workers could fill four wagons per day, that would be five thousand seven hundred sixty cubic *dhirā* of sand per day. Estimating the amount of sand to be removed at two hundred eighty-eight thousand cubic *dhirā*, he was astonished to realize the task could be completed in just fifty days.

Alhasan continued to occupy his mind with planning the excavation of the Sphinx, even discussing it with Al-Ghazi and Al-Jarjarai. This time, if he presented a plan to Al-Hakim, it would be complete to the smallest detail.

"Why do you care so much about it?" asked Al-Jarjarai.

"It's a marvelous work," said Alhasan. "There is genius in it."

"Genius!" said Al-Jarjarai "It's an idol. If it were up to me, I would cover it completely."

"Idol, temple, tomb, or sculpture—we don't know what it is, Al-Jarjarai. And we will not know unless we uncover it and explore it. There is nothing to fear from these ruins. The ancient gods have fled, but the genius of man endures."

"Your mind deceives you, Ibn al-Haytham," said Al-Jarjarai. "You cast your eyes upon the glories of the past, but you do not see the pit at your feet."

"Come now, Al-Jarjarai," said Al-Ghazi. "I didn't see anyone worshipping there. Did you?"

Al-Jarjarai said nothing.

"I don't think our friend is proposing a revival of idolatry."

"He might be a friend of yours, but he is no friend of mine. The Qur'an says, 'Leave alone those who take their religion to be mere play and amusement, and are deceived by the life of this world. But proclaim to them this: that every soul delivers itself to ruin by its own acts.'"

"And it will find for itself no protector or intercessor except Allah," said Alhasan, finishing the verse.

"That's enough, Al-Jarjarai," said Al-Ghazi. "I don't know the Qur'an as well as you and Ibn al-Haytham do, but I am certain it forbids false accusations. I can assure you that this man does not take his faith as a play or amusement. When we were in the desert, we were set upon by bandits."

"So I heard."

"So you heard. Well, you heard right. And you will hear more. After the fight, our soldiers were burying the dead. Ibn al-Haytham was badly wounded, but he stopped the gravediggers. Do you know why? He stopped the digging because the graves were not perpendicular to the Qibla. He had me fetch his astrolabe so he could calculate the Qibla exactly, so that all might be buried appropriately. Do you hear what I am saying? All. Our men and our attackers. For what?"

Al-Jarjarai said nothing.

"For what, Al-Jarjarai?" shouted Al-Ghazi.

The scouts riding ahead turned and looked back.

"For play? For amusement?"

Al-Jarjarai just shrugged.

"I will not have you insult this man."

"I don't take orders from you, Al-Ghazi. I serve at the pleasure of Al-Hakim."

"We all serve at the pleasure of Al-Hakim," said Al-Ghazi. "And it is his wish that Ibn al-Haytham survey the Nile. Under my command. Whatever this man wants, whatever he needs, we are to provide it to him. That is the word of Bi-amr Allah. And that is what we are going to do. I will not tolerate dissension in my ranks. If you wish to report that to Al-Hakim, go ahead. I will send two Mamluk guards to accompany you back to Cairo."

Al-Jarjarai said nothing, and the three men rode on in silence.

Alhasan marveled at Al-Ghazi's words. The soldier made it seem as though everyone—the cooks, the servants, the Mamluks, the engineers, and even Al-Jarjarai—were there to serve him. Of course they all served Al-Hakim, but Al-Ghazi's speech made him feel respected, almost important. He turned and looked over the cavalcade. Groups as small as this had changed history; that, he knew. Would this one? He suddenly felt a great responsibility. He would do his best for Al-Hakim. He would use everything he knew and every talent he had to attack this problem. That is all he could do.

On the twenty-first day of the expedition, the caravan reached the village of Dendera. With plenty of time before sunset, Alhasan decided to look around for ruins. There were no pyramids, but a local villager—an old man with thinning gray hair and bushy, black eyebrows—told Alhasan about an ancient temple nearby. The man, dressed in rags, offered to lead him to the site. They walked through a maze of small buildings made with mud bricks until they came to a vast courtyard with a large, stone building at the end. The man left Alhasan at the courtyard, saying that the ruins were cursed.

Paying no attention to the old man's superstitions, Alhasan walked across the courtyard. The temple was beautifully preserved and covered with elaborate carvings. Fascinated by the strange markings, Alhasan walked around the outside of the building, studying them. On the back of the temple was a deeply carved frieze depicting several figures. *If this is the temple Tiberius completed, that might be Cleopatra with the young Caesarion,* Alhasan thought, gazing at the figure of a woman in an elaborate headdress, holding a staff and standing behind a young boy. *I remember reading about it.*

Alhasan made his way around the rest of the building, stopping now and then to admire different carvings. When he returned to the front, he entered the temple. The walls inside were covered with carvings as well. He was captivated by the tall, thin figures, some with the heads of dogs. The ceiling was painted with a procession of colorful figures against an azure background, although the scene had been blackened with soot, probably from burning incense. As Alhasan studied a frieze on the wall above the entryway, he noticed the old man who had guided him to the temple coming across the courtyard with two younger men, also dressed in rags. Even from a distance, Alhasan could see that the young men had daggers drawn.

Chapter Eighteen

Instinctively Alhasan felt for the dagger on his belt and touched the purse that held the emerald ring. Two against one—perhaps three against one. He stood no chance in a fight. He retreated into the shadows of the temple and looked for another way out.

Quickly but quietly he passed along a colonnade. A hallway led to the left. He ran a few steps down it before realizing it ended in rubble. He retraced his steps to the main chamber. Footfalls echoed through the temple as the bandits ran inside. Alhasan removed his sandals to make less noise.

He hurried along the colonnade toward the front of the temple, the hushed voices of his pursuers coming at him from different directions. Without looking back, he assumed the thieves had split up. He might have a chance against one at a time.

Near the back of the temple, light poured in through a window high on the wall to his left. Water must have seeped under the casement, because the plaster below it had fallen away, exposing water-stained, stone blocks. Knowing the blocks would be covered with plaster, the mason had left them rough-hewn, even jagged. Alhasan tucked his sandals into his belt and grasped the blocks with his hands. Finding a toehold, he lifted himself off the floor.

The footfalls were coming closer, but the pursuer must have turned down the dead-end hallway. Alhasan found another foothold, and another. One more step, and he would reach the window.

"Got him!" yelled a voice below.

Alhasan felt a rough hand grab his ankle.

Never pull away, Al-Ghazi had once told him.

In an instant, Alhasan lowered his body and kicked down with his left foot. His ankle slid through the bandit's grasp, and his heel struck the man on the bridge of the nose. The bandit fell backward, cursing.

Alhasan raised his left foot out of the bandit's reach and searched for a toehold. The bandit jumped up, but his fingers only grazed Alhasan's right heel. At last Alhasan found a crack. He pushed himself up just as a dagger clanged against the stone below. He reached up with his right hand, grasped the window ledge, and gave it tug. It was solid.

Finding a toehold with his right foot, Alhasan pushed himself high enough for his chest to be level with the casement. With both hands on the window ledge, he pulled himself halfway out of the window.

The ground was at least thirty *dhirā* below. The temple had been built on an outcropping, and jagged rocks ringed the building. Alhasan rolled on his side and looked up. The curved ledge of the roof was no more than three *dhirā* above the top of the window. Alhasan rolled onto his stomach and swung his legs onto the window ledge. The window was not high enough for standing, but he could kneel inside its frame.

The bandit below was joined by his accomplices. Yelling and cursing, they began to hurl pieces of plaster at Alhasan. One piece hit him in the ribcage. Another struck him on the leg. He held up a hand to protect his face, but it was only a matter of time until they hit him in the head.

Grasping the inside edge of the top of the window frame, Alhasan stood with his head and shoulders outside the temple wall. The ledge at the top of the wall curved toward him. He could reach it, but he doubted if he could pull himself up. He looked at the rock below. A fall would kill him.

A large piece of plaster hit him on the right thigh. His foot came off the window ledge, but he hung on with his hands. The bandits noticed this and began to pelt his fingers with shards of plaster.

Frantically Alhasan searched for a foothold outside the building. He noticed a bit of mortar missing between two blocks halfway up the left side of the window. He sidled over and raised his left foot until he found the crack with his toes. His foot slid far into the opening, braced on all sides. He brought his left hand out, knowing that if the bandits hit his right hand, he likely would fall. He reached up and grasped the ledge. He pulled on it, and it held. He whispered a prayer and let go of the inside of the window with his right hand, throwing his weight to his left side. He reached up, grabbed the ledge with his right hand, and steadied himself. He pushed himself up from the toehold, his right leg swinging free. He placed his elbows on top of the ledge and grasped the inside edge with his hands. He swung his right leg up and onto the ledge and then rolled onto the roof. He heard the bandits running through the temple, shouting. *There must be a way up*, he thought.

He ran across the roof, looking for a way down. A small room stood in the middle of the roof. He ran over to it, pushed the door open, and went inside. The room was dark, and it took a moment to see anything. It appeared to be a small chapel. Alhasan searched the floor, but he could not find a passageway to the temple below. He looked up. The ceiling was decorated with unusual carvings, but it offered nowhere to hide. He edged back to the door and looked around outside. He could see the thieves climbing a broken wall that led to the roof.

He ran to the back of the temple and looked down. Two sculptures of lions' heads and front paws projected from the stone wall. He heard the voices of the bandits as they neared the roof. There was only one place to go.

He lay with his belly on top of the ledge and let his legs dangle over the side. He looked down to make sure he was aligned with one of the lion sculptures. As the bandits clambered onto the roof, Alhasan slid over the edge, hanging by his fingertips. He felt for the lion's head with his toes. Nothing. His grip began to give way. "God is great," he whispered as he let go.

He fell for a long moment until his feet landed on the lion's paws, buckling his knees and causing him to fall forward against the beast's stone head. He grabbed the sculpture and held on.

The bandits ran across the roof. A voice echoed from inside the small chapel. *They would have found me there,* Alhasan thought.

He glanced down. It was too far to jump.

The bandits continued to shout to one another. One ran up to the ledge above him. Alhasan pressed his body against the wall and looked up. He could see the bandit's arm and hand against the blue sky, pointing toward something. Alhasan looked over his shoulder and saw three horses riding toward the temple. A bit of light flashed from the chest of the dark horse in the center. It was Al-Ghazi.

The thief's arm disappeared, and the rooftop became quiet. Alhasan stood on the lion's head, but he could not reach the ledge. He turned around so he was facing away from the temple and sat on the stone sculpture.

Al-Ghazi was still some distance off. Alhasan saw the bandits run down the hill from the temple and disappear into the maze of mud huts. He was safe, but he dreaded what Al-Ghazi would say when he discovered him perched high on the temple wall.

Chapter Nineteen

"Well, well, well. The grandson of the lion, seated on the head of his namesake!"

Al-Ghazi's perfect teeth shone in the bright sunlight as he laughed.

"Do you want to tell me how you got up there? Or, better yet, can you tell me how you plan to get down?"

Chagrined, Alhasan could only shrug.

Al-Ghazi turned to the Mamluk guard at his side. "Go get one of the wagons. Load it with tents, carpets, and anything else that will break his fall when he jumps." He turned to Al-Jarjarai. "And bring his mount."

"I was attacked by bandits," Alhasan said after the Mamluk and Al-Jarjarai had ridden away. "Two young men with daggers and an old man with gray hair and bushy eyebrows. They ran down there."

He pointed to the cluster of mud huts.

"What did they take?" asked Al-Ghazi.

"Nothing. I eluded them by dropping onto this...." He did not know what to call it. "Ornamentation."

"I see. And what are we supposed to do with these thieves who took nothing? Try them ourselves, or take them back to Al-Hakim?"

Alhasan did not know what to say.

"Well, at least you escaped," said Al-Ghazi. "A feline move. I wish I could have seen it."

The Mamluk returned with a wagon, and Al-Jarjarai led the gray. Before he jumped, Alhasan tossed Al-Ghazi his everyday dagger and the one the grave robber had dropped.

"Where did you get this?" asked Al-Ghazi, admiring the ancient weapon's jeweled sheath.

"Outside the Great Pyramid," Alhasan said. "A grave robber must have dropped it in the sand."

Even from nearly thirty *dhirā* up, Alhasan's landing was well cushioned.

"Let's get back to camp," said Al-Ghazi.

"You go ahead," said Alhasan. "There's a chapel inside I want to see."

"You must be joking. I can't do that."

"I know you are responsible for my welfare, and I know I nearly—I know I got into trouble, but I also am the person the caliph entrusted...."

Al-Ghazi raised his hand. "Enough, Mathematician."

"I'm serious, Al-Ghazi."

"Enough! All I meant is that I am not going to leave you here alone. I will stand guard. You go inside and do whatever it is that you think will please the caliph." He took the gray's reins from Al-Jarjarai. "You two go back to camp."

As Al-Jarjarai and the Mamluk rode away, Alhasan walked around the outside of the temple, looking for the place where the bandits had climbed to the roof. He found a stairway leading to a terrace and then followed the thieves' path up the broken wall. When he got to the roof, he walked over to the small chapel. It was late afternoon; the sun would set in less than an hour.

He entered the ancient sanctuary. The sun outside was not as bright as before, but he still had to wait for his eyes to adjust to the darkness. He went to the center of the room and looked up. A carving of a woman stretched across the ceiling. Perfectly preserved, the sculpture was amazingly detailed, right down to the lines etched into the palms of the woman's hands and across the joints of her fingers.

Alhasan turned his attention to the carving next to the woman. It was a large circle filled with engravings of human beings, animals, and combinations of both. He studied each figure carefully. Something caught his attention: Amidst the lion, sheep, bull, and other animals was a large scorpion. Beside the scorpion, a centaur held a bow and arrow. *It's a map of the heavens*, Alhasan thought. *Scorpio, Sagittarius, Leo, Taurus, Capricorn*. Some of the figures were unknown to him, but their sizes and positions corresponded to the other Greek constellations.

Four standing Egyptian women or goddesses seemed to hold up the heavens. Alhasan smiled to himself. All the ancient people believed that gods, goddesses, or giants held up the heavens. He knew differently. "God is the One Who raised the heavens without any pillars that you can see," said Sura Thirteen of the Qur'an.

The stars and planets are held in the heavens by an invisible force, thought Alhasan. *I do not know what that force is, but whatever it is, it is real and sensible.*

Alhasan wished he had paper to make a rubbing of the planisphere above him so he could compare it to the Greek maps of the heavens he had in his study in Basra. He admired the carvings a while longer before turning to go. On his way out, he glanced at the life-sized female form on the ceiling. *God willing, I will find a mate before I pass from this life.*

He rejoined Al-Ghazi outside, and they returned to camp, arriving just in time for evening prayers.

Riding through the desert the next day, Alhasan thought about the ancient depictions of the constellations on the ceiling of the chapel. *The stars are not people, nor are they animals, nor are they gods,* he thought. *Whatever they are, they are sensible objects, part of nature.*

"Deep in thought, again, Mathematician?" asked Al-Ghazi. "Thinking about your cat-like escape?"

"No."

"Then what are you thinking about today?"

"Nothing that would interest you, I'm sure."

"I'll decide what interests me," said Al-Ghazi. "Actually, many of your thoughts interest me. I have always wondered what a madman thinks. Besides, we have hours to go before we make camp."

"I am thinking about the stars."

"In broad daylight? That *is* mad."

Al Jarjarai, riding at Al-Ghazi's side, chuckled.

"As I said, I didn't think you would be interested."

"No, I am. Go on."

Alhasan regarded Al-Ghazi suspiciously.

"I was only joking about the madness," said the North African.

"That temple I visited yesterday: On the ceiling of one chamber was a carving that turned out to be a map of the heavens. I wish I could have copied it. Some of the shapes were the same as the ones we know—the scorpion, the lion, the bull."

"The shapes in the stars look the same to everyone."

"Yes, some of them do."

"That bothers you?"

"No. What bothers me is that no one seems to know—or care— what the stars actually are."

Al-Ghazi said nothing.

"The Greeks believed their gods cast beings into the heavens to give them immortality, and those immortal beings are the stars. But the stars are not living beings. They are objects. They appear to be arranged in shapes, but the ancient people who made that map saw different shapes than we do."

"What do you think they are?"

"I don't know. But it troubles me that the people who study the stars never seem to ask this question."

"What do you mean? Like whom?" asked Al-Ghazi.

"Claudius Ptolemy, for one," said Alhasan. "He described the circumstances of the heavenly bodies, their relative ordering, their distances from each other, the magnitude of their bodies, their different motions, and the varieties of their shapes, and he did it with utmost precision, but he never ventured to say what the stars actually are. Even

worse, when he describes their procession through the heavens—which
he does with mathematical precision—his calculations are based upon
the motions of imaginary points on the circumferences of imaginary circles. But the stars are not imaginary. They are real. Part of nature."
Alhasan gestured toward the Nile. "Like rivers, mountains, waterfalls,
clouds, or lightning."

"Or the sun," said Al-Ghazi.

"Or the sun. They glow of their own accord, but their colors fluctu-
ate. They are so small that it seems if you had a broom long enough, you
could sweep them all into an area smaller than the sun."

Al-Ghazi turned to Al-Jarjarai. "Ride ahead and find a suitable place
for midday prayer," he ordered.

After the police secretary rode off, Al-Ghazi resumed the conversation. "I will tell you something, if you won't laugh at me," he said.

"Go ahead. I won't laugh."

"That's true: You never laugh," said Al-Ghazi, barely suppressing a
laugh of his own. "One night I was riding in the Nile Delta when I came
upon a swamp. There was no moon that night, and I carried no torch.
Looking out at the swamp, I saw a bluish-green light floating above the
rushes. It hung in mid-air, burning from within, like a star."

"Why would I laugh at that? It sounds fascinating."

"Because I haven't told you the whole story."

"Go ahead."

"I couldn't take my eyes off the glowing object. Do you know how
your eyes start to play tricks when you look at something for a long
time?"

"Yes."

"Well, I kept staring at the green globe, and it seemed as if I could
see faces floating to its surface and then receding—human faces, appearing and disappearing."

"That is strange."

"One was a woman's face, the most beautiful face I had ever seen, or
have ever seen since. She stared at me with unearthly eyes. I got down
from my horse and waded into the bog. As I approached the ball, it

receded. I stepped further into the swamp, sinking up to my ankles in ooze. Something told me to go no further. When I stopped, the ball stopped. I took a step backwards, and it came closer. Finally, I spoke to the woman. She started backwards and disappeared into the sphere of light. I stepped out of the swamp and waited, but she never reappeared. The light drifted away and suddenly went dark."

Alhasan waited, but it seemed Al-Ghazi had finished.

"I suppose you feel embarrassed that you spoke to the figure in the globe, but I don't know why you should. You were confronted with something real, a sensible object. It was really there, right?"

"Yes."

"It was real, and you observed it carefully. Lacking experience with such things, you tried to move closer. That didn't work. You spoke to it. Considering what you were seeing—the woman's face—it makes per-fect sense."

"Perhaps," said Al-Ghazi. "But this ball of light—hovering in place—perhaps that is what a star is, but at a great distance. It looked like a star right before it vanished."

"I see what you mean." Alhasan paused, debating whether or not he should say what was on his mind. Finally he confided: "I didn't tell you something, either. When we were at the Pyramids, I thought I saw a ghost come out of the tomb. It was moving toward me, so I spoke to it."

"What did you say?"

"I said, 'Peace be upon you.'"

"What did it say?"

"It didn't say anything. It turned and ran. It was not a ghost at all. It was a grave robber."

"Ha, ha, ha," bellowed Al-Ghazi.

As usual, Alhasan had no idea why Al-Ghazi was laughing.

"You're lucky he didn't cut your throat."

"I suppose I am. But my point is that, confronted by something unknown, I, too, spoke to it."

"So I am as mad as you are—ha, ha, ha."

Alhasan shrugged. "You always make a joke out of what I say."

"How else to pass the time in this desert?"

Alhasan rode along in silence.

"Don't be angry with me, Mathematician. I understand what you are saying, and I appreciate it. Believe me, I have never told anyone about what I saw in the swamp. But I told you, because I knew you would believe me."

"I am glad you told me about it," said Alhasan. "It gives me something to think about." He paused before adding, "This world is full of mysteries."

Chapter Twenty

Alhasan heard the cataracts before he saw them. At first, it sounded as though a merchant were pouring a sack of beans into a wooden bowl. As the caravan drew nearer, it sounded more like a rockslide rattling down a ravine. As the sound grew louder, an invisible mist reached the travelers, cooling their faces. As the caravan swung to the east to approach the river, a rainbow appeared over the cataracts.

"Look," said Al-Jarjarai. "The rainbow was God's sign to Nuh that there would never be another great flood, but here, perhaps, it is a promise that the life-giving flood will recur each year."

"I see we have two theologians in our party," said Al-Ghazi. "I didn't realize that surveying a river called for so much spiritual expertise."

"Have you studied theology?" asked Alhasan, trying to make peace with Al-Jarjarai.

"Yes, I have," said Al-Jarjarai.

"Where?"

"Why, at the House of Wisdom," said Al-Jarjarai. "I thought you knew."

"No, I didn't. And who was your teacher?" asked Alhasan.

"Abdelali Haddaoui," said Al-Jarjarai proudly.

"Abdelali, my old friend," said Alhasan. "I assume you never expounded on rainbows to him."

"Why not?"

"Because Abdelali Haddaoui would never countenance such a thought."

Al-Jarjarai looked offended.

"Come now, Mathematician," said Al-Ghazi. "I know Haddaoui is your friend, but you cannot know for sure what he would countenance and what he would not."

"Perhaps I have outgrown his teachings," said Al-Jarjarai.

"Ridiculous," said Alhasan.

"Why?" asked Al-Jarjarai. "Abdelali Haddaoui said you did. He said you came to the House of Wisdom as his student and left it as his teacher."

"I'm not sure you should compare yourself to our honored guest," said Al-Ghazi. "I heard him lecture at the House of Wisdom. He was spellbinding." The North African shot Alhasan a mischievous glance. "In fact, you might say he left his audience in disbelief. Am I right, Mathematician?"

Alhasan said nothing.

"Well, he left me in disbelief, I can assure you!"

"Rainbows appear everywhere," said Alhasan. "They are part of nature, not signs from Allah."

"Heresy," said Al-Jarjarai.

"Read the Book," said Alhasan. "God's promise to Nuh was given in words, not in a sign. Allah said only that the rainbow would remind Him, Allah, of the covenant He made with Nuh. And even then, Allah spoke only of rainbows that form in the clouds, not the ones that appear in a mist. You should avoid attributing your own thoughts to your Maker."

"Rainbows are miraculous, and miracles are God's domain, not Man's," said Al-Jarjarai.

"Rainbows are part of nature," repeated Alhasan, "and they can be understood by Man."

"You and your Mu'tazilism. No wonder Abdelali Haddaoui liked you," said Al-Jarjarai. "Well, things are changing, Ibn al-Haytham. Mu'tazilism is falling out of favor. Quickly. You, Abdelali, all of you questioners—you're on your way out!" He kicked his horse in the ribs and galloped away.

Al-Ghazi shook his head as the young man rode off. "I will never understand these pedagogical differences."

Alhasan gave the soldier a puzzled look.

"Ha, ha, ha—I thought you might like that word. My wife taught it to me."

Alhasan watched Al-Jarjarai ride away. "That young man has strong opinions. I wonder if it's true, about the spirit of inquiry."

"Things change, especially at court," said Al-Ghazi. "I have seen scholars praised one day and damned the next, all on the word of an adviser."

"I suppose you are right."

They rode on quietly as Al-Jarjarai disappeared behind an outcropping at a bend in the road ahead.

"I suppose you plan to study the rainbow, once you have solved the riddle of the stars," said Al-Ghazi, his eyes on the colored mist hanging above the river.

"If Allah grants me time to do it, yes."

Once the caravan reached the cataracts, Alhasan saw what was causing the noise he had heard from afar: Smooth depths of blue-green water swirled over rocky precipices, crashing onto boulders below and churning through narrow channels of stone.

Alhasan hoped to close off the Nile here, like putting a stopper in a bottle, but the great river spread out over the rocky terrain, creating countless islets and innumerable channels between them.

"Is this the place to make a permanent camp?" asked Al-Ghazi.

"I'm not sure," said Alhasan. "It depends on what is upstream from here."

"Then we will set up a temporary camp, and you can travel further south tomorrow," said Al-Ghazi. He turned to the driver of the first wagon. "There's a level spot between the rocks over there. Make camp there."

Alhasan and Al-Ghazi looked out over the rushing waters.

"What do you think?" Al-Ghazi asked Alhasan. "Can it be done?"

"I don't know," said Alhasan. "What worries me is that the people who built the Pyramids had the knowledge and skill to build such a dam, and yet they did not do it. I don't know if they refrained out of superstitions about the river, as I told Al-Hakim, or because they believed it could not be done."

"I hope, for your sake, it's the former. The caliph expects you to succeed."

Alhasan spent the next two days riding upstream from the cataracts, exploring them from the bank of the river.

"One site in particular intrigues me," Alhasan told Al-Ghazi. "There is a large island in the middle of the river. I would like to visit it, to see it close up."

"Very well," said Al-Ghazi. "I will have Al-Jarjarai secure passage for you."

"I would like the engineers, the surveyor, and the mathematician to accompany me."

"Very well."

Two days later, Al-Jarjarai presented two rowboats the locals used to navigate the river.

"Who will pilot the boats?" Al-Ghazi asked Al-Jarjarai.

"I will pilot one, and Tariq will follow me."

"No," said Al-Ghazi. "We need men who know the river."

"We can do it," said Al-Jarjarai.

"Bring me the men who sold you the boats."

"But Al-Ghazi," said Al-Jarjarai. "We are not crossing the sea."

"Bring them before midday prayer."

A brief audience with the boatmen about the river's currents convinced Al-Ghazi that each boat needed at least four locals—a pilot, a coxswain, and two oarsmen. With the larger crews, the expedition needed four boats instead of two.

The boats and crews secured, Alhasan and his assistants set out for the island. The waters were rough; only the quick reactions of the pilots, coxswains, and oarsmen prevented the boats from capsizing or running aground.

When the first boat reached the island, the pilot climbed the face of the outcropping, tied a rope around a boulder at the top, and let a line down to the passengers in the boat. Alhasan followed the pilot, and, one by one, the rest of the party climbed up the cliff.

Alhasan looked at the channel between the island they occupied and an islet to the east. He conferred with the engineers about the feasibility of breaking off parts of the island to fill the fast-flowing channel.

"We need to know the depth of the channel," said one of the engineers.

"I brought a measuring rod," said Alhasan. "It's tied in sections to the side of my boat."

"I will get it," said the engineer.

"It would be best to take measurements all the way across the channel," Alhasan told the pilot of his boat. "Is there any way to rig ropes between the islands so someone can take the measuring rod over the water?"

From the other side of the island came a scream. Everyone on the promontory rushed to see what had happened. A body was face-down in the water: It was the engineer who had gone to get the measuring rod. Rather than being swept away by the water, he remained in one place, but the force of the current kept him submerged. His robe billowed around his body, making him look less like a person than an underwater plant.

"His foot is stuck," yelled the oarsman in the boat.

The oarsman fashioned a loop with a rope and slipped it around his shoulders and chest. The coxswain looped the other end of the rope around the stem of the boat's prow. By then the oarsman was already in the water, drifting toward the engineer. When he reached the body, he dived down. The coxswain wound the rope around the stem so it wouldn't run out further. Alhasan held his breath to estimate how long the oarsman could remain underwater.

An inky stain spread through the water, enveloping the two men, making them invisible to Alhasan and the others at the top of the cliff. The onlookers stared at the cloudy water, but nothing happened. Alhasan couldn't hold his breath any longer; he took a gulp of air. It was taking too long.

Suddenly, two heads broke the surface of the water. The engineer was coughing, but alive. The oarsman had his arm around him. The coxswain and the other oarsman in the boat pulled on the rope, hauling the two men toward them like a catch of fish. When the engineer reached the side of the boat, the coxswain pulled him aboard. Blood spewed from the end of one of the engineer's legs.

"Tie it off, tie it off," shouted the pilot from the cliff above.

The coxswain cut a length of rope and wound it around the engineer's ankle. He then cut off a piece of the engineer's robe to dress the wound. As the boat rocked with the current, a pool of blood sloshed back and forth across the bottom of the hull.

"He had to lose his foot to gain his life," the pilot said. "He probably didn't feel the cut. The cold water numbed his leg."

The grisly scene in the boat and the near loss of life distracted almost everyone from the original mission. Since the engineer was alive, Alhasan wanted to continue working, but he knew he was the only one who did.

"We will return tomorrow and rig the lines between the rocks," the pilot told Alhasan. "For now, let's return to shore."

When the expedition returned to camp, Al-Jarjarai accosted Alhasan. "You almost sent a man to his death, and for what? Only to prove your boast about taming the Nile."

Alhasan said nothing, and the young police secretary walked away.

"Don't listen to him," said Al-Ghazi. "Every mission involves risk. I explained that to everyone before we began. No one was forced to come along. They all volunteered."

"He was retrieving a measuring rod for me."

"It does not matter. It was an accident. It was not his time."

"Thanks be to Allah," said Alhasan.

"Yes," said Al-Ghazi. "Allah is merciful."

"We must reward the oarsman," said Alhasan. "He risked his life to save a stranger."

"That is true," said Al-Ghazi. "I will direct the paymaster to give him a reward. What do you think an engineer's life is worth?"

Even without looking at Al-Ghazi's face, Alhasan could tell this was one of his jokes.

"Wait," said Alhasan. He knelt in the sand and wrote out a complicated equation. When he finished, he stood up and regarded his work. "With this set of givens and factors," he said at last, "I would say an engineer is worth four times the value of a captain of the guard."

"Ha, ha, ha," boomed Al-Ghazi. "I see you have acquired a sense of humor at last. Egypt truly is the land of wonders."

Chapter Twenty-one

As promised, the local boatmen rigged ropes between the two islands in the Nile. Four lines—two for the feet and two for hands—stretched between the rocky cliffs. In addition, the boatmen fashioned two safety lines to go around the waist of the man who would venture over the water. Each rope was looped around one of the hand lines to prevent the man from falling into the river, in case he lost his grip. Finally, two boatmen would accompany the man with the measuring rod—one in front of him and one behind—to steady the lines as he crossed.

"Please exercise the utmost caution," Alhasan told the party before they embarked on their mission.

Again the boatmen navigated the waters expertly, bringing their craft to the same spot where the party had landed before and where the engineer had fallen into the water. This time a rope ladder hung down the side of the cliff to aid in climbing to the top.

The heights safely scaled, Alhasan surveyed the rigging and climbed out on the ropes to test the strength of the lines.

"We need one more line, a baseline, taut and level between the islands, to establish a constant to compare to the measuring rod," Alhasan told the pilot. "Tie it to a stake in the ground, so we can raise it or lower it if necessary."

The baseline readied, Alhasan stood with his feet on the ropes. "Harness me to the lines," he said.

"Your Excellency," said the boat pilot, "I urge you to let another member of your party go out on the ropes."

"I cannot ask them to risk their lives for my endeavor."

"Let me do it," said the surveyor. "You are far too important to take such a risk."

"Your life is of equal value as mine," said Alhasan. "Perhaps greater, as you have more years ahead of you, God willing."

"God willing, I do," said the surveyor. "But I could not accomplish in ten lifetimes what you have accomplished in one. And, God willing, you will accomplish even more."

"Your Excellency, you should not take risks that jeopardize the entire expedition," said the pilot. "Besides, I assure you the lines are quite safe. Your assistant will be fine."

"Your logic is sound," Alhasan said to the pilot. He turned to the surveyor. "Go ahead."

Outfitted in the harness and equipped with the measuring rod and a plumb bob, the surveyor followed one of the boatmen out, over the water. First, he went the center of the channel and tied the plumb bob to the baseline rope to make sure the rope was level.

"It's not quite perpendicular," he called, looking at the junction between the rope and the plumb bob. "Raise your end."

The engineers raised the end of the rope. The surveyor motioned for them to keep going. They raised it more, and the surveyor motioned for them to stop.

Satisfied the line was level, the surveyor returned to the nearest bank and began to measure the depth of the river bottom at regular intervals, using the plumb bob to make sure the measuring rod was perpendicular to the baseline. He called out the measurements as he went, and the mathematician wrote them down. Slowly the surveyor worked his way across the channel. The current was strong, and the deeper the measuring rod went, the more the rushing water pushed it off the perpendicular. When this happened, the surveyor corrected the angle and repeated the measurement.

"The current is bending the measuring rod," Alhasan observed to the mathematician. "We will have to adjust for that when we do our final calculations."

While the surveyor measured the width and depth of the channel, Alhasan had the engineer and one of the boatmen measure the area and height of the island. "Perhaps there is enough stone on this island to fill the channel," Alhasan said to the engineer.

With the boatmen steadying the lines, the surveyor crossed the channel and returned without incident. The measurements complete, the party returned to camp.

Alhasan, the engineers, the surveyor, and the mathematician conferred. There seemed to be enough stone on the island to fill the channel to a height two *dhirā* above the present level of the river.

"It's a good start," said Alhasan, "but we will need more granite. As we stop the river, the level will rise."

"There is a granite quarry on the other side of the river," said one of the engineers. "The locals say its stone was used to build the Pyramids of Giza."

"I wonder if there are any masons in the area. It would be interesting to know how long it takes to quarry a two-*dhirā* stone cube and move it to the river," said Alhasan. "We could calculate how many blocks we need and multiply that number by the time and manpower required to put a block in place."

The next day, Alhasan explained his quarrying plan to Al-Ghazi. The captain of the guard dispatched Al-Jarjarai to find a mason.

It took two days, but Al-Jarjarai found an old man who had worked in the quarry. "The stonecutter says it takes four men—one to hold the chisel and three to hammer it—to make the holes they need to split the rock. He said a team of four could cut a block in three days and transport it from the quarry to the river in two."

"Does he have a team to cut a block?" ask Alhasan.

"I didn't ask him," said Al-Jarjarai.

"Why not?"

"It's obvious, isn't it? He already knows the answer. There isn't any need to quarry a block."

"Of course there is."

"I am telling you, the man worked in a quarry for twenty years. He is certain of his estimate."

"Men are certain of many things before they are proven wrong."

"That's your Mu'tazilism, Ibn al-Haytham. You don't believe in anything or anyone, except yourself."

"Al-Jarjarai," Al-Ghazi began.

"Wait, Al-Ghazi," said Alhasan. "It's true. I doubt. I doubt because I seek the truth. Doubt has served me well. Now, just imagine if this stonecutter's estimate—based on his recollection, his assumptions, his pride, or even his desire to impress—imagine if it is off by a day. No, not even a day, half a day. We might need two hundred fifty thousand blocks for this dam. His estimate would be off by more than one hundred thousand days. If we have two hundred fifty teams working—one thousand stonecutters—the estimate still would be off by five hundred days. That's almost a year and a half."

"Ask the mason to cut a block for us," said Al-Ghazi. He turned to Alhasan. "One block, or more?"

"At least three," said Alhasan.

"Ask the mason to cut three blocks for us. Negotiate a price. Have him begin as soon as possible."

"This is madness," said Al-Jarjarai. "Al-Hakim will hear how you wasted his treasure."

The next day, Al-Jarjarai returned with a price, and Al-Ghazi accepted it. The stonecutter and four of his sons spent the next two days locating a section of the quarry suitable for conducting the test. For centuries local residents had thrown refuse into the quarry. Debris dotted the stair-stepped pit. The mason and his sons cleared an area close to the river and marked the stone to be cleaved from the face of the rock.

The next morning the test got underway with Al-Jarjarai overseeing the work. Alhasan remained in camp with the engineers and the mathematician, working on estimates of how much stone would be needed to build the dam. Shortly before noon, one of the Mamluk guards rode into camp, shouting for Al-Ghazi.

"Captain, Captain," called the Mamluk, "come quickly."

"What is it?" said Al-Ghazi, emerging from his tent.

"Disaster, disaster. A man is hurt. Come quickly."

Al-Ghazi mustered the remaining Mamluk guards and ordered them to follow him to the quarry. Feeling responsible, Alhasan saddled the gray and followed.

By the time Alhasan reached the quarry, Al-Ghazi already had taken charge of the rescue, ordering ropes to be tied around a slab of granite that had broken loose and was crushing one of the workers. The medic was on one side of the man, and Al-Jarjarai was on the other. Two Mamluk guards had placed a lever at the side of the block, but they were unable to fit it under the stone. Alhasan felt useless.

The mason stood at the edge of the quarry with tears in his eyes. "My son, my son," he said over and over.

Alhasan stood next to the old man, trying to think of some way to comfort him. The young man was alive, but his legs were pinned under the granite slab. Rather than say the wrong thing, Alhasan remained silent. Remembering what he had seen other people do, he put his arm around the mason's shoulders. The old man went limp, and Alhasan struggled to keep him on his feet. The stranger looked him in the eyes.

"My son," he said.

"They will get him out," said Alhasan, not knowing if it was true, but praying it was.

Al-Ghazi had the Mamluks stretch the ropes across the quarry to the side opposite from the men with the lever. He ordered the horses tied to the lines and every available man to take hold of the ropes. On his command, everyone pulled. The edge of the stone lurched up. One of the Mamluk guards pushed the end of the lever under the block. The other guard slid loose stones beneath the slab to keep the edge in the air.

"Slowly release the lines," commanded Al-Ghazi.

The ropes went slack, and the block remained braced.

"On my command, pull again," called the captain of the guard.

The medic and the Mamluk guards grasped the lever.

"Ready?" asked Al-Ghazi.

The men nodded.

"Pull," he shouted, motioning to the guards on the ropes.

As men and animals tugged on the lines, the Mamluks and the medic pushed down on the end of the lever. The stone rose just enough for Al-Jarjarai to drag the worker to safety.

"Clear!" shouted Al-Jarjarai.

"Release the lines," commanded Al-Ghazi.

Alhasan tightened his grip on the mason's shoulder.

"He is free," he said.

The old man wiped tears from his eyes. "Praise Allah," he said.

Alhasan helped the mason down into the quarry. The young man was alive and, despite the pain, he was talking to his rescuers.

"My boy," said the old man, dropping to his knees beside his son.

"This is all your fault," said Al-Jarjarai, glaring at Alhasan.

"My fault?" said Alhasan. "It was an accident."

"There would have been no accident if you had listened to me. But you doubted. And you insisted. And this is the result."

Alhasan stared at the young man's crushed legs.

"You are cursed," said Al-Jarjarai. "You are cursed and this mission is cursed."

Alhasan looked at the young police secretary. "It was an accident, Al-Jarjarai."

Later in the afternoon, Alhasan took a walk by the river. Watching the water flowing past, he reflected on the day's events, the accident, and the feasibility of his plan. He sat on a rock, picked up a loose pebble, and tossed it into an eddy near the shore. He thought of the young man in the quarry and engineer who fell into the river. Responsibility rushed over him like a current, holding him down, making it difficult to breathe. He found another pebble and tossed it into the water. How many stones to make a dam? How many lives?

Hearing voices behind him, he turned and saw a group of Mamluks coming toward him. Al-Jarjarai was in the lead.

"There he is—the idolater," said Al-Jarjarai.

Alhasan stood, and the Mamluks surrounded him.

"What is this about?" asked Alhasan.

"This mission is cursed," said Al-Jarjarai. "One man lost his foot and another might lose a leg—all because of you."

He turned to the Mamluks.

"This man visits pagan tombs, worships in their chapels, and surrounds himself with their books. He pretends to be devout, but he secretly keeps counsel with ancient spirits. His evil is upon all of us. You saw. One man almost perished in the river. Another almost died today in the quarry. These are signs. If we ignore them, someone will die. We must end this mission now. And rid ourselves of this polytheist."

"Seize him! Kill him!" shouted the Mamluks.

"Stop!" commanded a voice from behind. It was Al-Ghazi on his black stallion.

The Mamluks froze in place.

"We will have justice, Al-Ghazi," shouted Al-Jarjarai.

"What kind of trouble are you stirring up, Al-Jarjarai?" asked Al-Ghazi, dismounting.

"Only what is deserved by this idolater."

"Idolatry is a serious charge."

"It is the appropriate charge, Al-Ghazi. You have ignored the signs, but I have not."

"I have been in the company of this man for months, and I have never seen him miss prayer, except when he was ill."

He turned to the Mamluks.

"You have seen him calculate the Qibla for prayer. I have seen him do it for the burial of bandits who attacked us and nearly killed him.

"What evidence do you have for this alleged idolatry, Al-Jarjarai, except for his interest in people of the past—and an argument you lost about Nuh and the Flood?"

"I have this!" said Al-Jarjarai, reaching under Alhasan's vest and pulling the jeweled dagger from his belt.

He held it up for the Mamluks to see.

"A golden idol," cried Al-Jarjarai, "proof of his devotion to the false gods of the accursed tombs."

"Idolater!" shouted the Mamluks. "Kill him!"

"Stop," ordered Al-Ghazi, taking the dagger from Al-Jarjarai's hand.

"You are right, Al-Jarjarai. This mission is cursed, but not because of Alhasan."

He turned to the Mamluks.

"It is this dagger that is accursed," he declared, holding the ancient weapon aloft.

He walked through the crowd of soldiers so all could see the golden figure on the handle. The Mamluks parted, afraid of being too near the idol. Al-Ghazi passed through the throng and took a few more steps toward the setting sun. He turned toward the group.

"The curse ends here!" he shouted.

With that, Al-Ghazi threw the dagger over the heads of the soldiers, Al-Jarjarai, and Alhasan. It landed in the river with a splash and disappeared among the cataracts.

"This mission is over," said Al-Ghazi. "We leave for Cairo in the morning."

Chapter Twenty-two

The room was dark when Alhasan awoke. He lay with his eyes open, staring at the ceiling, which was dimly lit with moonlight. Suddenly, he remembered the trial before Al-Hakim, the pronouncement of his madness, the order that he be placed under house arrest. Exhausted and defeated, he had collapsed onto this mattress. The sweet scent of straw enveloped him. How long had he slept?

He made his way toward the end of the room, where it adjoined another—the one with the door through which he had entered. He noticed something on the floor in front of the door and walked over to investigate. It was a tray with a bowl in the center. The bowl was dark, filled with food. He tried to open the entry door, but it was locked from the outside.

He carried the tray to the center of the room. Three rectangles of moonlight illuminated the carpet. Alhasan glanced at the window high on the wall. It was barred.

He placed the tray on the carpet and sat on the only cushion in the room. He lifted the bowl and sipped the broth. It was molokhia, the Egyptian stew made with jute leaves. Cold, but flavorful. He took another sip and began to eat.

Al-Ghazi had brought him to this place after the trial. That was hours ago. He had missed prayers at evening and nightfall; he would have to make up for them later. As he finished the stew, he decided to explore his quarters.

The two rooms—the one with the mattress and the one in which he was standing—made up the entirety of the house. Joined at the corner, the rooms formed a right angle. Judging from the position of the moon, the room he was in ran north and south; the other, east and west.

Across from the entry door, a second door led to a courtyard, bounded with high walls on the north and west sides. Alhasan noticed that someone—probably Al-Ghazi—had placed his sandals outside the door to the courtyard. Steppingstones led to a well in the center of the garden and beyond to a small lean-to covered with palm fronds in the northwest corner—the latrine. Alhasan put on his sandals and inspected the well. The moon was bright, and the scholar's head and shoulders cast a shadow on the silvery water below. He lowered the bucket to the water, let it fill, and hauled it up. He cupped his hands in the water, praised God, and took a sip. It seemed potable. He took two more sips, praising God with each one.

His thirst satisfied, he inspected the garden. The sandy soil was rife with weeds. A grapevine clung to life along the northern wall. Saplings grew from the stump of an olive tree near the western wall. Perhaps the tree had been cut down to discourage previous inmates from trying to escape.

A red tile walkway bordered the garden along the sides of the house. The northern end of the tiles had once been the floor of an outdoor kitchen. A short, broken wall ran along the tiles, dividing them from the garden. The northern wall was blackened with soot. Weeds sprouted in the remnants of an abandoned hearth.

Alhasan looked at the night sky. This much he had—his old friends, the celestial travelers. He recalled his last calculation of the Qibla and looked for Al-Jabbar, The Giant, whom the Greeks called Orion, above the roof of the house. He positioned himself so Saiph was aligned with the doorway leading inside. He picked out a spot on the far wall, directly below "the sword of the giant." He walked inside, never taking his eyes off the spot, and dug his thumbnail into the plaster, marking the Qibla. It was the best he could do without his astrolabe. Lacking his prayer rug, he dragged the carpet over so it was aligned with the Qibla and began to make up for his missed prayers.

The next morning, Alhasan awoke to the call of the muezzin. He smiled. The singer had a rich, clear voice—the finest he had heard since leaving Basra. He shut his eyes and listened, enchanted and inspired. He went outside to the well, washed, and returned to commence his morning prayers.

Afterwards, he returned to the garden, sat on the clay tiles with his back against the wall, and watched crimson clouds dissipate to pink and finally to gray.

He thought about his audience with Al-Hakim the day before. The testimony of Al-Jarjarai had been damning. Al-Ghazi had said something in his defense, but Al-Hakim had cut him off. The caliph then questioned him directly—about the accidents at the cataracts, the dagger he had found outside the Great Pyramid, his sitting on the lion's head on the side of the Temple of Hathor, and even about Ptolemy. The questions about Ptolemy had seemed to do the most damage. Al-Ghazi had tried to keep him from answering by discreetly shaking his head "no," but Alhasan had no choice. He was a scholar, and he had a duty to reveal the weaknesses in Ptolemy's work. That enraged Al-Hakim. Alhasan tried to explain himself, but the caliph wouldn't listen. "You're mad!" the caliph thundered. And with that, he ordered Al-Ghazi to lock him up.

Alhasan heard a rustling inside the cell. He got up and looked inside. Someone was sliding another tray of food under the entry door. He slipped off his sandals and ran across the room.

"You there! Wait!" shouted Alhasan.

He listened. Light, quick footsteps hurried away. He picked up the tray. It held a bowl of foule and a plate of hot flatbread. The food smelled delicious.

As he was finishing his morning meal, someone knocked at the door.

"Ibn Al-Haytham!"

It was a woman's voice.

"Ibn Al-Haytham, this is Mourad Al-Ghazi's wife. Please come to the door."

"I am here," said Alhasan.

"Have you eaten the meals I sent to you?"

"Yes."

"Please slide the empty trays under the door."

Alhasan fetched the trays and did as he was asked.

"Thank you for the food," he said as he watched the second tray disappear. "It was delicious."

"Thank you," said Al-Ghazi's wife. "Now, when you finish a meal, leave the tray partly under the door. Someone will retrieve it."

"I will," said Alhasan. "I have a question: Is the water in the well safe for drinking?"

"Yes," said Al-Ghazi's wife. "The last person imprisoned here drank it for three years."

"Three years?" said Alhasan. "Was he mad?"

"No. He was an enemy of the caliph."

"Do you know when will I be released?"

"No."

"I can't be here for three years!"

"For now, be patient. The caliph is angry that you did not make good on your claim about controlling the Nile, and he is convinced you are mad."

"May I have my chest with my books and papers?"

"No. The secretary of the police took them."

"Al-Jarjarai?"

"Yes. Mourad asked to bring them to you, but Al-Jarjarai refused him. He is quite powerful now that he has gotten you imprisoned."

"I need my Qur'an and my prayer rug, at least."

"I will see what I can do. But please, do not talk to my daughters when they deliver your meals. You only frighten them."

"Of course."

"And remember to leave the trays by the door."

"I will. And again, many thanks for the meals," said Alhasan.

"It is an honor to have one of the world's great minds living among us," said Al-Ghazi's wife. "I am sorry that it is under these circumstances."

"Thank you," said Alhasan, surprised at her words. True, she was a doctor and well read, but he always was surprised when strangers knew of him or had heard of his work.

"Goodbye," said Al-Ghazi's wife.

"Goodbye," replied Alhasan.

He listened to the footsteps fade away. They were slightly heavier than the footfalls he had heard earlier.

He looked around the room. He had nothing to do. No books, no papers, not even his Qur'an. Nothing but blank walls. He went back to his mattress. It was softer than the carpet he had slept on during the journey from Basra. He lay down and listened to the sounds outside. A faraway rooster crowed, and another answered. A peddler with a cart of jangling pots and pans called out his wares. A group of boys laughed and shouted as they ran down the street playing *dahrooy*, the metal hoop clanging as they hit it with sticks to keep it rolling.

After midday prayers, one of Al-Ghazi's daughters slid a tray with bread, goat cheese, grapes, and honey under the door. After evening prayers, she took it away and replaced it with one bearing roasted chicken and couscous. Alhasan's confinement was lonely, but the food was good—as good as Nada's.

The meal consumed, Alhasan went into the garden and sat on the red tiles. His back against the wall, he drew his legs up to his chest and wrapped his arms around his knees. He awaited his first crepuscular visitor. It was Capella, cream white in the amethyst sky, the shoulder of Auriga. Another quarrel with Ptolemy. The Alexandrian claimed in *Almagest* that Capella represented the Amalthea, the she-goat that suckled Zeus. Alhasan preferred the original Greek version, with Capella representing Auriga's left shoulder and the triangle of stars below it representing three kids he cradled in his left arm. There was something magical about the old Greek story, in which neither the identity nor the destination of Auriga was known. A few lines of poetry formed in Alhasan's mind:

> Soundlessly Auriga drives
> his undrawn chariot
> through unfamiliar territory,
> a landscape so desolate
> he suspects he has strayed
> into some secret region the gods have crafted
> for the punishment of outcast souls.

Alhasan got up, found a sharp rock in the garden, and returned to the tiles. He etched the words into the soft, red clay. He continued:

> The land holds no wildlife
> but birds. What birds there are
> hang in the air,
> out of his line of vision.
>
> The unmarked road itself is smooth—
> too smooth for his liking.
>
> The useless reins lie slack in his hands.
>
> In his crooked, left arm, three kids
> struggle against his ribs
> and nibble at his fraying vest.
> Occasionally one bleats, sensing
> that in all the time spent traveling
> it has not moved even one step nearer
> the shriveling teats of its tethered mother.
>
> Though the air is devoid of moisture,
> Auriga tastes neither dust
> nor the film on his teeth.
> He is concentrating, as ever,
> on the name that drops from time
> to time through his memory
> like a meteor, fading
> before he is able to make it out,
> vanishing without his having gleaned
> even a clue about his destination
> or any given that might suggest
> whether the goats he holds are for market,
> consumption, or sacrifice
> (and, if sacrifice, to whom).

Suspended between bull and queen,
warrior and the Dioscuri—figures
he neither sees nor hears—
isolated, unstoried,
heroic in his aimlessness,
Auriga coasts above us,
mirroring our fitful gestures,
reserving our generation
a place in the stars.

Alhasan bent down and blew the dust from the tiles. He reviewed the lines.

I must get my writing materials, he thought. *I will go crazy without them.*

He smiled at the absurdity of the thought.

"A madman going crazy," he said aloud. "That's what I am, Auriga: a madman going crazy."

Capella, The Kids, and the rest of Auriga gleamed overhead. As Alhasan got up to go inside, a meteor blazed across the sky.

"Until we meet again," said Alhasan, winking at the heavens. "Until we meet again."

Chapter Twenty-three

E arly the next morning, Alhasan heard the evening's food tray being taken away and a new one sliding under the door. Foule and bread, again, but it smelled delicious. "Thank you," said Alhasan, forgetting that he was not supposed to speak to Al-Ghazi's daughters.

When he removed the tray and carried it to the carpet, he heard a scraping sound on the threshold. He turned around and saw another tray sliding under the door. It was covered by his prayer rug. In the middle of the tray was his Qur'an.

"Thank you. Bless you," said Alhasan.

"You are welcome," said a girl's voice before her footsteps hurried away.

After eating his foule, Alhasan washed and sat in the courtyard with his Qur'an. He eagerly read *sura* after *sura*. Before he knew it, the muezzin was sounding the call to midday prayer.

Shortly afterward, his lunch arrived. He rushed to the door.

"Thank you," he said as politely as possible.

"You are welcome," said the small voice.

He passed the afternoon reading the Qur'an. At sunset, the scene was repeated: call to prayer, prayer, a meal delivered, "thank you," and "you are welcome."

The next day Alhasan embraced the Qur'an with the same fervor as he did on the day it was returned to him. At last he had something to occupy his mind. As the days passed, he read the scriptures all the way through, over and over. When he was young, he had memorized nearly half of the *suras*. He decided to memorize all of them.

He would employ the technique devised by the ancient Greek poet Simonides called the mind palace. He noted the positions of various objects in his cell—the rug, the cushion, the table, the chair, the lamp, the window, the door. He went into the garden and did the same thing: the well, the bucket, the grapevine, the wall, the hearth. He placed imaginary objects between the real ones until he had one hundred fourteen objects—one for each *sura* of the Qur'an. He memorized the positions of the objects until he could close his eyes and picture each one, starting at the entry door and going around his confines.

He then attached the names of the *suras* to the objects in a way that meant something to him. When he pictured the door, he thought of the *sura* called "The Opening." When he pictured the well, he thought of "The Cave." Sometimes the associations were silly. For "The Heights," he imagined an open Qur'an floating near the ceiling. Around the room and the garden he went, attaching a *sura* to each object. As he memorized a *sura*, he associated it with the object.

Within two weeks, he had memorized all the *suras* with less than ten verses. Within a month, he had memorized the *suras* with less than twenty verses. Day by day, week by week, he added more verses. As the first anniversary of his confinement approached, he hurried to complete his mental challenge. When the big day arrived, he began reciting the Qur'an after morning prayers and continued all day and into the evening. Before the muezzin's call to nighttime prayer, Alhasan recited the last verse of the last *sura*.

Every morning, Alhasan would choose an object and recite a *sura*, just to make sure he did not forget a single verse of the holy book. To keep his mind active, he embarked on a new challenge. Rather than going around the room and reciting the *suras* in order, he skipped around. He even memorized the number of each *sura* and each verse.

As he became proficient, he devised a game: He would think of two numbers at random and then recite the *sura* and verse associated with them. As he played the game, he developed an even deeper love of the beauty and wisdom of the holy book.

He also kept his mind occupied by watching the nightly procession of stars and planets across his small patch of sky. One night, in the second year of his captivity, Alhasan sat in the courtyard with his knees drawn up to his chest and his back against the wall, waiting for a planet to rise above the roof of his cell. Tonight it would be Mars. The evening before, Regulus was a full thumbnail above the roofline when Mars appeared. Tonight, the red planet should trail "the heart of the lion" by no more than the distance between the tip of his thumbnail and its lunula.

Alhasan thought of his old friend Rashid Al-Bariqi and their arguments about Ptolemy. Alhasan knew that Ptolemy had already worked out the position Mars would be in tonight. Alhasan's observation was not meant to challenge those findings. It was just something to do, to pass the time, to greet an old friend on his journey through the heavens, like hailing a passing ship in the open sea. The fact that Mars was about to sail into Leo, the constellation of the animal associated with Alhasan's family name, made it all the more enjoyable.

Perhaps Al-Bariqi was working his way through *Rising and Setting of Fixed Stars* and observing the same sky. Perhaps he was even thinking of him. Although much older than Alhasan, Al-Bariqi was his best friend—always there to hear him out, offer encouragement, share a meal, or go for a walk. Perhaps he was his only friend. Of course, Alhasan had no way of knowing if Al-Bariqi was still alive. Assuming he was, he had no idea if he ever would see him again.

Just then, the red planet peeped over the roofline. Alhasan held up his thumb to measure the distance between it and Regulus. The planet was right where it was supposed to be. Alhasan felt as he had when he was a boy, when the night's luminous travelers were his only friends.

As Alhasan sat watching the evening sky, a strange noise reached his ears. At first it sounded like the cheering for a horse race, but mixed in with the shouts of men and women were the screams of terrified children and something else—a feral shriek, as if a jackal, its claws on the neck of its living prey, shrilled its killing call as its victim sounded its dying cry.

The distant noise seemed to be coming nearer. Alhasan then heard a rumbling sound nearby. Someone was pounding on his door.

"Madman!" screamed a girl's voice.

The voice came from the street outside his cell.

"Madman, please!"

It sounded like the girl who said "you are welcome" every day.

"What is it?" shouted Alhasan as he rushed to the door. "What's wrong?"

"The caliph has ordered the slaughter of all the dogs in Cairo," cried the girl.

"What? What makes you think that?"

"My father told us. He was ordered to lead a party to round up the dogs and kill them. Please, Madman. Help me."

"I don't understand. What do you want me to do?"

"They are going to kill my Barakesh, my puppy. I have been raising her, and now they are going to kill her."

"But what can I do about it?"

"You can hide her. They will never look for her in there."

"Hide her? How?"

"I have a rope. You can pull her up through the window."

"But the bars."

"She will fit between them. Please, Madman. They're coming!"

"Yes, well, tie a loop around her chest."

"I already have the rope around her neck."

"No, no, that won't do. Take the long end of the rope and loop it around her chest, behind her front legs. Can you do that?"

"Yes," said the girl, "but we don't have time."

The noise on the street was coming nearer.

"Now run the end of the rope through the loop you made around her neck."

"Hurry, Madman."

"Do that and throw the loose end to me."

Alhasan dragged his table over to the wall beneath the window, climbed onto the tabletop, and reached between the bars into the street. "Throw the end of the rope here," he said, waving his hand.

The girl tossed up the end of the rope, but it fell short.

"This way," shouted a soldier down the street. Alhasan heard hooves clattering down the cobblestones toward his cell.

"Madman!" the girl screamed.

"Again. Throw it here."

The rope hit Alhasan's wrist, and he pinned it against the wall. He slid his hand across the rope until he was able to grasp it. He pulled until he felt the weight of the dog at the end.

"You, there," a soldier shouted from down the street.

"What?" said the girl.

Hand-over-hand Alhasan hauled in the rope until he saw the dog's head outside the window. He reached out and guided the animal between the bars. As Alhasan pulled the dog through the opening, it gave a small yelp.

Two mounted soldiers stopped in the street outside the cell.

"What are you doing?" asked one of the soldiers.

"I am feeding this prisoner," said the girl.

"You're doing what?"

"Do you know who I am?" said the girl. Without waiting for an answer, she continued, "I am the daughter of Mourad Al-Ghazi, the captain of the guard of Caliph Al-Hakim. It is my duty to feed the madman, Ibn Al-Haytham, who is inside this room under house arrest. Surely you have heard of him."

"Yes, of course," said the soldier.

"So, do I need your permission to feed this prisoner, or is my father's order enough?"

"Of course it's enough," said the soldier. "But what did you pass to him?"

"A roasted goat, if that's any business of yours."

"I thought I heard a dog," said the other soldier.

"Do you understand Arabic or not?" said the girl. "I said the prisoner is a madman. He howls and raves like a beast, especially when he is fed."

"I see," said the soldier, uncertainly.

"You should go home now," said the first soldier. "We are rounding up the city's dogs. They are running in packs, and the streets are not safe."

"Thank you," said the girl. "I was just leaving."

Inside his cell, Alhasan held the dog's muzzle under his arm and listened until the soldiers were gone. He climbed down from the table and carried the dog to the courtyard. He did not want its feet to touch the inside of the house and make it unclean. He let the dog down in the garden and tied the rope around a tree. He left the dog, but she immediately began to bark.

"Quiet, Barakesh," said Alhasan. "Do not be like your namesake." He untied the small dog and let it loose in the courtyard. It ran around the garden, sniffing at the plants and urinating in the sand.

Alhasan sat down with his back against the wall. Mars was high in the night sky, burning brightly. The cries of dogs, the shouts of soldiers, and the terrified screams of children filled the night.

The dog ran over to Alhasan, wagging its tail.

"Barakesh. That's a big name for small dog."

The puppy flopped down on the tile next to Alhasan and laid her muzzle on his thigh. The scholar reached down and patted her head.

"I guess the stars aren't my only friends after all," he said.

Barakesh rolled on her side and began to lick Alhasan's fingers.

"You are lucky you belong to that girl," said Alhasan. "She is resourceful. And brave."

He smiled to think how the girl talked back to the soldiers.

"She saved your life. Yes, she did," he said, patting the dog on the stomach.

"I hope she knows what she's going to do with you."

Chapter Twenty-four

The next morning, the girl arrived with Alhasan's breakfast as usual and slid the tray under the door.

Alhasan was waiting inside.

"Ow, ow, owwwwwww," he howled. "Ow-ooooooooo."

The girl laughed.

"Fool gets his foule," barked Alhasan. "Fool gets his foule. Ow-ooooooooo."

The girl laughed again.

"I am sorry, Madman," said the girl. "I had to tell them something."

"Yes, of course," said Alhasan. "I am only joking. It was quite clever, really. I would never have thought of something so clever."

"How is my Barakesh?"

"Your Barakesh is fine. My robe is in tatters, but your Barakesh is fine."

The girl laughed again.

"I brought her some food."

She slid a small, wooden bowl under the door.

"This looks better than my foule," said Alhasan.

"It is parts of a sheep you would not want to eat," said the girl. "Besides, foule has beans. It is good for the brain."

"So, you are going to cure the fool with foule?"

"I am going to keep the great mathematician's brain healthy."

"The great theologian, you mean. All I have done for two years is read and memorize the Qur'an."

"Then you must be able to recite all of it," the girl joked.

"Yes, I can," said Alhasan.

"Are you serious?"

"Completely. Would you like a demonstration?"

"Yes."

"What is your birthday?"

"The twenty-fifth day of Shawwāl."

"Shawwāl is the tenth month. The twenty-fifth verse of the tenth *sura* is: 'And Allah invites to the Home of Peace and guides whom He wills to a straight path.'"

"Say that again."

"'And Allah invites to the Home of Peace and guides whom He wills to a straight path.'"

"That's impressive. How about the tenth verse of the twenty-fifth *sura*?"

Alhasan closed his eyes and pictured the Qur'an next to Euclid's *Elements*, which was emblazoned with the number twenty-five.

"'Blessed is He who, if He willed, could have made for you something better than that—gardens beneath which rivers flow—and could make for you palaces.'"

"I will check those when I get home."

"How will you do that?"

"I will look them up."

"In the Qur'an?"

"Of course in the Qur'an. Where else?"

"You mean, you can read?"

"Read. Write. Even count," laughed the girl.

"But how? I mean, where did you learn?"

"My mother taught me. She taught all of us. She is a famous doctor."

"Yes, I know," said Alhasan. "So, what has she taught you?"

"Reading and writing first. Then numbers. Then she began to lecture about the human body, how it is made, the parts, what they do, and then about the art of healing."

"And did you write these lectures down?"

"Yes. She made us."

"That is good. That is what the good student does, not only to absorb and understand the lecture, but to preserve it so others can read it. In this way, the student is like a midwife, helping to bring the teacher's thoughts into the world, allowing his—or her—ideas to live long after the teacher is gone. The good student does this not because he has to, but out of respect and even love for the teacher."

"So, Madman, I see you are a poet as well as a mathematician and a theologian."

"I write poetry, yes," said Alhasan, confused by the change in subject. "But what I mean is that we each have responsibility to spread knowledge. The lecture and copying is the best way yet devised to spread the wisdom of scholars, although I have often wondered if there might not be a better way."

"Like what?"

"I once made a water clock for the governor of Basra."

"Yes, Father told us. I said, 'If a man can do a thing like that, can he really be mad?'"

"What did your father say?"

"He said he never saw the clock himself and didn't know if it really worked or was just a made-up story of Basra, like the flying carpets of your Al-Jashyari."

"It works," said Alhasan a bit defensively. "It was keeping perfect time the last time I saw it."

"So what does that have to do with copying a lecture?"

"Well, I like to tinker with things. I like to build machines. Have you ever seen a drum up close?"

"Yes."

"Have you ever seen a drum with sand on the drumhead when it is being played?"

"I suppose."

"What did the sand do?"

"It hopped around, of course."

"Of course, because...."

"Because the drumhead is shaking."

"Right. Now, have you ever seen sand on the drumhead when it is not being played, but there is a loud sound nearby?"

"No."

"Well, it vibrates, as if it has been struck lightly."

"I see."

"And if there is sand on the drumhead, it dances around."

"So?"

"So a drumhead will vibrate up and down with sound of the human voice. Now, if you were to attach one end of a light bar to the center of the drumhead, that bar would move up and down as the drumhead vibrates, correct?"

"Yes."

"And if you balanced a pen on a fulcrum placed midway between its two ends, and attached the bar from the drumhead to the end of the pen, then the bar would make the pen tilt up and down as the drumhead vibrates."

"Like the bones of the human ear!"

"Like what?" asked Alhasan.

"Mother says there is a small membrane deep in the ear that is like the head of a drum. Attached to the back of this drumhead is a small bone, and that bone is connected to several more bones that are hinged, like your bar and lever. The physician Masoudi described it all in the *Complete Book of the Medical Art*."

"Masoudi? Ah, yes, Ali ibn Al-'Abbas Al-Majusi. I met him at the House of Wisdom in Baghdad. My friend Adelali Haddaoui introduced me to him."

"Masoudi says that air enters the ear until it reaches the membrane covering the opening and that the membrane responds to vibrations of the air. The movement of the membrane is transferred to the bones, and then to the nerve that goes to the brain, allowing us to hear."

"Fascinating."

"So, go on. The drumhead moves the pen up and down."

"Yes. Now imagine placing a parchment scroll against the end of the pen. If you pass the parchment across the point of the pen when it is moving up and down, the pen would draw a wavy line on the parchment. That line, properly read, would contain every word spoken by the scholar. Imagine speaking to a room full of these devices, with each one capturing your every word. A copyist could make several copies of a work at once simply by reading it aloud."

"I see."

"The problem is that a pen will run out of ink. I haven't solved that problem yet. A reserve of ink, I suppose, connected by a tube—but the tube would have to be flexible, so it did not disturb the balance of the pen. If the ink runs out, even for a few moments, much would be lost."

"What if the pen had no ink?" asked the girl.

Alhasan paused to think.

"If the pen had no ink, it would scratch the surface of the parchment."

"Exactly. And if the parchment were covered with a coating of something, like wax?"

"The pen would scrape the line into the wax."

"So you would never run out of ink."

"That is brilliant," said Alhasan. "Brilliant."

"Thank you," said the girl. "Well, you work on your invention, Madman. I have to go."

"Wait!" said Alhasan. "I am sorry, but what is your name?"

"My name is Sadeem bint Mourad," said the girl.

"Sadeem? Is that Arabic?"

"Yes," said the girl."

"I have never heard that word before."

"Sadeem is the vapor that lies in the low regions early in the morning."

"It is a beautiful image," said Alhasan. "And a beautiful name."

"Thank you," said Sadeem. "Even coming from a madman, that is nice to hear."

Alhasan heard the girl's steps trailing away.

"I have to go to the market before I go home," she called. "Mother will wonder where I am. Take care of Barakesh!"

"I will," said Alhasan, although he was sure she was out of earshot.

He took the bowl of sheep viscera into the garden and set it on the sand. The dog attacked the meat as if it might escape.

"Yes, I will take care of you, as surely as they are taking care of me," said Alhasan.

The meat consumed, Barakesh licked the bowl, pushing it around in the sand.

"I never did ask what she is going to do with you," said Alhasan. "But knowing that girl, she will have a plan."

Chapter Twenty-five

"Ow-ooooooo," called Sadeem when she arrived the next morning with Alhasan's breakfast.

"Ow-ooooooo," responded Alhasan, smiling at the joke.

Sadeem slid the tray under the door.

"The foule smells wonderful. Please tell your mother how much I enjoy it."

"She doesn't make the foule anymore," said Sadeem.

"She doesn't? Then who does? Your sisters?"

"No."

"Who then?"

"Ow-ooooooo," called Sadeem from the street.

"You?"

"Yes."

"It is delicious."

"Thank you," said Sadeem.

"How long you have been making it?"

"I always helped my mother make it, but I have been making it on my own for the last six months."

She slid another bowl of meat under the door for Barakesh.

"What is your plan for the dog?" asked Alhasan.

My plan?" repeated Sadeem. "My plan is to leave him with you until the caliph has forgotten his decree and dogs return Cairo."

"That could take years."

Sadeem laughed. "Don't be ridiculous, Madman. It won't be more than a few weeks. Three months at the most."

"So you will bring her food every day?"

"Yes."

"Can you bring an empty bowl for her water?"

"Yes, I will. By the way you were right: I checked those verses in the Qur'an, and they matched what you said."

"Yes, I checked them, too, just to make sure."

"My sister's birthday is the twenty-third day of Dhu al-Qi'dah."

"Twenty-three and eleven—two prime numbers," said Alhasan.

"Yes, it would make a great day to get married."

"What do you mean?"

"Two prime numbers—indivisible, except by themselves and one. Understand?"

"The marriage cannot be divided?"

"Yes," said Sadeem. "So, what is it?"

"What is what?"

"The twenty-third verse of the eleventh *sura?*"

"Oh," said Alhasan. He closed his eyes and pictured the garden. He saw a rainbow and the number eleven. "'Indeed, they who have believed and done righteous deeds and humbled themselves to their Lord—those are the companions of Paradise; they will abide eternally therein.'"

"That is amazing, Madman."

"The mind is capable of more than most people imagine."

"How do you do it?"

Alhasan explained about placing objects in a memory palace and associating them with the things to be remembered.

"I will have to try that," said Sadeem.

"Now, may I ask you a question?" asked Alhasan.

"Go ahead."

"How far have you gotten in your mathematics? You know what prime numbers are, so you must know multiplication and division."

"Mother introduced me to Euclid's *Elements* two years ago."

"I see. May I ask how old you are?"

"Yes, you may."

Alhasan waited, but Sadeem said nothing. "How old are you?" he asked at last.

"I said you could ask. I didn't say I would answer."

Alhasan was embarrassed. "I understand," he said at last.

"I am joking, Madman," said Sadeem. "I just turned fourteen."

"On twenty-fifth day of Shawwāl," said Alhasan.

"That's right."

"Your education is progressing quickly."

"I suppose it is. I got bored with my studies, so I joined my older sisters. My eldest sister, Rania, is four years older than I am. She was sixteen when we started on *Elements*. Hadil was fifteen. Mother was unsure about my joining them, but so far I have been able to keep up."

"If you would like some help, I know something about *Elements*."

"Father said that you supported yourself by making copies of it."

"Yes, that's true. So, if you have questions, I can help."

"Thank you, Madman."

That afternoon, after delivering lunch, Sadeem asked Alhasan about a problem in *Elements*. He was thrilled to hear the words of the Greek master being read aloud by the young student. He was about the same age as Sadeem when his private tutor, Alijan Al-Harrani, introduced him to Euclid. He remembered how happy he had been in those days. He envied Sadeem the path of discovery that lay before her.

The next day, Sadeem returned with more questions about *Elements*, and again the day after that. Each day, Alhasan sat by the door and discussed geometry with the young woman. He looked forward to it, and the days when she did not need help were a disappointment. Still, he was proud that his young student was making progress on her own. He recalled the words of Al-Jarjarai: "Abdelali Haddaoui said you came to the House of Wisdom as his student and left it as his teacher."

The goal of the teacher is to make himself useless, thought Alhasan. *If I do my job well, the day will come when she will not need me. And then one day, perhaps, she will become my teacher.*

One afternoon, after the tutoring session was over, Sadeem said, "I can take Barakesh, now. Father thinks it is safe."

Alhasan felt a pang of regret. He had come to enjoy the dog's company, and he would be sorry to see her go.

"Did you bring the rope?" asked Alhasan.

"Yes," said Sadeem.

Alhasan climbed atop his table, reached into the street, and caught the rope. He took it to Barakesh, who was asleep in the shade by the well.

"Time for you to go home," said Alhasan, rousing the dog from its slumber.

He fashioned a harness around Barakesh's chest with the rope, picked her up, carried her into the house, and climbed onto the table.

"Are you ready?" he called to Sadeem.

"Ready!"

Alhasan set Barakesh on the casement between the bars. The dog's eyes were locked on his own.

"Good dog," said Alhasan.

With one hand firmly on the rope, Alhasan pushed the dog's hindquarters toward the street and over the edge of the casement. Barakesh got a frantic look in her eyes and dug her claws into the window ledge.

"It's okay, Barakesh," said Alhasan. "Remember, this is how you came in here. You like this wall."

With that, Alhasan pushed the small dog back and off the casement, until she was dangling by the rope. Carefully he lowered the animal down the wall.

"She's gotten big," called Sadeem.

Alhasan felt the rope go slack as Sadeem took the dog in her arms.

"I've got her," she called.

Alhasan let go of the rope.

"Thank you, Madman!" called Sadeem. "Thank you for taking care of her."

"You are the one who fed her every day," Alhasan said. "And you are the one who saved her life."

"I couldn't have done it without you," said Sadeem.

Alhasan smiled. Perhaps it was true.

Sadeem often brought Barakesh along when she brought Alhasan his lunch and stayed for her lessons. Sometimes Alhasan would put his fingers under the door, and Barakesh would lick them.

Day by day, week by week, Alhasan helped Sadeem navigate her way through *Elements*. He enjoyed how Euclid had structured his lessons, and how the young woman's mind unfolded to accommodate them, like the bud of a rose accepting a bee. One afternoon, almost a year after they had begun, Alhasan sat by the door discussing Sadeem's latest proof when the young woman interrupted him.

"Madman, I am sorry to say this, but you do not smell nice. Do you wash yourself?"

"Of course I wash myself," said Alhasan. Embarrassed, he stood up and moved away from the door. "I perform ablutions every day."

"I mean, do you wash your whole body?"

"Why, yes. Sometimes. Why?"

"Then it must be your clothing. Do you wash it?"

Alhasan paused, embarrassed. "No. I have no soap for washing."

"Then give it to me. I will wash it."

"But I have only this one robe."

"Take it off, and your undergarments, and pass them under the door. There must be a blanket on your bed. Cover yourself with that until I get back."

Alhasan undressed in the bedroom and wrapped the blanket around his waist. He stuffed his undergarments inside the robe and returned to the door. As he began to slide his robe over the threshold, he realized that not only was the garment soiled, but it had a large hole under the armpit. He felt a knot in his stomach as Sadeem dragged it under the door. She said nothing, but he was mortified.

After she left, Alhasan went to the well, lowered a bucket to the water, hoisted it up, and set it on the well wall. He removed the blanket from his waist, lifted the bucket overhead, and poured the water onto himself. It was cold. Alhasan shivered as the water streamed down the back of his neck and raced in rivulets down his chest. He took a handful of sand from the garden, wetted it with water from the bucket, and used it to scrub his body. With nothing but time, he carefully laved the granules over every bit of his skin. He did this over and over, until his skin was red with scrubbing. He then hoisted another bucket and dumped it over his head. He got another bucketful of water and did it again. He had not lied to Sadeem. He had rinsed his body before. But this was the first time he had washed himself thoroughly with sand.

"I have neglected my cleanliness," he thought to himself. "I must take better care of myself."

He picked up the blanket, but before wrapping himself in it, he raised it to his nose. It smelled terrible. He did not want it to touch his freshly scrubbed skin.

He looked around the courtyard. The grapevine against the northern wall had large leaves and long tendrils. Alhasan pulled off some of the leaves and tied them with a tendril to fashion a loincloth. "I look like Adam," Alhasan joked to himself.

In the morning, Sadeem arrived with his breakfast. "Ow-ooooo," she cried, sliding the tray under the door.

"Ow-ooooooo," called Alhasan as he picked up the tray and took it to the carpet.

"Go to the window and catch the rope again," said Sadeem.

"Why?"

"I washed your robe. I don't want it to get dirty by pushing it over the threshold."

Alhasan once again moved his table under the window, climbed on top of it, and reached into the street. Sadeem hit his hand with the rope on the first try.

"Carefully," she called from below.

Alhasan pulled on the rope until he saw the top of his robe, dazzling white in the bright sunlight, outside the window. He reached out and lifted the garment over the casement, between the bars.

"Be careful," said Sadeem. "You don't want it to tear it again."

The robe was immaculate, radiantly white and soft, and the hole under the arm had been mended like new. But there was something else: It smelled wonderful. Alhasan closed his eyes and pressed the fabric to his face. He was enveloped in the musky scent of oud. For a moment, he forgot where he was.

"This scent...." he stammered.

"Yes," said Sadeem. "I went to the market and asked the spice merchant what scent came from the Abbasid Caliphate. He gave me a small piece of wood and told me to let its smoke permeate the robe. Do you like it?"

"It's, it's—" He broke off. He couldn't allow her to hear his voice quaver. He took a deep breath, and then another.

"Madman?"

Alhasan cleared his throat.

"The scent is wonderful. You have no idea what it means to me."

Against his will, his voice had cracked. He took a deep breath to regain his composure.

"How can I ever repay you?"

"No need," said Sadeem. "You may be a madman, but you are a man, after all. You should smell like a man, not like a beast."

Alhasan didn't know what to say.

"Throw the rope back down," Sadeem said. "There's more."

Alhasan untied the rope, laid his robe on the tabletop, and dropped the end of the rope back down to Sadeem. He could feel her tugging on the rope as she fastened something to it.

"Bring it up," she called at last.

This time the bundle was gray, not white. Alhasan pulled it through the window.

"This is not my robe," Alhasan said.

"No, it belonged to my brother. Mother gave it to me. I altered it to match the size of yours. Your undergarments are inside."

As Alhasan untied the bundle, a packet dropped to the tabletop. Alhasan picked it up and held it outside the window."

"What is this?" he asked.

"It's a cake of soap, all the way from Aleppo. It's for your body. Use it, and tell me when you need another. Don't bother with the laundry. I will take care of it from now on."

"Thank you," said Alhasan.

"Try on the robe and see if it fits. I am making you another, so you can change your clothes more often. But first I want to make sure I have the right size."

Alhasan climbed down from the table, took his undergarments and the new robe into the bedroom, removed the vernal loincloth he had fashioned, and put on the clothing.

"It fits," he said, returning to the great room.

"That's all?" said Sadeem.

"It fits well," said Alhasan, realizing he might have sounded ungrateful, even though his heart was overflowing with gratitude. "It fits well and it smells wonderful. You really are too kind."

"It's nothing, really," said Sadeem. "It's the least I could do."

"Wait," said Alhasan. "Would it be possible—I hate to impose— but next time you do the laundry, could you wash my blanket as well?"

"If it's not in tatters." Sadeem laughed.

The sound of her laughter touched Alhasan to the core. This must be the sound an angel makes, he thought to himself.

Although embarrassed by the smell of the blanket, he tied it to the end of the rope and lowered it through the window to the young woman in the street.

"I will take care of it," said Sadeem. "Now eat your foule before it gets cold."

"Ow-ooooooo," called Alhasan.

"Ow-ooooooo," Sadeem replied.

Alhasan changed out of the robe Sadeem had made for him and into the one he had brought from Basra. He smelled the fabric again. It had the same aroma as it did when Nada had laundered it and scented it.

After breakfast, Alhasan sat on the cushion below the window with his back to the wall. He closed his eyes for a moment and fell asleep.

He was walking down a street in Basra—not his street, another street—when he realized he could jump onto a rooftop as easily as climbing a stair. He walked across the city, leaping from one rooftop to another with no effort. When he reached the market square, he leapt down. He bought a packet of pounce from one merchant and a bit of oud from another. As he approached the government offices, he leapt onto a terrace. Three civil employees were taking their afternoon meal. "Peace be upon you," he said to the astonished clerks, then leapt to the roof. "I can fly," he thought, stepping off the roof.

He awoke. The sun was high in the sky, shining down onto his knees. The freshly laundered robe dazzled his eyes. He lifted a sleeve to his face and breathed in the scent of oud.

Home.

He let his arm fall to his lap. The impact loosened a few pieces of lint from his robe. The specks rose in the sunlight like sparks from a fire, spiraling skyward until they disappeared into the darkness beyond the shaft of light.

One mote drifted back down into the sunlight, shining like a star. Alhasan watched the particle descend. It was not just a dot, but a line— a long fiber, slowly spinning as it fell through the air. Just before it reached his knees, the particle reversed direction and began to rise. Alhasan watched it drift upward, turning around and around as it rose. When it reached the shadow, it disappeared as if it had never existed.

Alhasan waited. He sat still, not wanting to disturb the air. Gently breathing through his nose, he kept his eyes on the edge of the shaft of light. As he had hoped, the piece of lint returned, falling slowly through the air. Then, as if an invisible hand caught it, it began to rise again.

The heat from the sunlight must cause it to rise, like a falcon riding an updraft from the desert floor, Alhasan thought. *Once the fiber reaches the cool air of the shade, there is nothing to hold it aloft, so it drifts back down.*

He watched the mote rise through the shaft of light. It shone more brightly than Sirius. It was as bright as two or three stars strung together like beads—An-Niṭāq, An-Niẓām, and Manṭaqa, the String of Pearls that the Greeks called Orion's Belt.

He watched the cosmic necklace spin upward, but the moment it passed into the shadow, it disappeared again. He strained to see it. He couldn't believe that something so beautiful could simply vanish.

At that moment Alhasan had a thought so large, so stupendous, that he stopped breathing altogether. He sat motionless on the bench as the enormity of what he was thinking pushed its way into every recess of his mind.

Could it be? he wondered before the need for air shook him out of his reverie. He took a breath and looked around.

"Could it be?" he asked himself aloud.

He paused for a moment. He knew he had a choice to make, a choice that could change the course of his life. He felt like a falcon poised at the top of an updraft. He had spotted something far below. If he folded his wings and plunged toward it, there would be no turning back.

He knew without working it out that following this thought would consume untold hours, days, and years.

The thought pushed its way deeper into his mind. He felt his wings drawing in. The sky disappeared behind him and the canyon walls became a red blur as he fixed his mind on the thought below. It had scampered out of its burrow and into the light. In a moment he would taste its blood.

Chapter Twenty-six

L ight causes vision.
Just three words, but, if true, they would displace volumes of arguments and centuries of discourse.

Light, not the form of a thing, enters the eye, causing a sensation that the optic nerve carries to the brain.

Light, not a ray from the eye, travels through the air in straight lines, enabling sight.

The mote of dust was visible because it reflected light, like a strand of pearls. When it passed into shadow, it disappeared.

It had no form that penetrated the pupil.

There were no rays emanating from his eyes to find it in the darkness.

Light alone makes things visible.

Euclid's geometry, so perfect in its description of sight, was correct. It was wrong only about the source of the rays. They did not originate in the eye and travel outward to a point on an object. They originated from a point on an object and traveled into the eye.

But how?

Alhasan glanced around the room. Suddenly it did not make sense. Every point of every surface giving off rays that entered the eye? How?

He closed his eyes and imagined a lamp in the center of the room. Its flame gives off rays in every direction. If you walk around it, you can see it from every point in the room. The rays illuminate every surface of every object in the room—at least the surfaces facing it. If a ray strikes an object, it stops. It does not pass through it, unless the object is transparent or translucent, like glass. Surfaces on other side of the object are dark, hidden by its shadow. The light rays travel in straight lines; they do not curve around objects and illuminate the other side.

One flame can light an entire room. Even when the wick burns down, the reduced flame illuminates every corner of the room, sending out rays in every direction before it burns out and dies. Then darkness.

Alhasan imagined the mote of dust—not the entire mote, but one end. No, one point on one end. Sunlight strikes it. What if it reflects that light in all directions? Not behind it, of course. That lies in shadow. But in all other directions. One point giving off hundreds, millions, countless rays. One ray, originating at that point, travels through the air, through the pupil, and strikes a point at the back of the eye. One point to one point. And the next point on the fiber does the same. Countless rays emanate from that point, but one ray, parallel to the first ray that entered the eye, passes through the pupil and strikes a point in the back of the eye adjacent to the point struck by the other ray. And so on down the length of the fiber. Each pearl on the necklace sends a ray to the eye. Adjacent points at the back of the eye absorb the rays. These points stimulate the optic nerve. The brain registers a tiny string of points—the mote is seen.

Alhasan opened his eyes and looked at the wall. Every point on the wall is reflecting rays in every direction. One point sends out a ray that travels through the pupil to the back of the eye. Point to point. The point is seen. Countless points giving off countless rays, but a subset of these enter the eye. Point to point. Vision.

Still, it seemed unlikely.

A falcon glides on an updraft. Points of light from a creature scampering across the desert floor reach the falcon's eye. It detects the movement, folds its wings, and dives.

Alhasan looked at his hands, the ridges on his fingertips, dozens of curving lines reflecting light to the eye.

So many points, so many colors, so many textures—all entering the eye. It seemed unimaginable.

But the geometry worked; that much he knew. The further an object is from the eye, the greater the convergence of the rays from its surface, so fewer rays pass through the pupil and strike the back of the eye. Therefore, the object appears small. That solved the mystery of mountains. The closer an object is to the eye, the less distance the rays have to travel, and the less they will converge. Since the rays cover a greater area at the back of the eye, the object appears larger.

The curvature of the eye must play a significant part. This would require a great deal of mathematical calculation, but it must play a part in how the visible world is conveyed to the brain.

So many calculations. So much to understand. And to explain.

Alhasan felt a great weight pulling him down. It was as if the falcon had snatched up not a mouse, but a rabbit, and was trying to fly to the top of the canyon with the entire weight in its beak. No, not a rabbit. A lamb. Perhaps a calf.

Alhasan smiled at the ridiculous image.

He looked around the room, his eyes taking in every nuance, every discoloration of the wall. Yes, it was a lot of work. But it all proceeded from a single organizing principle—light causes vision. He would start there.

The falcon would eviscerate its prey on the ground, muscle by muscle, ligament by ligament, bone by bone, and raise it, piecemeal, to its aerie on high.

Chapter Twenty-seven

"Ow-oooooooo," howled Sadeem as she approached the door of Alhasan's cell with his lunch.

"Ow-oooooooo," said Alhasan, returning the greeting.

"What is it?" asked Sadeem.

"What is what?"

"You sound different. Is something wrong?"

"No, nothing is wrong."

"Did something happen, Madman?"

"Yes, Sadeem, something happened. Something wonderful, something unbelievable has happened."

"What is it? Tell me."

"I can't. You will think I am mad."

Sadeem set the tray on the threshold and pushed it under the door.

"The one thing a madman should not be afraid of is appearing to be mad."

Alhasan smiled. "I can't. I don't know where to begin."

"What is it?" shouted Sadeem.

It sounded like she had stamped her foot.

"Alright," said Alhasan. "I will try."

His mind blazed with a thousand thoughts. He tried to think of just one, a starting point.

"You know the two theories of vision."

"Intromission and extromission."

"Yes. And they are?"

"Intromission says that objects give off forms or particles that travel through the air and enter the eye. Extromission says that the eyes send out rays that sense an object and transmit its appearance back to the eyes."

"Now, for any two competing theories...."

"It is either the case that one of them is true and the other false; or they are both false, the truth being other than either of them; or they both lead to one thing which is the truth."

"Correct," said Alhasan. He took a deep breath. "Sadeem, I know the truth regarding the competing theories of vision."

"It's extromission, of course," said Sadeem. "Euclid's geometry proves it."

"Almost, Sadeem. Almost. But in this case, the truth is other than either of them. In fact, it is so near to both of them that you almost could say they both lead to one thing, which is the truth."

"So what is that one thing?"

Alhasan looked around at the room. He knew it would sound mad, but he also knew it was true.

"Light causes vision."

Alhasan stared at the door, awaiting a response. It was the first time he had said the words aloud. He knew they sounded absurd.

"Light?" asked Sadeem.

"Light."

"Light makes things visible, but what does that have to do with sight? Mother has shown us the optic nerve. The eyes send something to the brain. Something must enter the eye, either the form of an object, or particles from it, or disturbances at the ends of the rays that flow out of the eyes."

Alhasan decided to try another approach.

"Euclid is right, Sadeem. His calculations regarding vision are perfect. He is only wrong about the source of the rays. They do not go out from the eye. They travel into it."

Silence.

"Imagine a lamp on a table in the center of a dark room," said Alhasan. "Now imagine placing an opaque cylinder over the lamp, tight to the table. What would happen?"

"The room would be dark."

"Yes. Now imagine making a single hole in the cylinder, the size of a single point."

"A point is imaginary."

"Alright, a small hole. What would happen?"

"Light would pass through the hole."

"And if the hole were the size of a single point?"

He waited.

"A single ray would pass through the hole."

"A ray of what?"

"A ray of light."

"And how do rays travel?"

"In straight lines."

"So where would that ray go?"

"In a straight line."

"Until?"

"Until it struck an object."

"Now, this is important: How much of the object would it strike?"

He waited.

"A single point."

"Yes! Point to point. Does that sound familiar?"

"It's Euclid."

"Yes! Now, imagine that the object the light ray strikes is the eye—the pupil of the eye. Both the intromissionists and extromissionists say that the pupil is diaphanous."

"The light ray passes through the pupil."

"And?"

"And travels through the vitreous material to the retina."

"It strikes the retina. How much of the retina?"

"A single point."

"Point to point."

"And you think that the light ray stimulates the retina, like a sound stimulates the ear?"

"Exactly."

"And the optic nerve carries that sensation to the brain."

"Yes. And what would you see?"

"A point of light."

"Correct. Now imagine a second hole beside the first. And a third and a fourth, all in a line. What does the brain see?"

"A line segment."

"A line segment of what?"

"Of light."

"Arrange the points on the cylinder into a triangle. What do you see?"

"A triangle of light."

"Now, remove the cylinder completely. What do you see?"

"The flame. The room."

"You see."

"Yes."

"That was not a question, Sadeem. It was a statement. You see."

"Yes. I see."

"That is how vision works. Euclid was so close. Light, not a ray from the eye, travels through the air in straight lines, enabling sight. Light enters the eye, causing a sensation."

"How can you be sure?"

"I need your help with that."

"What do you mean?"

"I have been thinking about this all morning. I have had a thousand thoughts. So many things I need to understand, to prove. I need a pen and ink. Please, Sadeem. I cannot do it all in my mind."

"It is forbidden."

"By whom?"

"By my father, and by the caliph."

"But not by Allah!" said Alhasan.

"I'm sorry, Madman."

Alhasan turned and walked into the courtyard. She was his only hope. But she was only a student, a child. Well, not a child. She was nearly fifteen. But he couldn't expect her to understand, or to disobey her father. He was a hard man.

"Madman," called Sadeem. "Madman, please. I'm sorry."

"It's alright, Sadeem. I understand."

"Madman, I need help with a proof."

"Read it to me."

Alhasan sat by the door and picked at the plate of food as he answered Sadeem's questions. He felt sick. The weight of his discovery was too much. It took his utmost concentration to help his student construct even the most elementary proof. Every word reminded him of his idea—an idea that must go unexplored until his release.

As Sadeem prepared to leave, Alhasan said, "Send your father. I need to talk to him."

"Yes, Teacher. I will ask him to come when he gets home."

Alhasan went into the garden and paced back and forth. It was too much. He looked at the sky. Clouds dotted the blue—some solid, some transparent. Each frothy swath reflected light rays in every direction, some of which entered his eye. It was too much. He went into his bedroom and fell asleep.

He awoke to the sound of knocking and the voice of Al-Ghazi: "Mathematician. My daughter says you want to speak with me."

"Yes," Alhasan called on his way to the door. "Al-Ghazi, I must ask you to appeal to the caliph on my behalf. It has been almost three years. I need to get out of here."

He waited anxiously. It was his last hope, his only hope.

"I will speak to Al-Hakim," Al-Ghazi said at last.

"Thank you," said Alhasan. "I can't take it in here anymore, Al-Ghazi. I have to get out. I have to go home."

He heard the clinking of the black stallion's silver breast collar as
Al-Ghazi turned his horse in the street. "Thank you," he called out
again, thinking how fortunate he was to know someone in Al-Hakim's
court.

He went into the garden and sat on the red tiles. He brushed a bit of
sand from a tile and looked up as evening sapphired the sky. "O Allah,"
he prayed, "I seek forgiveness for every sin I committed, about which, of
course, You know inside and out, from the beginning to the end of my
life, whether committed deliberately or intentionally, few or many,
abstruse or manifest, old or new, secretly carried out or openly done.

"Please, if it is Your will, soften the heart of Caliph Al-Hakim. Let
him have mercy on me and free me from this prison that I might better
serve you. I promise, if I am freed, I will spend every day in the explora-
tion of the insights you have revealed to me."

He prayed again later that evening and the next morning. Before
midday prayers, Al-Ghazi returned.

"I spoke with the caliph," said the captain of the guard. "I'm afraid
he showed no interest in releasing you. You raised his hopes about taming the Nile, and your failure to do so still rankles. In fact, he warned me
never to mention your name again."

A rising tide of nausea choked Alhasan. "Thank you for trying," he
whispered.

"I am sorry, Mathematician. I will try again in a few months," said
Al-Ghazi. "Perhaps after Ramadan he will be in a better temper."

"Do not put yourself in jeopardy," said Alhasan. "Your family
needs you."

That afternoon he excused himself from helping Sadeem. "I am not
feeling well," he told his student.

Sleep was his only escape from disappointment. He dozed off in
mid-afternoon.

It was night when he awoke. He had slept through the muezzin's
calls at sunset and nightfall. He laid out his prayer rug and made up for
the missed devotions. The prayers completed, he lit the lamp on his
table. The flame sent rays into every corner of the room.

The tray with his evening meal was by the door. He picked it up and carried it to the carpet. It was a new tray, darker than the one Sadeem usually brought. When he set it down, something rolled out from under the bowl. It was a thin metal rod.

Alhasan picked it up. One end was round. The other end was pointed. He touched the tip with his finger. It was sharp. He set it on the tray and picked up the bowl of molokhia. As he lifted it, he noticed that it left a ring on the tray. He reached down and touched the glistening circle. It was warm and sticky. He ran his hand across the tray. The entire surface was coated with wax.

He set down the bowl and picked up the metal rod. He placed the sharp end against the tray and dragged it toward himself. A small curl of wax arose from the point. Alhasan brushed it away, revealing a thin, shining line.

He could write.

Chapter Twenty-eight

S adeem slid Alhasan's breakfast under the door without a word.

"Ow-ooooooo," called Alhasan.

Silence.

"Ow-ooooooo, ow-ooooooo. The fool can write! The fool can write!"

"What are you talking about?" said Sadeem at last.

"Thank you, Sadeem. Thank you so much. You have no idea what you have done for me."

"I don't know what you are talking about."

"The wax. The tray. Thank you."

"Oh, that. I'm sorry. I spilled wax. I tried to clean it off, but I didn't have much time. I was in a hurry."

"It was brilliant. It works perfectly."

"Madman, stop your raving and eat your foule."

"Fool eat foule. Fool eat foule."

"I won't need your help today," said Sadeem, her voice trailing off as she began to leave.

"Sadeem, wait! I am serious. Thank you. I wish I could repay you for this kindness."

"Madman, I don't know what you are talking about, but whatever it is, your lessons are repayment enough."

Alhasan stood at the door, puzzled.

"I have to go, Madman," said Sadeem. "My sister lost her pottery stylus. I have to help her find it." A smile crept into her voice. "That girl would lose her fingers if they weren't attached."

By midmorning Alhasan had filled his wax tablet with the first principles of vision and the propagation of light. When the tray was covered with writing, he tried the stylus on the wall of his cell. He found that it cut into the plaster, so he transferred his writings from the tray to the wall, using abbreviations throughout to conserve space. The copy complete, he held the tray over his lamp to soften the wax. He smoothed out the wax by rolling a wet, ceramic cup over it, and it was ready to use again.

That afternoon, and every afternoon that week, Alhasan explained his morning's work to Sadeem. He wanted to know what made sense to her, and he especially wanted to know what did not.

"Something is bothering me, Madman," said Sadeem one afternoon.

"What is that?"

"You say that every point of a primary source of light gives off rays in all directions."

"Yes."

"And every point of every surface gives off reflected light rays in all directions."

"Yes."

"Then all these light rays, traveling in all these directions, must be intersecting."

"Yes."

"The air is awash with light rays."

"So it would seem."

"Yet we do not see them all."

"No."

"That seems impossible. It seems like lights and colors would mix in the air."

"And if they mixed in the air, they would reach the eye mixed," added Alhasan. "Thus neither the colors of the visible objects nor the objects themselves would be distinguished by the eye."

"Yes," said Sadeem. "Everything would be blurry."

Light rays must not affect each other when they intersect, thought Alhasan after Sadeem left. *Otherwise we could not see objects clearly.*

Simple observation showed this was the case, but how could he prove it? He paced around his cell. He needed to isolate a few rays of light and force them to intersect—but how?

He closed his eyes and pictured a lamp inside an opaque cylinder. He imagined a single opening, emitting a single ray. Enlarging the hole would emit a second ray, but the rays would not cross, because they would be parallel. But a second source of light, some distance from the first, would send out rays at a different angle. Two sources of light and one opening. Only a few rays of light from each lamp could pass through the aperture. Coming from different angles, they would intersect at the opening. The question was, if you extinguished one of the lamps, would the light from the other be affected?

Alhasan could hardly wait for nightfall. This time, instead of viewing celestial lights, he would observe earthly ones. The muezzin sounded the call to prayer at sunset. A few minutes after he completed his prayers, Sadeem arrived with his dinner. They greeted each other with howls, and then she left. The room grew darker as Alhasan tasted the stew. *Tharid*, thought Alhasan, *the favorite dish of The Prophet, peace be upon him.* He recalled the hadith: *"The virtue of 'A'esha as compared to other women, is like the virtue of Tharid as compared to the rest of the foods."* Alhasan understood. The mixture of lamb, broth, and bread was simple but delicious. He savored each bite.

At last it was dark. Alhasan lit his lamp, set his writing tray in the middle of the carpet, and took out his stylus. He placed the tip of the stylus in the center of the tray and struck the other end with a brick he had taken from the broken garden wall. One blow punctured the tray. He worked the stylus around in the hole to scrape away the burrs. He lifted the tray and held it up to the lamp. The hole was clean and round.

Alhasan placed the brick on the table and stood the tray on edge against it. He positioned the lamp across from the hole. The tray cast a large shadow on the wall. As expected, light rays admitted through the aperture lit the wall in the middle of the shadow. But the patch of light was not circular, like the aperture. It was oblong. And it was moving. Alhasan stepped closer to inspect the patch of light. He had expected rays traveling in parallel lines from the center of the flame to illuminate a small circular portion of the wall, in the shape of the aperture, as Theon of Alexandria had observed. Instead, the aperture was large enough, and the distance to the lamp great enough, to admit rays from the entire flame.

Rays from the top of the flame passed downward through the aperture, forming the lowest part of the illuminated patch on the wall. Rays from the bottom of the flame passed upward through the aperture and formed the highest part of the illuminated patch. When the lamp flickered, the light on the wall flickered as well. Rays from the right side of the flame appeared on the left side of the patch, and rays from the left side of the flame appeared on the right.

"Al-Kindi was right," Alhasan said to himself. "The entire flame is visible, upside down and backwards."

To test his hypothesis about the mixing of light rays, he needed a second source of light. That afternoon he had fashioned a small torch using a piece of grape vine from the garden as the stave and a strip of cloth from his blanket soaked in wax from the writing tray as the wick. He held the wick over the lamp to ignite it and then placed the torch into a cup. He placed the two sources of light at equal distances from the center of the aperture. Two patches of light—a bright one from the flaming torch and a dimmer one from the trimmed lamp—appeared on the wall.

Knowing the torch would not burn for long, Alhasan worked quickly. He placed the tray from dinner between the lamp and the aperture and observed the wall. The dim patch disappeared. The bright patch was unaffected. He crossed to the other side of the table and screened the torch from the aperture. The bright patch disappeared, and the dim patch remained as it was. He carefully watched the dim patch as he removed the screen from the torch. The illuminated patch did not change, even though light rays from the torch had intersected with those from the lamp.

He repeated the process over and over until the torch finally burned out. He sat down with his stylus and wrote in the wax:

> All the lights that appear in the dark place have reached it through the aperture alone, therefore the lights of those lamps have come together at the aperture and then separated after passing through it. Thus, if lights blended in the atmosphere, the lights of the lamps meeting at the aperture would have mixed in the air at the aperture and in the air preceding it before they reached the aperture, and they would have come out so mingled together that they would not be subsequently distinguishable. We do not, however, find the matter to be so; rather the lights are found to come out separately, each being opposite the lamp from which it has arrived.

He read the passage to Sadeem the next day.

"That is amazing, Madman. Truly amazing. You actually saw two flames on the wall?"

"Yes."

"And one was brighter than the other."

"Yes. Just as on the table."

"And the light from one did not affect the light from the other?"

"Not at all."

"So that explains why we see everything clearly."

"I believe it does."

That afternoon, Alhasan couldn't resist making another torch. When evening fell, he repeated the process, this time varying the distances between the lamps and the aperture, and between the aperture and the wall. Always the result was the same: The presence or absence of one light source did not affect the image projected by the other.

The next morning, Alhasan heard his student calling from down the street.

"Madman, Madman!" cried Sadeem.

Alhasan could hear the bowl and plate rattling on the tray as she ran toward his cell.

"Madman, it works! It really works!"

"What works?"

"The lamps, the hole, the wall! It works just like you said."

"I would not mislead you, Sadeem."

"I know that, Madman. What I mean is that I saw it for myself. It was astounding. Simply astounding. And what an uproar it caused."

She was laughing as she slid the tray under the door.

"What do you mean—uproar?"

"The way you described the lights on the wall—it all seemed so mysterious, so I decided to try it at home. Without Father knowing, I took his auger and made a small hole in the middle of my bedroom door. My sister Hadil and I waited until everyone was asleep, then we lit two lamps in my room. She stayed inside, and I went into the hallway. I closed the door, and there they were—two patches of light on the wall, just as you said."

"Yes."

"But that's not all, Madman. Beforehand I told Hadil to screen one lamp, and then to screen the other, just as you said, so I could see if there was any effect on the lights."

"And was there?"

"No. But that's not the best part."

"And what is the best part?"

"The best part was that Hadil was wearing a white nightgown."

"I don't understand."

"I saw her as she moved between the lamps! Her nightgown, her hair, her whole form."

Alhasan thought about this for a moment.

"The hallway must have been very dark," he said at last.

"Completely dark. And I could see her moving around in the bedroom. So I told her to change places with me, so she could see for herself. I put on a white nightgown, stood between the lamps, and waved to her."

"Could she see you?"

"Yes, she could see me. She saw me and she screamed!"

Sadeem burst out laughing. Alhasan couldn't help but smile.

"She thought she saw a ghost," said Sadeem. "She woke everyone up. Rania came running, and when she saw my form as I approached the door, she thought a ghost was coming after her."

Sadeem shrieked with laughter. Behind the door, Alhasan laughed aloud.

"Mother heard the commotion and came running down the hall as well. I opened the door, and the apparitions disappeared. Mother demanded to know what had happened. I explained to her that you were investigating light and vision, and that you had described how lamps sent rays in straight lines in every direction, and that a few rays of light admitted through a small hole would appear on the wall beyond. She didn't believe me, so I closed the door. Of course the lights appeared, just as before."

"So there were ghosts of lamps, but not ghosts of people."

"Correct. But Mother wanted to see the real ghosts."

"So you went inside."

"No, I had Hadil go inside and stand by the lamps. I stayed in the hallway with Mother."

"And did she scream?"

"No. She observed the image on the wall very carefully. Then she said, 'Alhasan is practicing magic. I forbid you from talking to him anymore. From now on, I will send his food with Rania or Hadil.'"

"Oh, no," said Alhasan. "I mean, that would be terrible for your studies."

"That is what I told her. And I told her that any man who has memorized the Qur'an and who can quote any *sura* when asked is incapable of doing evil. I said you are correcting what the world has wrongly believed about light and vision for centuries. I said that your demonstrations are true, not false; they are physics, not magic."

"And that convinced her that I could continue to tutor you?"

"No, it didn't."

Alhasan felt disappointed.

"But you are here," he said.

"Yes, this morning, while I was making your foule, Mother wanted to know what light had to do with vision. I explained that light rays pass through the pupil, as through the aperture in my door, and form an image on the retina, like the image on the wall. The optic nerve transmits this sensation to the brain."

"What did she think of that?"

"She said it makes more sense than rays flowing out of the eyes or forms entering into them."

Alhasan felt relieved.

"She said, 'That man is brilliant, but I forbid you—I absolutely forbid you—from performing that demonstration in our house again. And you are never to speak of it to your father.'"

"Your mother is wise," said Alhasan.

"Yes," said Sadeem. "Almost as wise as you are."

Chapter Twenty-nine

"I have been thinking about the demonstration you performed in the hallway," Alhasan told Sadeem at the conclusion of her lessons the next day.

"That was hilarious."

"Yes, but I was thinking about something. You were able to see the image of your sister clearly because the hallway was completely dark."

"Everyone saw the ghosts clearly," Sadeem laughed.

"Yes. Exactly. But since I used only my writing tray to screen the lamps, the room was filled with light, and the image on the wall was indistinct. I need something to block out the lamplight."

"Like what?"

"A piece of canvas from a tent or a sail, thick enough to keep out light and large enough to cover a doorway."

"I see."

"I also was thinking of something more serious. I need your opinion."

"I can't think of anything you would need my opinion about."

"Don't say that, Sadeem. Your analytical skills are formidable. You are the best student I have ever had."

"Are you serious, Madman?"

"Why, yes. I am completely serious. This discovery—it is the most serious thing I have ever encountered, and I need to discuss it with you."

"Go ahead."

Her words brimmed with confidence.

"Until you saw the lights on your wall, you did not believe me, did you?"

"I believed you saw something and that you knew what it was. Yes, I believed you."

"So, when you saw the lights for yourself, nothing changed?"

"No, everything changed!"

"But you already believed me."

"Yes, but then I saw it for myself. Everyone could see it."

She paused. "And I knew for certain you weren't mad."

"And your mother? You told her what I did, but she did not believe you until you closed the door."

"And then she believed you were a sorcerer!" Sadeem said, laughing.

"But when you explained how the eye worked, and you used the demonstration as an example...."

"She believed it."

"There is a power in these demonstrations that surpasses argument."

"Yes, there is."

"Do you know why?"

"Because you can see for yourself."

"That is part of it, but I think it is deeper than that."

"Is this a lecture by Ibn Al-Haytham the mathematician, the poet, the philosopher, or the theologian?"

"Perhaps all of them. Or perhaps the madman."

"Proceed, Madman."

"When you performed the demonstration, you eliminated me from the argument. You did not just see the result, you relived the experience. My words, my logic, my reputation as a mathematician or a madman—they no longer mattered. I did not matter. You interacted directly with light, with nature. You allowed the universe to speak for itself."

"And if the lights had not appeared on the wall, your words, your claims, and your excitement would have meant nothing."

"Exactly. You would have known I had erred. Authorities are not immune from error, Sadeem, nor is human nature itself. Only God is perfect. The seeker after truth must submit to Him and to His manifest laws in the universe, and not to the sayings of a human being, whose nature is fraught with all kinds of imperfections and deficiencies."

"You are saying that we must insist on demonstration."

"Yes. The seeker after truth is not the one who puts his trust in the authorities, but rather the one who suspects what he learns from them, questions them, and submits their sayings to demonstration. You also should suspect yourself as you perform your critical examinations so you avoid falling into either prejudice or leniency."

"I will, Madman."

"And I will, too, Sadeem. That is why I need your help. I have decided I will not put anything into this treatise unless I can prove it with mathematics or a true demonstration."

"That is an excellent idea."

"But there are many things I will need in order to do so."

"I see," said Sadeem. "Well, lucky for you, Rania is very forgetful. She is always leaving things in the oddest places."

"I see. Well, it would be shame if she were to misplace a straight metal tube, about one *dhirā* long, no wider than your little finger."

"Yes, that indeed would be a shame."

"But it must be straight. Whoever makes it must use a ruler to ensure it is perfectly straight."

"Of course."

A few nights later, Alhasan's dinner tray contained a bowl of molokhia, a plate of bread, and a perfectly straight, narrow copper tube. A few nights later, it contained a bowl, a plate, and a small roll of canvas. Over the next seven years, Sadeem's sister misplaced everything from a sheet of copper to a spherical mirror. With each lapse in Rania's memory, Alhasan was able to establish another physical proof about light and vision. The walls of his cell were covered with countless notations, diagrams, drawings, and proofs. When Rania got married, Hadil began to lose things. When Hadil got married, Sadeem herself became forgetful.

"I can only hope that you do not get married," said Alhasan.

"I have a suitor, Madman," said Sadeem.

"You do?"

Alhasan wondered if his voice sounded disappointed.

"Yes. Now that Hadil is married and I am twenty-two years old, my father is eager to marry me off."

"And do you love him?"

"Love him? I have not even met him! And I doubt if I will. I told my mother I could never marry anyone who cannot solve a quadratic equation."

Sadeem laughed. Her voice still rang like an angel's.

The next morning, Sadeem greeted Alhasan with a howl and then called him to the door.

"Madman, something has happened," she said in a hushed tone.

"What is it?"

"The caliph has disappeared."

Although her voice was low and conspiratorial, it seemed to have a hint of happiness in it.

"How do you know?"

"My father, of course. He said the caliph went out at night on his donkey, but he never returned. They have been looking for him all morning."

"He must be staying with someone."

"My father doesn't think so. He says the caliph never stays out all night. He always returns for morning prayers. He thinks.... He suspects foul play."

"Upon the caliph? That seems unlikely."

"Al-Hakim had enemies. Many of them. My father said he had more enemies than there are stars in the sky."

"That might be true, but taking the life of a caliph would require more than antipathy."

"Courage?"

"Not courage, Sadeem. Madness."

Sadeem slid the tray under the door.

"Do you realize what this means?" she said. "It means you might be freed."

Chapter Thirty

After breakfast, Alhasan heard an uproar in the streets. Cries of "The caliph is dead" echoed across the city. Men shouted, women wailed, dogs barked. Mounted soldiers rode down the street, calling for calm.

Alhasan went to the garden and prayed. He had waited ten years for this day. The caliph was dead. Alhasan prayed for his soul. And he prayed that his decree of madness was dead as well.

Sadeem arrived with Alhasan's lunch.

"I cannot stay," she said. "Father is coming to see you. He met with the new ruler about your situation."

"Who is the new caliph?"

"Ali az-Zahir, the sixteen-year-old son of Al-Hakim. But he is not the ruler. The caliph's sister, Sitt Al-Mulk, has taken charge. Ali bin Ahmad Jarjarai is her vizier. He has ordered the police to secure the city."

"Al-Jarjarai? Then I have no hope."

"There is always hope, Madman."

An hour later, Alhasan heard a knock at the door.

"Mathematician," shouted Al-Ghazi from the street, "our new leader, Sitt Al-Mulk, Regent of the Fatimid Caliphate, desires an audience with Ibn Al-Haytham, the Butcher of Basra."

"When?"

"In six days."

"Six days?" said Alhasan. "This is wonderful news."

"Al-Jarjarai advised her not to see you," said Al-Ghazi, "but I prevailed."

"I am grateful," said Alhasan. "I truly am."

Six days later, right after midday prayers, Alhasan heard the lock on his door unbolted. For the first time in ten years, the door swung open.

Al-Ghazi had aged. His beard had gone from black to gray; his cheeks, once ruddy and full, were pale and slightly hollow. Only his teeth were the same—white, straight, and evenly spaced.

"Why Mathematician, you hardly have aged at all," said Al-Ghazi. "Tutoring my daughter must have kept you young."

"Al-Ghazi, I must thank you for everything you have done for me. I know you appealed to the caliph on my behalf. And your wife and your daughters have left me wanting for nothing."

"You make it sound like you were my guest, not my prisoner."

"I don't know how to repay you."

"The caliph paid me for your safe delivery, don't you remember? And you have turned my Sadeem into a first-rate mathematician. With her knowledge of calculation, she could oversee the division of property in the ministry of justice or even work for the treasury. Perhaps it is I who owe you."

"Always joking," said Alhasan, embarrassed by Al-Ghazi's praise.

"You must come with me now," said the captain of the guard. "I will not bind you as a prisoner until we get to the palace. Remember, you must be on your best behavior if you ever hope to see your beloved Basra again."

"I will be," said Alhasan.

"Not a word about Ptolemy!"

Alhasan nodded.

As Alhasan rode behind Al-Ghazi on the black stallion, the trial was the furthest thing from his mind; the sights and sounds of the Cairo street overwhelmed him. For ten years he had seen nothing but the rooms and courtyard where he had been kept prisoner. Alhasan stared wide-eyed at everything he saw: children playing in the street, a black-and-white cat curled up on a window ledge, an old woman hefting an umber squash at a vegetable stall. He had forgotten the simple beauty of everyday life.

As they rode toward the caliph's palace, Alhasan noticed two young women walking toward them. Alhasan marveled at their lively, flashing eyes and smooth brows. Mesmerized by their beauty, he looked at them a bit too long. He met the eyes of one and then quickly looked away, realizing his rudeness. As they passed, he heard them whispering behind their hands. Strange, but the one who had met his gaze had raised her eyebrows, as if she were about to say something. People never failed to perplex him.

Before they entered the palace, Al-Ghazi bound Alhasan's hands behind his back. He took him by the arm and led him into the prisoner's dock, an alcove visible from the throne, but not from the rest of the hall.

"Your Regency, I present Alhasan Ibn Alhasan Ibn Al-Haytham," said Al-Ghazi. "He has been under house arrest for ten years by Caliph Al-Hakim's decree."

The late caliph's sister sat on the throne. Ali bin Ahmad Jarjarai stood at her side. Other advisers, scribes, and attendants stood before her in the hall. Al-Jarjarai bent down and whispered something into Sitt Al-Mulk's ear.

"The enemy of my brother and of Claudius Ptolemy," said Sitt Al-Mulk, mockingly.

Her entourage chuckled.

"He was not the late caliph's enemy, Your Regency," said Al-Ghazi. "Your brother found him to be mad, and he put him under my care until he came to his senses."

"And have you come to your senses, Ibn Al-Haytham?" asked Sitt Al-Mulk.

Before he could answer, Al-Ghazi spoke up.

"I can assure Your Regency that Ibn Al-Haytham is in complete possession of his faculties."

Sitt Al-Mulk cut him off.

"Al-Ghazi, you are here as my bailiff, not as his counsel. I want to hear from the great mathematician himself. Ibn Al-Haytham, are you well?"

"By the grace of God, I am," said Alhasan.

"And your mind is sound?"

"As sound as it was made."

Al-Jarjarai whispered in Sitt Al-Mulk's ear.

"Do you equivocate, Ibn Al-Haytham?" asked Sitt Al-Mulk.

"Not at all," said Alhasan. "I meant only that none of us are free from that human turbidity which is in the nature of man, but we must do our best with what we possess of human power. From God we derive support in all things."

"Your Regency, may I question the defendant?" asked Al-Jarjarai.

"Al-Jarjarai, this man may be standing in the dock, but he is not on trial. You heard Al-Ghazi. He has been ill. We are only seeking evidence of his recovery."

"Then may I question the patient, to elicit the soundness of his mind?"

"You may."

Al-Jarjarai stepped down from the podium and approached Alhasan.

"Do you know me, Ibn Al-Haytham?" he asked.

"Yes. You are Ali bin Ahmad Jarjarai. When we last met, you were secretary to the chief of police."

"Yes," said Al-Jarjarai.

"Before that," said Alhasan, "I believe you were Abdelali Haddaoui's prize student at the House of Wisdom. Or had you become his teacher?"

Al-Jarjarai gave Alhasan a menacing look.

"You remember our journey to the cataracts of the Nile?"

"Yes."

"Can you describe the purpose of that journey?"

"To determine the feasibility of building a dam on the Nile."

"And what was your conclusion?"

"I concluded it was feasible. I believe someday a dam will stand on the site I proposed."

Al-Jarjarai laughed, and Sitt Al-Mulk's scribes and attendants joined in.

"And how high above the river will this dam stand?"

"Approximately seventy *dhirā*."

"Seventy *dhirā*?" repeated Al-Jarjarai. "Higher than the minarets at the Mosque of Al-Hakim?"

"Yes."

The courtiers laughed again.

"And what did the caliph think of your plan?"

"I do not know."

"Why not?"

"He placed me under house arrest before I could present a detailed plan."

"He placed you under arrest? For what?"

"He said I was mad."

"He said you were mad, but that did not have anything to do with building a dam seventy *dhirā* high?"

"No."

Alhasan heard more laughter from the court.

"While we were on that journey, did you propose to excavate the Sphinx?"

"I did not propose it to Caliph Al-Hakim."

"Did you propose it to anyone?"

"I discussed it with Captain Al-Ghazi. You were there as well."

"And why would you like to expose this idol?"

"It is a wonder of the ancient world. It should be seen."

"Do you believe the stories about the ancient Greek Sphinx?"

"Of course not."

"Did you not say the Sphinx asked a riddle?"

"That is the legend."

"Didn't you make up a riddle about the Sphinx in the desert?"

"I did."

"Why?"

"It was an intellectual challenge, like a puzzle."

"And do you remember this riddle of yours?"

"The ancient riddle asked what creature walks on four legs in the morning, two legs at noon, and three legs in the evening. I asked, 'What creature calls out two times in the morning, four times at noon, and three times at sunset?'"

"And what was the answer?"

"One who submits to God."

"So you mock Islam with an idol's riddle."

Alhasan said nothing.

"Ibn Al-Haytham?" urged Sitt Al-Mulk.

"I was not mocking Islam."

"But if you do not mock Islam and revere pagan idols, why were you carrying a dagger from an ancient tomb?"

"I found it in the desert."

"Did you find it, or did you take it from a tomb?"

"A grave robber dropped it. I picked it up."

"Your accomplice?"

"He was a stranger. I tried to give it back to him."

"So, grave robbing is something you condone?"

"No."

"But you kept the pagan artifact?"

"Yes."

"And did you visit a pagan temple in Dendera?"

"I did."

"For what purpose?"

"To gain knowledge."

"To worship?"

"To gain knowledge."

"Pagan knowledge?"

"Knowledge is sought for itself. We have learned much from the pagan Greeks, Romans, Persians, and others."

"At the temple of Dendera, did you sit on a carving of a lion's head that projected from the side of the building?"

The courtiers laughed again.

"I took refuge there."

"You took refuge in a pagan temple?"

"Your Regency," broke in Al-Ghazi, "Ibn Al-Haytham was attacked by bandits. He had a duty to protect himself for the good of the mission. He escaped to an ornament on the side of the building. It took courage and dexterity."

"That is enough, Al-Ghazi," said Sitt Al-Mulk. "Do not interrupt again."

Al-Jarjarai continued his questioning.

"Did you tell Al-Ghazi and me that the temple of Dendera had a map of the heavens that you wished to copy?"

"I did."

"For what purpose?"

"For knowledge."

"Ibn Al-Haytham, can you tell this court—I mean, Her Regency—what you think of Claudius Ptolemy?"

The question rankled, just as Al-Jarjarai thought it would. Alhasan had been asked the same question ten years earlier, and his answer had enraged Al-Hakim. The scholar tried to think of something to say that would not be a lie. "He was the greatest astronomer of the ancient world," he said at last.

"Is that all?"

Alhasan thought of his discussion with Rashid Al-Bariqi ten years earlier—the very day that Mourad Al-Ghazi had entered his life. "His tables regarding the positions of the heavenly bodies, their magnitudes and motions, have stood the test of time."

"But?"

"But nothing."

"Are they lacking anything?"

"No. Not for what they are."

"But what about for what they are not?"

Al-Ghazi sucked in his breath and looked down. Alhasan glanced at the soldier's face. He seemed to be suppressing a laugh.

"I do not understand the question," said Alhasan.

"No one understands the question," said Sitt Al-Mulk, laughing.

This time, her entourage laughed at Al-Jarjarai, not with him.

"Are you finished, Al-Jarjarai?" asked Sitt Al-Mulk. "So far, you have convinced me only that Ibn Al-Haytham is a man of great curiosity, which sometimes borders on the impious."

"I have only one more question, Your Regency."

"Proceed."

"Ibn Al-Haytham," said Al-Jarjarai, addressing the entire court, "you are a man of honor who is bound to tell the truth to this assembly."

"Yes," said Alhasan.

Al-Jarjarai approached the prisoner of Al-Hakim.

"Ibn Al-Haytham," he asked, "are you a sorcerer?"

Chapter Thirty-one

What does this man know? thought Alhasan. *And how does he know it? It couldn't be Sadeem; she would never betray me. Her mother? Perhaps, but why? Al-Ghazi never heard about the true demonstration in the hallway—at least that's what I was told.*

These thoughts raced through Alhasan's mind in less than an instant; he answered the question without hesitation.

"No," he said.

"Your Regency," said Al-Jarjarai, "I would like to call a witness."

Alhasan glanced at Al-Ghazi. His one-time nemesis betrayed no emotion.

"Proceed," said Sitt Al-Mulk.

Al-Jarjarai motioned to someone in the rear of the hall to come forward.

"Your Regency, I present Maged Ben Zereba, the husband of Al-Ghazi's daughter, Rania."

Alhasan tried to step forward to see the man, but Al-Ghazi held him in place.

"Face the throne, Mathematician. Do not turn away from Her Regency."

Al-Jarjarai stepped toward the witness.

"How do you know...," Al-Jarjarai caught himself before he said *the defendant.* "Ibn Al-Haytham?"

"I don't know him myself," said Maged Ben Zereba, "but my wife knows all about him. Her sister Sadeem has been his student for the last eight years."

"So your wife's sister must know him well."

"Very well. He tutors her every day."

Alhasan tried to glimpse his accuser again, but Al-Ghazi stood in his way.

"Not now, Mathematician," he whispered.

"And did your sister-in-law ever discuss Ibn Al-Haytham with your wife?" continued Al-Jarjarai.

"She did, many times."

"And did she say he schooled her in his arts?"

"She did. She said he called her his best student."

"Is there one story in particular you wish to tell Her Regency?"

"There is."

"Please proceed."

"My wife, Rania, said that late one night, when she was still living with her parents, she heard a scream in the hallway. It was her sister, Hadil. Hadil said she saw a ghost and pointed at the wall. As Rania came closer, she saw a spirit coming out of the wall toward her."

"Can you tell Her Regency what this has to do with Ibn Al-Haytham?"

"Yes, I can. Rania told me that she screamed, and that when she did, Sadeem came out of her bedroom, and the spirit disappeared. Sadeem said it was not a ghost; it was her. She said Ibn Al-Haytham had taught her how to send her spirit through a door and onto a wall."

"Let us understand. Your wife's sister said that Ibn Al-Haytham was her teacher, and that he had initiated her into the dark arts?"

"Nonsense," shouted a voice from the back of the hall.

Alhasan turned to see who it was, but Al-Ghazi held him in place.

"This is all a sham, Your Regency."

Alhasan recognized the voice. *It's Sadeem.*

"And who might you be?" asked Sitt Al-Mulk.

"I am Sadeem bint Mourad, the daughter of Mourad Al-Ghazi and Khadija bint Muhammad, and the student of the greatest teacher and scholar in the world, Ibn Al-Haytham."

"The sorceress herself," said Sitt Al-Mulk. She turned to her entourage. "My brother used to say that holding court was a bore, but this is turning out to be one of the most interesting afternoons of my life."

"I am no sorceress," said Sadeem, "and Ibn Al-Haytham is no sorcerer. He is the kindest, most patient, most devout, and most brilliant man in the world. He has solved the mystery of vision that has eluded scholars for centuries, and he has devised a method of proving the truth about the real world with the same precision and certainty that geometry does about imaginary points, lines, angles, surfaces, and solids."

"He must be a sorcerer," laughed Sitt Al-Mulk. "You clearly are under his spell."

Al-Jarjarai and the courtiers chuckled.

"Mock me if you wish, Your Regency, but I can quickly prove how devout he is."

"Please proceed," said Sitt Al-Mulk.

"Your Regency, may I ask what day and month you were born?"

"Unusual request, but yes. I was born on the seventh day of Rajab," said Sitt Al-Mulk.

"The seventh day of the seventh month?"

"Yes."

"Two prime numbers," said Sadeem.

"What's that?" asked Sitt Al-Mulk.

"Nothing, Your Regency," said Sadeem. "Ibn Al-Haytham, can you hear me?"

"Yes," said Alhasan.

"Ibn Al-Haytham, what is the seventh verse of the seventh *sura* of the Holy Qur'an?"

Alhasan pictured an open Qur'an hovering near the ceiling of his cell.

"'Then We will surely relate their deeds to them with knowledge,'" recited Alhasan, "and We were not at all absent.'"

Sitt Al-Mulk looked at her advisers. "Is that correct?" she asked.

"Yes," said one of the scribes, an open Qur'an in his hands.

"The seventh verse of the seventh *sura*," scoffed Al-Jarjarai. "Anyone can memorize seven *suras*. How about the one hundred-and-seventh verse of the one hundred-and-seventh *sura*?"

The hall grew quiet. The scribe riffled through his Qur'an. Al-Jarjarai began to smile. Suddenly, Alhasan's clear, strong voice rang out from the alcove:

> Woe unto those who pray
> But are heedless of their prayer—
> Who make a show of their deeds
> And withhold simple assistance.

"There are only seven verses in the one hundred and seventh *sura*," added Alhasan. "Those are the last four, ending with the seventh."

Members of the court talked among themselves, but Al-Jarjarai silenced them.

"Quiet," he shouted. "No one doubts that Ibn Al-Haytham is a savant, but the madhouses are full of savants. The question before Her Regency is whether or not he is a teacher of the dark arts, as Maged Ben Zereba has testified."

"And I am here to testify that Ibn Al-Haytham never taught me about spirits, or magic, or any dark arts," said Sadeem. "He taught me only Euclid's *Elements* and Al-Khwarizmi's *Compendious Book on Calculation by Completion and Balancing*."

"A female mathematician. That is even rarer than a sorceress," joked Sitt Al-Mulk. The courtiers laughed.

"Tell me," said Sitt Al-Mulk, "are you able to solve problems using Al-Khwarizmi's method?"

"I am."

"I understand this is very useful for governance—for the division of property and land, and for estimating expenditures."

"That is what I understand as well," said Sadeem.

"Intelligent, well spoken, pleasant to look at. How old are you, Sadeem bint Mourad?"

"I am twenty-two, Your Regency."

"Are you married?"

"No."

"It seems like you would be an excellent partner for my young nephew, the new caliph. What do you say, Sadeem bint Mourad? Will you accept Ali az-Zahir as your husband?"

"I am honored by the mere suggestion, Your Regency," said Sadeem, "but I am sorry, no."

"Don't worry," said Sitt Al-Mulk conspiratorially. "He is only sixteen, but he will be well schooled in the marital arts."

A few members of the entourage chuckled.

"Your Regency misunderstands," said Sadeem, embarrassed.

"Modesty. I like that," said Sitt Al-Mulk. "But why would a young woman like yourself refuse such an offer, which is far above your family's station, if I may be honest?"

"I cannot marry the new caliph because...."

"Yes?"

"Because I have given my heart to another."

Sitt Al-Mulk laughed, and everyone joined in—everyone except for Al-Ghazi and Alhasan.

"You will marry the caliph. That is my decree," said Sitt Al-Mulk. "Al-Ghazi, you served my brother well. I expect you to talk some sense into your daughter."

"I will, Your Regency," said Al-Ghazi.

"Now, about Ibn Al-Haytham," Sitt Al-Mulk said to Sadeem. "Your brother-in-law—it's her brother-in-law, right?" she whispered to Al-Jarjarai.

He nodded.

"Your brother-in-law has testified that Ibn Al-Haytham taught you the dark arts, but you object to this charge. Explain yourself."

"What my brother-in-law described, and what my sister misapprehended, was nothing more than a demonstration of light and optics," said Sadeem. "It was physics, Your Regency, not sorcery."

Standing in the dock, knowing full well that sorcery was a capital offense, Alhasan could not help but smile at his student's well-chosen words.

Al-Jarjarai was smiling, too.

"So you admit that the scene described by your brother-in-law actually happened," he said.

"It happened," said Sadeem, "but not the way he described it."

"Then help us to understand," said Al-Jarjarai. "You were in your bedroom, is that correct?"

"Yes."

"Behind a door?"

"Yes."

"A solid door?"

"A solid door with an aperture."

"With an aperture."

"Yes."

"What is an aperture?" asked Sitt Al-Mulk.

"A very small hole, Your Regency," answered Sadeem.

"How large was this aperture?" asked Al-Jarjarai.

"No larger than the width of my little finger," said Sadeem.

"And while you were behind this solid door—with an aperture— your spirit in appeared the hallway, is that correct?"

"No. My image appeared."

"Your image appeared, and your sister saw you?"

"Yes," said Sadeem.

"Sorceress!" shouted one of Sitt Al-Mulk's advisers.

"Witchcraft, sorcery," shouted others.

Al-Ghazi released Alhasan's arm and raced to his daughter's side as the advisers crowded around her. Alhasan strained to see his student, but the courtiers stood in the way, shouting at Sadeem and threatening her.

"Enough!" shouted Sitt Al-Mulk.

The entourage quieted down.

"Take her away. Take all of them away, except Ibn Al-Haytham."

His sword drawn, Al-Ghazi escorted his daughter away from the mob. Maged Ben Zereba followed. For the first time, Alhasan saw his student, but only from behind.

"I'm sorry, Madman," cried Sadeem as her father led her away. "I am sorry."

Alhasan heard his beloved student begin to cry. As her sobs echoed through the hall, he could think of only one thing to say.

"Ow-ooooooo," he called out from the alcove. "Ow-ow-ooooooo."

"Ow-ooooooo," answered Sadeem as her father led her into the street.

"Come forward," said Sitt Al-Mulk, motioning to Alhasan.

He approached the throne.

"Ibn Al-Haytham," said Sitt Al-Mulk, "despite this outrageous and childish display of, of childishness, I find that you are sound of mind. However, I also find that you are a menace to the Fatimid Caliphate. I therefore order you to be returned to the Abbasid Caliphate immediately."

She turned to Al-Jarjarai.

"Have Al-Ghazi escort him out of the caliphate."

"Your Regency," said Alhasan, "I am grateful for my release, but may I have a few days, perhaps a week, before I go? I need to write down the discoveries I made during my captivity—equations, diagrams."

A look of disgust crossed Sitt Al-Mulk's face. "You will leave immediately. You are a blot on my brother's shining legacy. You, your failures, and your so-called discoveries cannot be forgotten quickly enough."

Al-Jarjarai seized Alhasan by the arm and led him away from the throne.

"That is enough for today," Sitt Al-Mulk said to the assembly. "This council is adjourned."

Al-Jarjarai led Alhasan down a series of corridors to the office of the chief of police.

"Find Al-Ghazi, the Captain of the Guard, and bring him here," Al-Jarjarai told one of the officers.

Al-Jarjarai pushed Alhasan into a small room adjoining the police chief's office. He opened a cabinet, removed Alhasan's cedar chest, and set it on a table.

Al-Jarjarai opened a large log book and turned the pages until he came to the one he was looking for. He opened Alhasan's cedar chest and removed the articles one by one, checking each against an entry in the log book.

"Everything is here except for a prayer rug and a copy of the Holy Qur'an," he said. "It appears Al-Ghazi took them ten years ago."

"Yes, Al-Ghazi gave them to me. They are in my cell," said Alhasan.

Al-Jarjarai called a scribe.

"Make a note that all of Ibn Al-Haytham's personal effects have been returned to him," said Al-Jarjarai.

As the scribe wrote in the log book, Al-Jarjarai repacked the chest.

"You are fortunate," he said to Alhasan. "If Al-Hakim were here, he would have found you guilty of sorcery."

"I doubt that," said Alhasan. "Despite his temper, Al-Hakim was an intelligent man who loved learning. He would have listened to a rational argument rationally."

"He would have had your head!" roared Al-Jarjarai. "My only regret would have been that I could not have wielded the sword myself."

"I do pity you, Al-Jarjarai," said Alhasan, "not for losing your hand, but for losing your reason."

A few minutes later, Al-Ghazi arrived at the door.

"Sitt Al-Mulk has banished Ibn al-Haytham from the caliphate," said Al-Jarjarai. "You are to take him away immediately."

"Can I at least be unbound?" asked the scholar.

"No," shouted Al-Jarjarai. "You will remain a prisoner until you reach the border of the caliphate."

Al-Ghazi picked up Alhasan's cedar chest.

"Let me give you a hand with this," said the North African, smiling mischievously. "Is it alright if I give him a hand, Al-Jarjarai?"

The chief of state glared at the captain of the guard.

"His hands are tied," Al-Ghazi said to Al-Jarjarai, "so I will give him a hand. Unless you wish to."

He smiled at Al-Jarjarai and headed out the door. Alhasan followed.

"You should not antagonize Al-Jarjarai," Alhasan told Al-Ghazi.

"I have nothing to fear from anyone who cannot handle a sword and a dagger at the same time," said Al-Ghazi.

As if to prove his point, Al-Ghazi put down the chest and untied Alhasan's hands.

"Thank you," said Alhasan, rubbing his wrists.

When they reached the street, Al-Ghazi said, "You wait here, and I will get you a mount."

"The gray?"

"I am afraid the gray died a couple years ago. I will bring you my new dappled gray instead. He is young and full of spirit."

"Al-Ghazi," said Alhasan.

"Don't worry, you can handle him."

"No, there's something else. I would like to see my cell again. My Qur'an and my prayer rug are there."

"Fine. I will give you a ride that far and then go on to my home to retrieve your mount."

Al-Ghazi gave Alhasan a boost onto the black stallion's back and then handed him his cedar chest, which he balanced on his lap. Walking, not galloping, they rode through the city. When they reached Alhasan's cell, Al-Ghazi dismounted first, set the cedar chest on the ground, and helped Alhasan down.

"I will be right back," said Al-Ghazi, climbing into his saddle.

"Wait, Mourad," said Alhasan. He opened the chest, took out his purse, and rummaged through its contents.

"I want Sadeem to have this," said Alhasan, handing Al-Ghazi the emerald ring he found outside the Pyramid.

"Are you sure?" asked Al-Ghazi, holding the ring up to the light. "This stone looks valuable."

"It never brought me any happiness," said Alhasan. "Perhaps it will bring some to Sadeem."

"That is very generous, Mathematician."

"Tell her I appreciate what she tried to do for me today and that I have never been more proud of her."

"I will."

"And tell her that I wish her nothing but happiness with her beloved."

"I will," said Al-Ghazi, tucking the ring into his purse. "There is something you should know, Mathematician. Sadeem thinks very highly of you. I am sure she would wish the same for you."

Alhasan wanted to say thank you, but all he could do was nod. As Al-Ghazi galloped away, the physicist picked up his chest and pushed open the door of his cell. The interior was a blur of blue and white. For the first time in his adult life, Alhasan had tears in his eyes.

Chapter Thirty-two

*T*his *day has been tumultuous*, thought Alhasan. *No wonder I am emotional.*

He wiped his tears with the cuff of his robe. The scent of oud permeated the fabric.

I wish her all happiness. I do.

He retrieved his prayer rug and Qur'an and carefully placed them in the cedar chest. Ten years earlier he had done the same thing, not knowing where he was headed nor how long he would be gone. Now he was going home—not that he actually had a home. He had told Nada it would be hers after three years. It had been ten. *She might have five children by now—or more,* he thought. He smiled to think of a bustling family living in his former quarters.

Perhaps Ali Farooqi was right. He had come to Egypt as required. Perhaps the caliph would reward him with a position in the government. Almost immediately, Alhasan discarded the thought. He would rather copy books than serve as a minister of anything.

He looked around the room. His writings covered the walls. Seven years of work. Now he would have to leave it behind. He stared at the proofs, equations, and diagrams he had scratched into the plaster, trying to commit as much as possible to memory. He grabbed his wax tablet and stylus and began jotting down the most difficult proofs—the ones that had taken the most time. Within a few minutes he had filled the entire writing surface. *It's useless,* he thought. *There is too much.*

He heard two horses clip-clopping up the street and stopping outside his door. One snorted and must have shaken its head, because Alhasan heard a metallic clinking. *It's the black stallion's breast collar,* thought Alhasan.

"Mathematician, it's time," called Al-Ghazi. "Let's go."

Alhasan looked at the stylus and remembered the first time he saw it, rolling out from under his bowl. *Her sister will never miss this,* he thought, slipping the secret gift into his purse.

"I am coming, Mourad," said Alhasan.

"Stop calling me Mourad," said Al-Ghazi. "You make me sound like your friend, instead of your guard."

Alhasan handed the North African his cedar chest and writing tray.

"What is this?" asked Al-Ghazi, holding up the metal tray and peering through the small hole in the middle.

"It is a door to the spirit world," said Alhasan. "Ghosts fly in and out of it."

"Perhaps you are mad after all," said Al-Ghazi, placing the tray on top of the cedar chest and fastening both to the hindquarters of the dappled gray.

"Mourad, please. Allow me to buy paper, ink, and pounce. I need to write down some of the equations I scratched into the walls inside. It will only take a few hours."

"We don't have a few hours, Mathematician. Sitt Al-Mulk wants us out of the city now."

"Then just an hour. Please."

"I am sorry, Alhasan. We must leave."

The North African checked the dappled gray's girth strap and then gave his charge a boost into the saddle.

"We will walk at first," said Al-Ghazi. "Your mount is trained to follow mine."

It had been ten years since Alhasan had ridden a horse by himself. He tried to get comfortable in the saddle and remember what to do.

When they reached the first corner, Al-Ghazi turned right. Alhasan laid his reins against the left side of his horse's neck, and it turned as well. Alhasan glanced over his shoulder to look at his cell one last time. A woman was standing at the doorway, looking inside.

"Sadeem!" shouted Alhasan, but his horse had already turned the corner.

"You're not going back," said Al-Ghazi, wheeling his horse around and grabbing the dappled gray's bridle.

"Understood," said Alhasan. He remembered Sadeem's words at the trial: *I have given my heart to another.*

They rode along the street, the scuff-and-clop of horses' hooves the only sound.

"Did she like the ring, Mourad?" Alhasan asked at last.

"She must have, Mathematician. She cried when she saw it."

It was a tumultuous day for her as well, thought Alhasan.

That evening they made camp outside Ismailia. It was a clear night. It had been ten years since Alhasan had seen more than the patch of sky visible from the garden of the house where he had been imprisoned. He had forgotten how beautiful the entire sky could be. Countless stars sent rays of light down from the heavens, through the atmosphere, and into Alhasan's eyes, creating an infinitely complex, glittering image on his retinas and in his brain. He smiled. Understanding this process made him feel closer to the One who created it all.

Late the next morning, he and Al-Ghazi stopped at an oasis on the road to Jerusalem.

"Mathematician, I am going to leave you here," said Al-Ghazi. "Just follow this road to Jerusalem. Once there, ask for the road to Damascus. When you get to Damascus, see if you can join a caravan to Baghdad. It would be safer than riding alone, although I don't think any bandits would bother with you by yourself. I don't think they have much use for Euclid. But take this sword just to be safe."

He handed Alhasan his scimitar.

"What are you going to do?" asked Alhasan.

"I am going home," said Al-Ghazi. "I am too old to make this journey again. Besides, you don't need me to find your way."

"But what about the remittance? The five thousand dinars."

"I doubt if anyone remembers that codicil, but if they do, I will send a courier, someone I can trust. I can count on you to vouch for it, correct?

"Of course you can. But what about Sitt Al-Mulk and Al-Jarjarai?"

"I will circle into Cairo at night. No one will see me, except, perhaps, the ghost of Al-Hakim. I will stay at home for two or three months. No one will expect me back before that. Then I will retire on the money Al-Hakim paid me. I refuse to work for his ridiculous sister or for that child they call the new caliph."

"Your son-in-law to be."

"Ha, ha, ha," bellowed Al-Ghazi. "You don't know Sadeem. She is more stubborn than you can imagine. Once she makes up her mind, that is the end. She will not marry anyone she does not love, least of all that twit. Ha, ha, ha!"

Al-Ghazi's booming guffaws frightened two black starlings out of a tree. His laugh was contagious. Alhasan smiled at the idea of Sadeem refusing the young caliph.

"That girl swears she will not marry anyone who cannot solve a quadratic equation! See what you have done? You have kept me from being the caliph's father-in-law."

The black stallion watered, Al-Ghazi prepared to leave.

"I have something that belongs to you," said Al-Ghazi, reaching into his saddle bag. He pulled out the golden dagger that Alhasan had picked up outside the Pyramid.

"But you threw that into the Nile."

"I did?"

"Yes, I saw you do it."

"Did you?"

"Yes."

"You are certain that you saw me throw this dagger into the Nile?"

"Yes."

"No errors of vision?"

Alhasan recalled the scene. Al-Ghazi stood with his back to the setting sun and held the dagger aloft.

"The sun was behind you. I saw you in silhouette."

"Everyone saw me in silhouette, even that idiot Al-Jarjarai—ha, ha, ha, ha!"

He handed the dagger to Alhasan.

"You see? You weren't the only one who learned something at the House of Wisdom."

Alhasan smiled. "That was a good trick," he said. "That was a very good trick."

"Thank you. Coming from a sorcerer, that is high praise indeed. Ha, ha, ha."

Alhasan placed the dagger in his belt and bade Al-Ghazi farewell. He found a shady place under a date palm and watched the North African ride away. For the first time in a week, he relaxed. What a whirlwind it had been—the tumult in the streets when Al-Hakim did not return, the trial before Sitt Al-Mulk, the sudden banishment with barely enough time to collect his things.

He thought about all he had left behind—seven years of diagrams, calculations, and notes etched into the walls of his cell. He had a sinking feeling as he realized that he would never remember all the things he had worked out.

"No," he said aloud, "I can remember. I must remember. I will start with the first principles, the first true demonstrations. I will start working it out, and it will all come back to me."

Even as he said it, he knew it wasn't true. Of course he could make a start, and he still remembered the most important discoveries, but the equations about reflection; refraction; concave, convex, and spherical mirrors—much of it would be lost. He thought of the excitement he had felt when he stumbled upon one property or another and worked it out mathematically. He barely understood it at the time, and he certainly would not remember it.

The lost work wasn't the only thing bothering him. "I had a life!" he shouted to no one in particular.

Startled, the starlings hopped away into the sun and then quickly returned, their yellow beaks open as they tried to cool themselves from the heat.

He would rise early and wash. At the call of the muezzin, he would say his morning prayers. Not long afterwards, Sadeem would arrive with his breakfast, usually foule, but she made it so many ways he never got tired of it. She called it food for his brain. As he ate, they would discuss the prior day's findings. These talks had a way of getting him so excited that sometimes he would leave his tray half-finished and go back to work. Often he talked as he worked, never quite sure if Sadeem was there or not. Sometimes she would answer, but other times there would be silence, and he would realize she had slipped away, probably to go to the market or to do her chores.

After midday prayers, she would arrive with his lunch—usually molokhia. "It's spicy, to keep you young," she would joke. He smiled as he thought about Sadeem's teasing jokes and sayings. *She was the best assistant I ever had*, he thought to himself.

Over lunch he would tell Sadeem about his morning's work. She would ask him questions. Sometimes they were so incisive that he would jump up to scratch them into the wall so he would not forget them. In fact, he had devoted one entire wall to her questions alone. The discussion of the morning's findings would go on as he sipped the hot broth and ate the wonderfully cooked meat and vegetables. He explained everything to her, and she never once acted bored. What a strange young woman.

For the second time in his adult life, tears welled up in his eyes. What was wrong with him? Was he becoming feebleminded? Of course he would miss Sadeem, but there would be other students and other assistants when he got back to Basra. If Kareem kept up with his studies, he could become Alhasan's assistant.

He wiped the tears from his cheek with the cuff of his robe. He remembered the first time Sadeem laundered his robe, the way it smelled of oud, and how a speck of lint became airborne, drifting upward into the light, changing his life. Or was it Sadeem's kindness that changed his life, that made him notice the mote and encouraged him to think about it?

When he finished lunch, he would give Sadeem her daily lessons. When they first started, he had helped her with Euclid's *Elements*. Surprised at her grasp of geometry, he proceeded to teach her Al-Khwarizmi's method of calculation by completion and balancing. She became proficient at it. Indeed, there were times when she returned the next day to tell him that she had used Al-Khwarizmi's method on his prior day's work and come up with a different result. Often—well, almost always—she was right. Her corrections made a difference, enabling him to move forward without losing valuable time working with incorrect assumptions.

The lessons completed, Alhasan would nap. Sometimes he would return to work in the late afternoon, but more often he would retreat to the courtyard and watch the clouds catch fire as the sun sank in the west. Just before evening prayers, Sadeem would return with his dinner. She could never stay long, as her father would be home and would question any delay in her return. Alhasan would eat his dinner alone, but he was always grateful for the careful preparation of his food.

He had been fortunate. The time spent under house arrest had been the most productive years of his life. Now it was over. And his work was gone.

"I will go back for her!" he said aloud. He meant to say he would go back for "it," for his work, but somehow he said "her" instead.

He realized it was true. It wasn't the work he missed. It was Sadeem. He missed her, and he couldn't imagine living without her.

He jumped to his feet and looked at the dappled gray, which was nibbling grass growing at the base of another palm.

"You can't go back, you fool!" he shouted at himself. He began pacing back and forth. The starlings took to the air and then circled back and landed in the tree.

"You heard her. She told Sitt Al-Mulk that she couldn't marry the young caliph because she had given her heart to someone else."

It didn't matter. He would go back, and he would ask for her hand in marriage. At least she would know how he felt about her. *Let her read the book of my heart,* he thought. *If she rejects me, at least I will know. Certainty, I can live with.*

He lifted the reins over the head of the gray and laid them on its neck. Holding the saddle with both hands, he put one foot on the stump of a long-dead palm frond, boosted himself up, and put the other foot in the stirrup. He climbed into the saddle and pointed the gray back toward Ismailia.

Al-Ghazi had galloped away, disappearing from sight long ago. There was little chance of overtaking him. Alhasan tried to form a plan. *Al-Ghazi said he would circle back to his house at night and remain there for a couple of months. Circle back. There must be a road on the outskirts of Cairo. But where is the house?* Alhasan thought about the geography of city. He recalled the long ride from Al-Khandaq into the heart of the city and the palace of Al-Hakim. From the palace, they had ridden directly south toward his cell, making a short jog west before turning south again. That was the corner where he had seen Sadeem standing outside his cell. Remembering the scene, Alhasan felt a clot in his chest. He had wanted to go to her then, but Al-Ghazi had stopped him. What would the North African say when he showed up at his door? How would he convince the soldier to listen? He would have to find a way.

When Al-Ghazi had left his cell to get the gray, he had headed south down the street. The house couldn't be far; the food Sadeem brought was always hot, and she came by foot. Alhasan thought again of his student, the way her laughter rang out from the street, how she had questioned him, how she had believed in him, and how she had spoken at his trial, trying to save his life.

Alhasan rode on. The sun climbed higher overhead. It soon would be time to pray. He needed something for a boost back into the saddle. He saw a palm in the distance and continued on. When he got to the tree, he dismounted and unfastened the rope that held his prayer rug to his horse's back. As he began to calculate the Qibla, he noticed a small, dark figure far down the road, with a bright light flashing at its center. Even at a great distance he could make out Al-Ghazi's black stallion

with its silver-plated breast collar. *Now what does he want?* Alhasan wondered. Whatever it was, he felt relieved. He would be able to discuss his
marriage proposal sooner rather than later.

He unrolled his rug in the shade of the palm and then stepped into
the sunlight. He pulled his dagger from his belt and plunged it into the
soil so it was perpendicular to the ground. When its shadow moved
under the hilt, he pulled it out of the ground and slid it into its sheath.
He stood behind his prayer rug, crossed his arms, and began to pray.

Alhasan was well into the fourth Rakat when he heard the clinking
of Al-Ghazi's silver harness. He closed his eyes to concentrate, sat back,
and recited the Tashahhud and the Taslim.

The prayer completed, Alhasan opened his eyes. He was looking
directly at the side of Al-Ghazi's horse, but instead of the North African's thick boot, he saw a woman's slender foot in a beaded sandal. He
raised his eyes, following the shape of the woman's leg under her black
robe. Looking higher, he saw a slim forearm wrapped in jeweled bracelets and a delicate hand holding the leather reins. He admired the woman's hand for an instant and then looked at her face.

She was extraordinarily beautiful, with a small chin; a straight, narrow nose, tending slightly toward the aquiline; full, shapely lips; and
widely set, almond-shaped eyes, lightly outlined with blackened pencil,
the way the Egyptian women made them up. Suddenly, Alhasan realized
he had seen her once before. It was the young woman he had passed in
the street on the way to his trial, the one who had met his gaze.

"Who are you?" he asked.

The woman smiled.

"Madman" was all she said.

Chapter Thirty-three

I t was just one word, but Alhasan knew that voice like no other. For eight years he had listened to it, questioned it, and waited for it every morning, noon, and night. The young woman's fine features dissolved into a watery blur as tears filled the scholar's eyes.

"Sadeem," he said at last.

He wiped his eyes and looked down, embarrassed.

"What are you doing here?" he asked.

"Madman, you left something behind," said Sadeem in a smooth, even voice. "I thought I should bring it to you."

Alhasan looked up at his student and then glanced at the cedar chest, strapped to the back of the dappled gray.

"No, I don't think so," he managed to say. "I have everything I came with."

Sadeem reached into a leather pouch slung around the horse's neck and pulled out a large, thick book.

"You left without this," she said, handing him the book. Her jeweled bracelets sparkled as they slid down her forearm and came to rest on her slender wrist.

Alhasan stood and took the book from her hands. He didn't recognize it. He opened the leather cover to read the title.

"*The Optics*," he read aloud.

He looked up at Sadeem and managed a smile.

"I'm sorry," he said, closing the book and handing it back to his student. "I didn't bring Euclid's *Optics* with me."

Sadeem smiled. Alhasan noticed that she had inherited her father's perfectly straight, pearl-white teeth.

"Look again," she said, with a teasing lilt in her voice. "It isn't Euclid's *Optics*."

Alhasan opened the book and read the full inscription:

The Optics
of Alhasan Ibn Alhasan Ibn Al-Haytham of Basra,
completed on this, the fourth day of Dhu al-Qi'dah,

in the year 411

Alhasan looked up at Sadeem.

"I don't understand," he said.

His student just smiled.

He looked back at the book and began to turn the pages. He saw a diagram of a copper tube with the flame of a candle at one end. A few pages later, he saw a drawing of a copper sheet with a small aperture and two sources of light on a table. He turned the pages more rapidly. He saw curved mirrors, spherical mirrors, with all with mathematical descriptions carefully written in clear, elegant calligraphy.

"It's all here," he said.

"Yes," said Sadeem. "It's all there."

"But how? When?"

"Every night, when I went home after bringing you dinner, I would write down the day's findings. When we discussed them in the morning, I was reading them back to you, double-checking to see if I had gotten them right."

Alhasan thumbed through the manuscript.

"After the trial, when Father took you away, I returned to your cell to copy the missing drawings, diagrams, and equations. I think you saw me. I heard you call my name, but I didn't see you."

"But why did you do it?" he asked.

"Because you told me to," said Sadeem. "Don't you remember? 'It is what the good student does: Preserve the teacher's words so other scholars can read them. The good student does this not because he has to, but out of respect and even love for the teacher.'"

"Yes, of course. I remember saying that. But I believe I was talking about your mother's teachings."

"You were. But how much truer is it when the teacher is not just your tutor, or even your mother, but your beloved?"

Alhasan looked up at Sadeem.

"Your beloved and your betrothed," she said.

"I don't understand," said Alhasan.

"You gave this ring to my father, didn't you?" said Sadeem, reaching her hand across her lap so Alhasan could see the emerald ring he had plucked from the sand outside the Pyramid.

"Yes."

"And it was intended as your *mahr*, to seal our engagement."

Alhasan didn't know what to say.

"My father said you asked for my hand when you gave it to him."

"I told him that I wished you nothing but happiness with your beloved."

"Yes, and I told him you are my beloved."

"But you told Sitt Al-Mulk...."

"I told her I couldn't marry the caliph because I had given my heart to someone else. That was true. I had given it to you."

"But your father never said anything to me."

"He thought nothing could be done. Sitt Al-Mulk had ordered me to marry the caliph. And you were banished from the caliphate. He thought there was no hope for our marriage."

"But there is always hope."

"Yes, Madman, there is always hope."

"And now?"

"And now, it depends on whether or not you want me."

Alhasan's mind was racing. A few minutes earlier he was riding back to Cairo to ask for her hand in marriage; now she was here, in front of him, telling him they were already engaged. He blinked his eyes to see if he had fallen asleep in the shade of the palm tree. He looked up at Sadeem. She was still there. More beautiful than ever.

"Do you want me, Madman?" she asked softly.

"I want you with all my heart," said Alhasan. "Just now I was riding back to Cairo to ask for your hand. I realized...." He paused to take a deep breath. "I realized that I cannot imagine life without you."

"If you're sure," said Sadeem, with a teasing tone in her voice. "I mean, it didn't seem like you were that sure a moment ago."

"I have never been more certain of anything," said Alhasan.

"Then let's start the wedding!" boomed a voice behind him.

Alhasan turned around to see Al-Ghazi standing beside a bay horse, helping a woman down from its back. The woman's fine features reminded him instantly of Sadeem. Beside them stood a handsome young man holding the reins to a gray colt.

"Madman, meet my mother, Khadija bint Muhammad, and my brother, Nasrin," said Sadeem.

"It is an honor to meet you," Alhasan said. "Face to face, I mean," he said to Sadeem's mother.

"Mother and I rode out with Nasrin to find you," said Sadeem. "I told her I couldn't marry the caliph, and, more importantly, I couldn't let you leave without me. Mother understood, and she agreed. When we met Father on the road, he gave me his horse, so I could catch up to you."

"Are we going to have a wedding, or not?" boomed Al-Ghazi.

"It is the fifth day of Dhu al-Qi'dah," Alhasan said to Sadeem.

"Five and eleven. Two prime numbers," said Sadeem, smiling.

"Indivisible," said Alhasan.

"Indivisible," repeated Sadeem.

As modest as she was beautiful, Sadeem dismounted on the far side of the black stallion. She slipped the reins over the horse's ears and walked around in front of it, stopping a few steps away from her betrothed. Alhasan realized she was at least as tall as he was.

"I'm not very tall," he said.

"I knew how tall you were," said Sadeem. "I've done your laundry for years. It's not your height that matters, it's the size of your—"

"Sadeem!" roared her father.

Sadeem giggled.

"I was going to say, heart, Father. The size of his heart."

"Ha, ha, ha," boomed Al-Ghazi. "That's good. I thought you were going to say the size of his brain."

"Mourad doesn't trust anyone with a brain bigger than his," said Khadija bint Muhammad, "which includes most of humankind."

Everyone laughed, even Alhasan. For once, the expression on his face matched the joy in his heart.

He stepped closer to Sadeem and looked into her eyes.

"I love you," he said. It was the first time he had ever said those words aloud.

Sadeem's eyes sparkled.

"And I love you, Madman."

"Nasrin will preside over the ceremony," Al-Ghazi declared. "Mathematician, can you get your Qur'an?"

"Of course," said Alhasan. He handed *The Optics* to Sadeem and retrieved the holy book from his cedar chest.

"Do you know the wedding verses?" Al Ghazi asked.

"Yes," said Alhasan. "O mankind, fear your Lord, who created you from one soul and created from it its mate and dispersed from both of them many men and women."

"No, no," said Al-Ghazi. "Nasrin will read them if you tell him which ones they are."

"Oh, of course," said Alhasan, slightly embarrassed. He handed his Qur'an to Sadeem's brother. "It's Surat An-Nisā', verse one."

Nasrin found the page.

"Next, Surat 'Āli 'Imrān, verse one hundred two."

Nasrin marked the first page with his finger and looked for the next verse.

"It begins, 'O you who have believed, fear Allah as He should be feared.'"

Sadeem glanced at her mother and smiled.

Nasrin found the page and marked it with his next finger.

"And finally Surat Al-'Aḥzāb, verses seventy and seventy-one.

He turned to Al-Ghazi. "There is one hadith as well."

"Do you know it?"

"Yes."

"Is it long?"

Alhasan pauṣed for a moment. "It is three sentences—about sixty words."

"Sadeem, are there any blank pages in that book of yours?" asked Al-Ghazi.

"Yes, Father, there are twenty pages at the back for notes."

Al-Ghazi turned to Alhasan. "Write the hadith in the book so Nasrin can read it."

Alhasan retrieved his pen, ink, and pounce from his chest. Sadeem handed him *The Optics*, and he copied out the hadith:

> By Allah! Among all of you I am the most God-fearing, and among you all, I am the supermost to save myself from the wrath of Allah, yet my state is that I observe prayer and sleep too. I observe fast and suspend observing them; I marry woman also. And he who turns away from my Sunnah has no relation with me.

He sprinkled pounce over the page and waited for the ink to dry. It did not take long in the desert heat. He blew away the powder and handed the book to Nasrin.

"Let us begin," said Al-Ghazi.

The family gathered in the shade of the palm tree.

"Alhasan Ibn Alhasan Ibn Al-Haytham, I give you my daughter in accordance to the Law of Islam in the presence of the witnesses here with the dowry you already have provided. And Allah is our best witness."

"Mourad Al-Ghazi, I accept marrying your daughter, giving her name to myself in accordance to the Law of Islam, in the presence of the witnesses here with the dowry agreed upon. And Allah is our best witness."

Al-Ghazi turned to Nasrin and nodded.

"There is none worthy of worship except Allah and Muhammad is His servant and messenger," said Nasrin, with the others joining in. Nasrin then read the three passages from the Qur'an. He closed the holy book and turned to the page Alhasan had written in the back of *The Optics*. After reading the hadith, Nasrin said a prayer for the bride and groom, their families, and the Muslim community.

The ceremony concluded, Khadija bint Muhammad hugged her daughter, and Mourad Al-Ghazi kissed Alhasan on both cheeks.

"Congratulations, My Son," Al-Ghazi said.

"I am afraid you have traded a rich caliph for a poor scholar," said Alhasan, trying to make a joke.

"I have traded a fool for a man of genius—the only man my Sadeem would be happy with."

Al-Ghazi turned to Nasrin. "Give me that book," he said, pointing to *The Optics*.

Nasrin handed the book to his father, who took out his dagger and opened the book to the back.

"May I?" he asked, holding the dagger up to one of the blank pages.

Alhasan nodded. The captain of the guard made an incision down the center of the book and removed the page.

"May I have the pen, ink, and powder?"

Alhasan handed the writing materials to his new father-in-law.

Supplies in hand, Al-Ghazi spread the blank page flat on the back cover of *The Optics* and began to write. Alhasan looked at Sadeem, but she simply shrugged. Long minutes passed.

"We will come to Basra in a few months, when the weather has cooled," said Sadeem's mother.

"Will you, Mother?" asked Sadeem. "That would be wonderful!"

The note completed, Al-Ghazi sprinkled the paper with pounce and waited for it to absorb the ink.

"Sadeem, this letter is for you—and only you—to open when you get to Baghdad. Understood?"

"Yes, Father."

Al-Ghazi blew the dried powder from the page and carefully folded it.

"In Baghdad," he repeated, handing the letter to Sadeem.

"In Baghdad," said his daughter.

Chapter Thirty-four

It took the newlyweds just over two months to make the trip to Baghdad, and that included a two-week stay in Jerusalem to see the holy sites and celebrate their honeymoon. After ten years in prison, Alhasan had no money, but Sadeem's mother, believing that she and her daughter would catch up to the exiled scholar, had brought along a bag of silver dinars as a gift for the young couple.

"This money is from my midwifery," Khadija bint Muhammad told her daughter, "the fruits of my labors and the labors of many women in Cairo."

Sadeem repeated the joke when she showed the money to Alhasan outside Jerusalem. He could tell from Sadeem's expression that she expected him to say something.

"Your mother is very generous," he said.

"That was a joke, Madman. Her labor as a midwife? Their labor giving birth?" She raised her eyebrows.

"Oh, I see. Your mother makes jokes, just as your father does."

"Yes, my handsome Alhasan."

She paused.

"I understand that joke," said Alhasan. "You are making a pun on my name."

"Yes, but you are supposed to laugh at it, not analyze it."

"What do you expect from a Madman?" said Alhasan, trying an old joke from their time in Cairo.

Sadeem smiled. "Don't worry, Madman. I will help you with humor. If someone says something and I laugh at it, just laugh along. I will explain it later."

Alhasan always felt ill at ease among people, but with Sadeem he felt at peace. It was as if she brought along the safety of the prison where they had met and kept it wrapped around him. Only now she was on the inside, beside him.

When they reached Damascus, Alhasan suggested that they skirt the city. When Sadeem asked why, Alhasan concluded that Al-Ghazi had never told his family the story of his ill-fated engagement, nor of how he had nearly killed a man while delirious. Still, he did not want to lie to Sadeem.

"I am anxious to get to Baghdad," he said. It was the truth.

"I know," said Sadeem. "You want to discuss your discoveries at the House of Wisdom, don't you?"

"Yes, I do. I only hope that Abdelali Haddaoui is there to see it."

"I am sure he will be. You told me he had been teaching at the House of Wisdom for only five years when you arrived there as a student. He likely is no more than ten years older than you are."

Sadeem probably was right, but when you are sixteen, someone ten years older seems like they are from a different generation. Only later do you realize that ten years is barely anything. Alhasan watched Sadeem brush a strand of hair from her face, the bracelets at her wrist glinting in the sunlight. *What is age?* he wondered. *What is time?* Someday, perhaps, these terms would mean something to him, but for now they seemed as abstract and unreal as imaginary points on an imaginary plane.

Sadeem on her bay and Alhasan on the dappled gray caught up to a caravan outside Damascus. Mounted guards at the rear of the procession scrutinized them for a moment and dismissed them as harmless.

"We should see if we can join them," said Alhasan. "It would be safer traveling in a group."

He hailed one of the guards.

"Peace be upon you."

"And upon you be peace."

"Who is your leader?"

"His name is Djalea. He rides at the front, wearing the white turban of the Unitarians."

"Unitarians?"

The guard narrowed his eyes. "Where are you from?"

"We come from Cairo," said Alhasan, noticing the guard's white turban.

"Of course we know the Unitarians," said Sadeem. "And we are all saddened by the death of Al-Hakim."

"He is not dead, but in Occultation," declared the guard.

Alhasan started to say something, but Sadeem touched his arm.

"Many blessings upon him," said Sadeem. "My father was his captain of the guard. He served him faithfully for twenty years."

The guard's hard look softened.

"Where is this caravan going?" she asked.

"To Baghdad."

"May we pass to speak to your leader?"

"I will accompany you," said the guard.

Led by the guard, Alhasan and Sadeem rode past the long train of camels laden with baskets giving off the scents of herbs and spices; ox-drawn carts clattering with earthenware jars; a group of young men—perhaps pilgrims—on foot; two merchants in fine dress, on horseback; an old man in a faded gray robe with his head uncovered, Christian-style, on a pearl-gray donkey; a goatherd with a small herd; a horse-drawn wagon carrying stacks of wooden cages filled with chickens, roosters, ducks, and, at the top, a pair of peacocks, one male and one female; and four more guards on gray horses.

At the head of the cavalcade rode Djalea. Along with a white turban, he wore a simple woolen cloak with dark, vertical stripes; a black vest; and a sash of white linen with long fringe at the ends—the clothing of Lebanon. A leather sheath, holding a wooden lance, hung from his

saddle; another, holding a scimitar, dangled from his waist. He acknowl-
edged the couple's greeting and looked at them with mild interest.

"We would like to join your caravan," said Alhasan. "We can pay,
and I am handy with a sword." He patted the scimitar at his side.

Djalea glanced at the sword's well-worn grip and sheath. "Speak
with the paymaster about the fee and take up a position behind the forward guard." He regarded Sadeem's deft handling of the bay as they
rode along. "This is your wife?"

"Yes."

"She may ride at your side, but she must fall back with the wagons
if we are attacked."

"Understood. Many thanks."

Djalea pointed out the paymaster, and the newlyweds waited for
him to approach. A pair of leather saddlebags hung from the back of the
paymaster's mount. Iron chains lashed the bags to the horse's sides. The
price of joining the caravan was non-negotiable: five silver dinars.

"It is worth the safety and security," Alhasan said to Sadeem.

She agreed. She took the coins from her bag and handed them to
her husband to give to the paymaster. The paymaster held up one of the
coins and scrutinized its engravings, front and back. He hefted the coins
in his palm, and then nodded toward the train.

"Welcome to our caravan."

The couple took up a place behind the guards near the front of the
column. As the sun dropped toward the western horizon, Djalea led the
caravan off the road and into a flat area, broad enough for making a
camp. At the call for evening prayer, Sadeem joined a group five women
who had been riding on carts with their husbands. Alhasan got his
prayer rug and joined the men. The Christian in the gray robe stood
apart from everyone else.

When prayers were over, everyone except Alhasan and Sadeem
went about tasks that had been assigned. Sadeem joined the women
who were preparing food. Feeling awkward and out of place, Alhasan
wandered off to gather firewood. Even from the edge of the camp, he
could distinguish Sadeem's voice from all the others.

When the food was ready, Alhasan and Sadeem found a place away from the group where they could eat together.

"What are the Unitarians?" Alhasan asked. He had been wondering about it ever since they joined the caravan.

"Sometimes I forget that you were in prison for ten years," said Sadeem.

"What do you mean?"

"You were part of my daily life, so it seemed to me that you were just like everyone else—my family, my friends, the people at the market. Bringing you food every day, and especially when you began to tutor me, I came to think I was visiting you at your home. I didn't think of it as a prison cell. I knew you were working on your theories about light and vision when I wasn't there. You seemed like a normal person with a normal occupation. I forgot that you were isolated from everything. I guess I was the only source of news you had."

"You were."

"I never thought to tell you about the Unitarian movement. It did not affect my family—well, perhaps it affected my father in some official ways. Caliph Al-Hakim issued proclamations about the Unitarians, but that came later."

Alhasan wanted to interrupt, but he said nothing. He had listened to Sadeem enough over the years to know she would explain everything. He waited patiently and watched the reflection of the faraway fire dancing in his young wife's eyes.

"It began with a young scholar named Hamza ibn ʿAlī ibn Ahmad. He came to Cairo from the Abbasid Caliphate to study at the House of Knowledge, where he became known as 'Hamza the Fatimid.' He was very capable. His work brought him to the attention of Al-Hakim. The two began to meet, and Al-Hakim appointed him Head of Letters and Correspondence."

"I thought I had seen that name."

"You did?"

"Yes, it was on the letter your father delivered to the vizier of the Abbasid Caliphate, the one requesting my visit to Cairo."

"I see. So I owe a debt of gratitude to Hamza the Fatimid."

Alhasan understood. "As do I," he said, forcing an awkward smile.

"Hamza made the Raydan Mosque his headquarters. With Al-Hakim's support, he began to attract scholars from around the world to study with him."

"Did your father round them up?"

Sadeem laughed. "You must forgive Father for how he treated you."

"I forgave him long ago. Besides, I owe him a debt of gratitude, too."

Sadeem smiled.

"Continue, please," said Alhasan. "This is interesting."

"It is about to get more interesting," said Sadeem. "Hamza began to preach a new doctrine, which incorporated elements of ancient Greeks such as Pythagoras, Plato, and Plotinus. He called it Absolute Monotheism or Oneness. Father sometimes was standing guard at the palace when Al-Hakim met with Hamza. He said he thought Hamza's ideas were a corruption of Islam."

"I find them fascinating. Before I was a mathematician, I was a theologian. I attempted to reconcile the differences between the sects and discover the one true doctrine. But I failed."

"I know. Father told us you set off a riot at the House of Wisdom when you said there is no Ultimate Reality that can resolve the differences between the sects."

"It wasn't a riot."

He studied his wife's face. The beginnings of a smile crimped the perfectly smooth skin at the corners of her eyes into tiny creases of delight.

"You are teasing me again," he said.

Sadeem's smile grew, dimpling her cheeks and revealing her pearlescent teeth. He stared at her lips, deep red in the firelight. He wanted to kiss his wife.

Sadeem put a finger to his lips. "Later," she said, reading his thoughts. The creases at the corners of her eyes deepened and lengthened as her smile grew even more.

"Anyway," she continued, "Hamza was working on the same problem you were, and he brought in the philosophies of the Greeks and other mystical schools of thought. He preached a unity of belief. That is where the name Unitarians came from. He called for reforms, which some people did not like."

"Like what?"

"He spoke out against polygamy, remarriage after divorce, and other familiar practices. People began to threaten him and his followers, so Al-Hakim issued a decree protecting them and promoting free worship for all."

"He favored this Hamza."

"Yes. In fact, shortly afterward, Al-Hakim issued a decree that came straight from the teachings of Hamza. Al-Hakim referred to his decree as the 'divine call.' I forget everything it said. Mother and Father did not heed the call. They considered it extreme."

"How so?"

"Among other things, it said that pilgrimages, fasting, holy days, law, and rituals led people away from oneness with God. Hamza called his beliefs 'a spiritual doctrine without any ritualistic imposition.'"

"Amazing. I never knew any of this."

"I know. I'm sorry. I should have told you about it."

"No, I am glad you didn't. It might have distracted me from my work in optics."

"Yes, and, since you are a Sunni, I knew it had no relevance to your faith."

"That is true."

"Perhaps you noticed fewer people going to the mosques on Fridays."

Alhasan thought about this. "Yes, I did. I thought fewer people were living in the area and traveling past my cell."

"One of the things Al-Hakim called for was reading, prayer, and social gatherings on Thursdays instead of Fridays, and not in mosques, but in other meeting places."

"How strange."

"Yes, that is what my parents thought. We did not attend these gatherings. Well, Father might have attended one for show, but we continued to go to the mosque on Fridays. Shortly after issuing the divine call, Al-Hakim named Hamza the imam of the Unitarians."

Sadeem paused to eat, since she had been doing most of the talking.

"So when you gave condolences for the death of Al-Hakim, it was because he supported the Unitarians?"

"Yes, but not just that. Al-Hakim was able to issue the divine call because, of course, he was the Ismaili imam. But Hamza and his follow-ers considered him more than an imam."

She took another bite of the roasted goat, paused to chew, and then continued, "They saw Al-Hakim as divinely inspired, a link to what they called the Cosmic Intelligence."

"Al-Hakim was a man of great intellect," said Alhasan. "This must have appealed to him."

"Yes, he took it seriously. Father said he became even more with-drawn and ascetic."

"Is that why the guard objected when you said Al-Hakim was dead?"

"Yes. Before your trial, Hamza issued a proclamation that Al-Hakim was not dead, but had gone into Occultation. But it is more than that. We had to be careful with that guard. That is why I stopped you from asking questions."

"Careful about what?"

"I was not sure which group of Unitarians he belonged to."

"You mean the Unitarians are not united?"

Sadeem smiled.

"The new sect, bisected?"

Sadeem laughed. She had to put a finger to her lips to keep a morsel of food from falling out.

"Yes. And the differences spilled out into the streets."

"All while I was in prison, oblivious to everything going on around me?"

"Yes. You see Hamza had a follower, also from the East, named Ad-Darazī. At first he was a loyal disciple."

"They always are."

"He preached the Unity doctrine, but he came to the conclusion that Hamza was making mistakes leading the movement. Ad-Darazī thought he should lead the reforms and he gave himself the title 'The Sword of the Faith.'"

"What did Al-Hakim think of that?"

"I don't know, but Hamza told him, 'Faith does not need a sword to aid it.'"

Alhasan smiled. It reminded him of what his father had told him long ago.

"This made Ad-Darazī angry, and the rivalry grew. When Al-Hakim began to refer to Hamza as the 'Guide of the Consented,' Ad-Darazī began to call himself 'Lord of the Guides.'"

"Lord of the Guides? Without Al-Hakim's permission? That would be dangerous."

"Perhaps Ad-Darazī knew that, because Father said he began to meet with Al-Hakim on his own. He had written a book that expressed the unusual—most would say heretical—belief that God had been present in different men, beginning with Adam and continuing through the prophets, Ali, and his descendants, including Al-Hakim himself."

"He thought Al-Hakim was divine?"

"Yes, this is what he told the caliph and what he wrote in his book."

"What did Al-Hakim think? I suppose it is a short step from believing you are divinely inspired to believing you are divine."

"Father was not sure what he thought. He said Al-Hakim asked Ad-Darazī many questions about manifestation, incarnation, the transmigration of souls, and the like. You know my father; he listened, but he thought it was nonsense."

"What did Al-Hakim do? Did he proclaim his divinity?"

"No. At first he did nothing. He let Ad-Darazī preach. But Hamza criticized Ad-Darazī, labeling him a heretic and calling him 'The Insolent One' and even 'Satan.' Riots broke out when Ad-Darazī preached, and several of his followers were killed. Al-Hakim suspended the decree protecting free worship and had my father arrest Ad-Darazī."

"Hamza prevailed," said Alhasan, looking off at the fire. "Did Al-Hakim place Ad-Darazī under house arrest?" There was bitterness in his voice.

"No, Madman," said Sadeem, laying her hand on her husband's arm. "He had him executed."

Alhasan continued staring at the distant flames. Sadeem stroked his arm and looked up at his face. Tears glistened under his eyes. Sadeem hugged her husband's arm and put her head on his shoulder.

"I am so lucky," said Alhasan at last. He looked down, meeting Sadeem's eyes. "I am so blessed."

Chapter Thirty-five

Baghdad had grown tremendously in ten years. Alhasan did not recognize the outlying areas at all. He doubted if he could have found his way through the maze of mud huts and stone buildings without Djalea as a guide. Eventually the Abbasid scholar began to recognize some of the minarets, domes, and marketplaces. Excited, he pointed out the sights to Sadeem.

At last the caravan reached its final destination, the central marketplace where Abdelali Haddaoui had spotted Alhasan ten years before. Alhasan thanked Djalea for the safe conduct through the desert. He looked around and saw Sadeem talking to one of the women in the caravan. When she finished, she rode up to Alhasan.

"That woman, Ilham, asked us to meet her here tomorrow, and she will lead us to her house to share the evening meal," said Sadeem. "She said we are welcome to spend the night."

"How kind of her."

"She is talkative, but kind and sweet. Her husband is an apothecary. I think you will like him."

Alhasan tried to look appreciative, but inside he was nervous at the thought of making conversation with a total stranger.

"You will be fine," said Sadeem, sensing his unease. "He will be grateful to have a chance to do the talking."

"Fine," said Alhasan. "I am looking forward to it."

"You don't have to lie for my sake," said Sadeem. "I know it will be difficult for you. But don't worry. They will be pleasant. You will see."

Alhasan nodded.

"I know the way to Abdelali's from here," he said. "Assuming he is still there."

"Let's find out," said Sadeem.

After ten years in isolation, Alhasan found the sights and sounds of Baghdad jarring and confusing. Small piles of rubbish burned beside the road, sending up pale plumes of acrid smoke. Children who were not even alive the last time he passed through these streets darted in front of his mount. Vendors called to him to buy trinkets, fruit, and odd smelling cooked meats. At the same time, ghostly images from his past emerged from the aperture of memory and settled over the chaotic present. A knot formed in Alhasan's stomach. He longed for the solitude of his cell.

After a short ride, the newlyweds reached the bronze doors of Abdelali's home. A green patina highlighted the geometric designs embossed on the door. Everything seemed well kept. Hopeful, Alhasan knocked on the door. Abdelali's servant Essam answered.

"Peace be upon you."

"And upon you be peace."

"Essam, correct?"

The servant nodded.

"Can you tell me if your master is here?"

"He is. May I ask who calls?"

"Essam, it is I, Ibn Al-Haytham."

Essam's eyes widened. "Wait," he said. He turned and ran into the house. "Master!" he cried. "Master come quickly!"

Alhasan heard Abdelali's voice.

"What is it, Essam? I told you I did not wish to be disturbed."

The rest of the conversation was muffled. Then Alhasan heard footsteps running across the tile floor. Abdelali appeared at the door. His eyes opened even wider than his servant's had.

"I don't believe it," Abdelali whispered, gasping for breath. "Is it possible? Is it you, Alhasan?"

Alhasan managed a crooked smile. Abdelali lunged through the door and wrapped his arms around him.

"My friend, my dear friend, it is you," Abdelali said. "You are alive. Alive!"

"Alive and quite well, Abdelali."

His teacher stepped back and looked at him. "I heard you were dead. Everyone said so. I didn't want to believe it. I didn't want to!"

Alhasan felt his throat tightening.

"As you can see, I am not dead at all," he said.

Abdelali took a deep breath through his nose. His eyes searched Alhasan's face, taking in the change and the constancy.

"Alive," he repeated.

The surprise absorbed at last, Abdelali noticed Sadeem.

"And who is this lovely young woman?" he asked.

"This is my wife, Sadeem."

"Wife? Praise Allah! Blessings upon both of you." He placed his right hand on his chest. "I am Abdelali."

"I am Sadeem. I have heard much about you."

"Please, come into my home. Essam! The horses!"

The servant led the animals away and the newlyweds followed Abdelali into his home.

"Halima!" called Abdelali. "Halima, we have guests!"

Drawn by the commotion, Abdelali's wife was waiting in the entryway. "Alhasan," she said. "It is so good to see you. And who is this?"

"Alhasan has taken a wife," said Abdelali, unable to conceal the astonishment in his voice.

"Congratulations to you both. May Allah bless this union," said Halima, smiling with deep dimples in both cheeks.

"Thank you," said the newlyweds together.

"Come," Halima said to Sadeem. "How long have you been traveling."

"Two months," said Sadeem, following Halima down the hallway, "but only three hours today."

"Please, this way," Abdelali said to Alhasan, motioning toward the great room.

The two men sat on cushions.

"You must forgive me," said Abdelali. "It is a shock to see you. How long has it been?"

"Ten years."

"Ten years. And what have you been doing for ten years?"

"I surveyed the Nile, I memorized the Qur'an, and I wrote a rather lengthy treatise on optics."

"Optics. As you discussed at the House of Wisdom?"

"Yes. Abdelali, I have solved the mystery of vision."

"Have you? I am excited to hear about that."

"I am glad. I would like to give a talk at the House of Wisdom."

"Of course. I will arrange it."

"Abdelali, I want you to invite everyone."

"What do you mean, everyone?"

"I mean, not just scholars interested in optics. I want you to invite mathematicians, astronomers, physicians, even philosophers."

"I don't understand. Why?"

"Because I will discuss something even more important than my discoveries about optics."

"What is that?"

"I have developed a methodology that touches upon all the sciences, indeed upon knowledge itself."

Abdelali looked at the younger scholar carefully. "This is an enormous claim."

"It sounds enormous, but it is really quite simple. You will see."

"Alhasan, I do not wish to be embarrassed again."

"I understand. I can explain it to you now, if you like."

"Please."

Alhasan spent the next hour describing his true demonstrations— why he felt he needed them, how they worked, and why he believed they superseded logic and argument. "Man is flawed," he concluded. "Therefore, if we are to know the truth about nature, we must enter into a dialogue with the universe itself."

"This is fascinating," said Abdelali. "I am not sure I share your enthusiasm, but I certainly will not be embarrassed by its presentation at the college of our peers."

Alhasan and Sadeem spent the night in comfort and luxury. The next day, Abdelali began to make the arrangements for Alhasan's talk. Alhasan asked Sadeem to go to the marketplace to purchase items he would need for his presentation. Alone in Abdelali's study, Alhasan took sand, water, and a cloth, and began to rub the metallic backing off of a small convex mirror Sadeem had purchased in Cairo for one of his true demonstrations. By late afternoon, he was finished. He held his old writing tray up to one of Abdelali's windows and placed the glass disk next to the aperture he had made years before. He scrutinized the image that appeared on the far wall, as he moved the glass further from the aperture. "Perfect," he said at last.

Later that afternoon, Alhasan and Sadeem met Ilham at the marketplace and accompanied her home. Sadeem was right; Ilham's husband, Abdelilah, was pleased to have someone to talk to. Alhasan was intrigued by the processes the apothecary employed.

"I am giving a talk at the House of Wisdom tomorrow," he said toward the end of the evening. "I invite you to come. I am certain you will find it useful."

Alhasan and Sadeem walked home in the starlight. Alhasan looked up at the heavens and oriented himself in the street. There in the northeast shone Auriga. Alhasan smiled at the charioteer.

"I have been dreaming of speaking at the House of Wisdom ever since you told me Al-Hakim had disappeared," he said.

"I know you have," said Sadeem.

They walked the length of the street in silence.

"Can I tell you a secret?" Sadeem asked as they crossed the empty marketplace.

"Of course. You are my wife. You can tell me anything."

"I have been praying that this day would come for you ever since you told me about the two lamps and the aperture."

"You have?" said Alhasan, dumbfounded. "Your faith is great—greater than mine."

"Did you think God had forgotten you?"

"No. But I had resigned myself to the idea that I would never see Baghdad again."

"I never doubted you would return," said Sadeem.

They turned the corner and headed toward Abdelali's house.

"Do you want to know another secret?" asked Sadeem.

"What is it?"

"I never doubted that I would be here with you."

Chapter Thirty-six

Waking early, Alhasan stared at a small dome that protruded from the ceiling high above the bed in Abdelali Haddaoui's expansive home. Next to him, Sadeem slept on her right side, her left arm stretched across his chest. He turned his head and looked at his bride. Her right arm was crooked beneath her head, her delicate hand and wrist framing her face. A shock of mussed, dark hair lay across her brow. Her father had said that the face he saw floating in a sphere above a marsh was the most beautiful face he had ever seen, before or since, but that was ten years ago, before Sadeem had grown into a woman. Alhasan wondered what he would say now. He did not believe a face could be more beautiful than the one on the pillow beside him.

Alhasan did not want to wake his wife, but he was anxious to get up. Abdelali had scheduled his talk for the evening, as requested, but Alhasan wanted to get to the House of Wisdom early. He needed to set up the various devices he had created for his true demonstrations and make sure everything worked. He stared at the ceiling and listened to his wife's soft breathing. When he turned to look at her again, her eyes were open.

"What were you looking at?" she asked.

"First you, then the ceiling."

"What were you thinking about?"

"Angles of incidence and reflection."

Sadeem rolled onto her back and looked at the ceiling.

"From a curved surface?"

"Yes. I was imagining a single ray of light from the window—"

"And you wanted to know how to find the point on the curved surface where the light would be reflected into your eye?"

"Yes."

"Ptolemy's problem. You solved it."

"I did?"

"Yes. Your proof required six subsidiary lemmas. It was one of the things I had to copy from your cell after you were freed. I couldn't remember all of it, no matter how many times we discussed it."

"Six subsidiary lemmas. Too long and tedious. I should find a mathematical solution."

"I already did."

"You did?"

"Yes, using calculation by completion and balancing."

"You little genius," said Alhasan. "Sitt Al-Mulk was right." He raised the pitch of his voice to match the Egyptian leader's. "'You are a perfect match for the young caliph.'"

"I am sorry, Your Regency," said Sadeem, dramatically. "I have already given my heart to another."

"I will never understand why it was me," said Alhasan.

"Simple," said Sadeem. "You were the only man I knew who could solve a quadratic equation."

She leaned over and kissed her husband.

"Did you write your solution to Ptolemy's problem in *The Book of Optics*?" Alhasan asked.

"No. I wrote it in my diary," said Sadeem. "It's a secret."

"I told you last night, you can tell me your secrets," said Alhasan, taking her hands in his.

"I can, and I might," teased Sadeem. "But later. Today you have to prepare for your talk. You don't want to embarrass Abdelali."

"Do you think I might?"

"Of course not. I was joking. You will be brilliant."

She stood up and walked toward the washing room. Alhasan watched the flash of her ankles beneath the hem of her robe and then leaned back and stared at the ceiling. *Six subsidiary lemmas*, he thought. *I can't wait to see her solution.*

Later that morning, Alhasan took an assortment of optical devices to the House of Wisdom—lamps, mirrors, tubes, screens with apertures, and the glass disk he had fashioned from the convex mirror. Essam assisted him. They also took an auger, which Abdelali had agreed he could use on a wooden door at the rear of the room where the lecture was to take place. The door led to a scriptorium, where books that had been translated into Arabic were read aloud to calligraphers who copied the texts into new manuscripts.

Alhasan examined the thickness of the door and then paced the length of the meeting room to measure it. He did some quick calculations on a scrap of manuscript a copyist had discarded and then marked a place on the door for Essam to drill. As the head of the scriptorium read a treatise to the copyists, Essam bored into the wood.

In the lecture hall, Alhasan unpacked his lamps and devices and arranged them on two large tables. One apparatus was the straight copper tube he had brought from Cairo. Another was an opaque cylinder of the type he had described to Sadeem when he first explained his theory of vision. Next to it he laid the pottery stylus Sadeem had given him years before.

The drilling completed, Essam called to Alhasan. The mathematician placed a small copper disk with an aperture into the opening on the side of the scriptorium. He tried to fit the glass disk into the opening on the side of the door that faced the auditorium, but the hole was too small. Essam used the auger as a router to enlarge it. Spiraled shavings swirled to the floor as Essam worked the auger around the opening. Essam ran his finger around the perimeter to remove any burrs and stepped back. Alhasan pushed the convex glass into the opening. It fit.

Alhasan removed the glass disk and handed Essam a patch of leather. "Affix this over the opening. Tonight, you will stand here before the lecture begins. Be sure no one opens this door. When I say, 'now,' remove the covering from the hole."

Essam nodded. "I will."

"Try to appear relaxed and disinterested, as if this door were the only place in the world where you felt comfortable standing."

"I will."

With Abdelali's permission, Essam brought lamps from all parts of the building to the scriptorium. When he was done, he helped Alhasan hang a large sheet of white canvas at the front of the hall.

As Alhasan was raising the canvas to a precise position above the floor of the House of Wisdom, his wife was on the other side of the Round City, climbing the stairs to the palace of Caliph Al-Qadir. A guard stopped her at the door.

"I am here to see Caliph Al-Qadir's vizier," said Sadeem.

"On what business?"

"I am an emissary of the Fatimid Caliphate."

The guard looked surprised but allowed her to pass.

Inside, she made her way to the vizier's secretary and repeated her introduction.

"Just a moment," he said.

The secretary disappeared behind a curtain that hung at the rear of the chamber. A short while later he reemerged.

"This way," he said.

Sadeem walked through the opening of the curtain and down a hall to large, open door.

"Peace be upon you," said the vizier, walking toward her from the center of his chamber.

"And upon you be peace," said Sadeem.

"When I heard Ibn Al-Haytham had returned to Baghdad, I assumed someone would call on me from the Fatimid Caliphate, but I never expected it to be a woman, nor such a young and beautiful one."

"Thank you," said Sadeem.

"My name is Shafqat Ali Farooqi. And you are?"

"Sadeem bint Mourad."

"Mourad? Mourad Al-Ghazi?"

Sadeem smiled.

"Why, yes. Your smile answers for you."

"My father sends his greetings. He always speaks highly of you."

"That is wonderful. I hope he is well."

"He is, thank you."

"He sent you in his place?"

"He did. This letter will explain everything."

She handed Ali Farooqi the note her father had written on the page he had cut from *The Book of Optics* outside Cairo. Ali Farooqi unfolded it and began to read. Sadeem watched him carefully. When he finished, he looked up and smiled.

"Normally, I would ask to see proof that the asset lent to the Fatimid Caliphate had been returned, but in this case it will not be necessary. News of Ibn Al-Haytham's arrival and his talk at the House of Wisdom has spread throughout the city. I accept this letter—and your smile—as proof of who you are and why you are here."

Relieved, Sadeem smiled again.

"Prasanna!" the vizier called.

The vizier's secretary opened the door to the chamber.

"The chest," said Ali Farooqi.

The secretary left, and Ali Farooqi turned back to Sadeem.

"I assume you have a cart or a mount."

"I do."

"Five thousand silver dinars is quite heavy," said Ali Farooqi.

"Yes," said Sadeem. "I imagine it is."

Chapter Thirty-seven

As dusk descended upon Baghdad, Alhasan fitted his glass disk into the hole in the door to the scriptorium and then went inside and started lighting the twenty lamps Essam had collected.

"God is the Light of the heavens and the earth," Alhasan recited to himself. "The likeness of His Light is as a niche wherein is a lamp (the lamp in a glass, the glass as it were a glittering star)."

He prayed for God's help as he heard the murmur of the arriving scholars.

"Light upon Light," Alhasan continued. "God guides to His Light whom he will. And God strikes similitudes for men, and God has knowledge of everything."

The noise in the lecture hall grew. Alhasan had worked all his life to bring knowledge to his people. If he could convince these scholars that his findings about light and vision were correct and, more importantly, that his methods for discovering the truth were sound, he would accomplish that lifelong goal. But human hearts can be adamantine, and the strongest minds are the most difficult to bend. He would strike with the hammer of truth, but only The Compeller could provide the forge's softening fire.

The audience assembled, Abdelali began the proceedings. He welcomed the guests and introduced Alhasan by listing some of his noteworthy treatises. He then read a statement Alhasan had prepared:

My friends, Ibn Al-Haytham will begin his lecture by speaking
to you from another room. He asks that you remain calm. What
you are about to witness is physics, not magic. It represents
knowledge in its purest form—a dialogue with the universe
itself.

Abdelali paused while his assistants extinguished lamps around the
auditorium. The room darkened, Abdelali continued, "My dear colleagues, I now present Ibn Al-Haytham."

"Now!" said Alhasan.

Essam removed the leather patch from the opening in the door. The
light of twenty lamps reflected off Alhasan, who stood in the middle of
the scriptorium in a white robe and yellow turban. Light rays from his
turban passed downward through the aperture and were refracted
upwards by the curved glass. Light rays from his leather sandals passed
upward through the aperture and were refracted downward by the glass.
Light rays from every point on his body passed through the aperture and
the glass and into the auditorium. An image of the scholar, upright and
true, appeared on the large white canvas sheet hanging at the front of
the lecture hall.

The audience gasped, but the sound was nearly inaudible in the
center of the scriptorium.

"Greetings, my fellow seekers after truth," called Alhasan. The figure on the canvas sheet raised its hands in a sign of peace.

The audience gasped again. A murmur arose from the assembly.

"I am speaking to you from the room behind you. Please face the
back of the hall and regard the light shining from the center of the
door."

The crowd turned around and looked at the door.

"What you see is the light of twenty lamps located here in the scriptorium, shining through an aperture I made in the door. This aperture is
of such a size and located in such a position so that only light rays
reflected from my body and from the air immediately around me, traveling in straight lines, can pass through the door and onto the canvas
sheet. All other light rays are screened out."

He lowered and raised his hands.

"Whatever I do in this room is reflected from my body, through the aperture, and onto the sheet in your room. If I lower my hands," he said, lowering his hands, "you see it. Or if I raise my hands, you see it. Because your room is dark, only light passing through the aperture illuminates the sheet.

"Now, if anyone would care to assist me, please come to the door and place your hand over the opening."

A man near the back of the room did so.

"You will see that when the opening is covered, my image disappears from the sheet. Uncover the opening, and my image reappears. The image on the sheet is made with light—not magic, not spirits, nothing but light. Watch as I begin to extinguish the lamps."

Without leaving his place, Alhasan reached out with a candle snuffer and, one at a time, extinguished four lamps within his reach.

"You see, my image begins to fade, because less light is reflected from my form. I will extinguish all the lamps here in the scriptorium. Keep your eyes on the canvas sheet. The image will grow dimmer with each lamp I extinguish..."

Alhasan made his way around the scriptorium, putting out one flame after another until only one lamp was left burning.

"...until, finally, the image disappears altogether."

The last lamp in hand, Alhasan opened the door to the auditorium. As he walked into the room, someone by the aisle shouted "God is great!" By the light of the lamp he carried, Alhasan could see it was Abdelilah, the apothecary he had visited the night before.

"Magnificent!" shouted someone else in the audience.

"Praise Allah!" called another.

"God is great!" shouted another.

As Alhasan approached the front of the hall, scholars along the aisle reached out and patted him on the back. The cries of praise were deafening.

And then, above it all, Alhasan heard a single, high voice.

"Owwooooooooooo!"

Alhasan looked toward the left side of the hall. A small group of women stood in a screened-off area. There, in the first row, stood Sadeem with Ilham on one side and Halima on the other.

"Owwooooooooooo!" called Alhasan, doubting he could be heard over the tumult in the room.

The crowd quieted down, and Alhasan began to speak. "What you have witnessed is what I call a true demonstration. A true demonstration is a physical procedure conducted to test a supposition or hypothesis, or to illustrate a known law. The true demonstration you witnessed was designed to test whether or not rays of light reflected from a source on one side of a screen and passing through an aperture could be refracted by a piece of glass in such a way that a clear, upright image would appear on the other side of the aperture. I take it from your reaction that the true demonstration worked."

"God is great!" shouted someone in the back. Alhasan glanced at Sadeem. Her smile radiated across the room.

"As I came down the aisle," said Alhasan, "some of you clapped me on the back. I think you were conducting your own true demonstrations, to see if I was real and alive."

The audience laughed.

"I can assure you I am both."

He paused.

"I have been away a long time, held in captivity in a cell in Cairo. But I was never alone. The Lord was always with me. My ten-year imprisonment was His way of making sure I would solve the mystery of vision and discover the properties of light."

The audience nodded in approval.

"I was not doing very well...."

The memory of his solitude choked him like a rope. He paused and looked down. He took another deep breath and waited for the tightness in his throat to go away.

At last he looked up. "I was not doing well, so the Lord sent me an angel, a young student who changed my life—my wife, Sadeem."

He gestured toward the women hidden by the screen.

"God is great!" called out someone in the audience. "Praise Allah," shouted another.

"Yes, praise Allah," said Alhasan. "With His help, and with Sadeem's, I came to know the real value of true demonstrations. And that is, as Abdelali said in his introduction, to enter into a dialogue with the universe, and through it, with The Creator.

"Human beings, as we know, are fraught with all kinds of imperfections and deficiencies. As a result, when our inquiries concern subtle matters, perplexity grows, views diverge, opinions vary, conclusions differ, and certainty becomes difficult to obtain.

"That is why, if one's goal is discovering the truth about nature, one must eliminate human beings and their opinions as much as possible and allow the universe to speak for itself.

"I formerly composed a treatise on light and vision in which I employed persuasive methods of reasoning, but when true demonstrations relating to all objects of vision occurred to me, I started afresh. Whoever, therefore, comes upon the said treatise must know that it should be discarded. Even the most brilliant reasoning is worthless if nature does not support it.

"Tonight I will discuss how true demonstrations led me to discover many properties of light. But this method can be used to study anything in nature.

"Take any principle—anything you have wondered about—and imagine a way to test it. True demonstrations will guide you to the answer. They will enable you to distinguish the properties of particulars, finding what is uniform, unchanging, manifest, and not subject to doubt. Once this is accomplished, you can ascend in your inquiry, in a gradual and orderly fashion, criticizing premises and exercising caution in regard to conclusions—your aim in all that you make subject to inspection and review being to employ justice, not to follow prejudice, and to take care in all that you judge and criticize that you seek the truth and not be swayed by opinion."

A scholar in the audience rose to his feet. "If I understand you, Ibn Al-Haytham—and please correct me if I am wrong, for surely I must be—but it seems that you are asking this learned assembly to discard not just your former treatise on optics, but all the books here in the House of Wisdom."

The man swept his hand around the room, indicating the libraries, reading rooms, and storehouses of manuscripts beyond its walls.

"Under our patron, Caliph Al-Qadir, we have collected books from as far away as Al-Andalus, including the writings of Plato, Aristotle, Pythagoras, Archimedes, Euclid, and Ptolemy."

Members of the audience nodded in agreement.

"I myself have been teaching Aristotle in this very hall for twenty-five years," said the scholar. "Are you suggesting that we discard the knowledge of the ancients, which has endured for centuries?" The man smiled at his colleagues. "Unless, of course, it passes a 'true demonstration?'"

He laughed, and a few chuckles arose from the crowd.

"I was one of your students, Mohamed Emara," Alhasan replied to his former teacher, "and when you taught me what Aristotle had done, I became engrossed in my desire to understand philosophy wholeheartedly. Aristotle discussed the nature of the physical world. He analyzed the terminology of logic and divided it into primary kinds. Furthermore, he analyzed those aspects which are the material and elemental bases of reasoning, and he described their classes. This analysis is essential for the discussion of truth and falsehood."

Mohamed Emara nodded.

"Because of Aristotle, I saw that I can reach the truth only through concepts whose matter is sensible and whose form is rational."

Mohamed Emara and a few other scholars voiced their approval.

"But," said Alhasan.

The audience grew quiet again.

"But," he repeated, "the seeker after truth is not one who studies the writings of the ancients and, following his natural disposition, puts his trust in them, but rather the one who suspects his faith in them and questions what he gathers from them, the one who submits to argument and demonstration.

"Thus the job of one who investigates the writings of scientists, if learning the truth is his goal, is to make himself an enemy of all that he reads, and, applying his mind to the core and margins of its content, to attack it from every side.

"He should also suspect himself as he performs his critical examination of it, so he may avoid falling into either prejudice or leniency."

The scholars debated these words in muffled tones that began to rise. Suddenly, a woman's voice rang out from behind the screen, "'Authorities are not immune from error, nor is human nature itself.'"

Alhasan looked over and saw his wife, standing.

"'Only God is perfect,'" Sadeem continued. "'The seeker after truth must submit to Him, and to His manifest laws in the universe, and not to the sayings of a human being.'"

The crowd grew quiet, and Alhasan continued his lecture. He began his discussion of optics by restating the competing theories of vision—intromission and extromission. He described his own theory of vision as a unification of these theories, with light rays instead of forms entering the eye, but traveling through the air in the same straight lines and forming the same visual cone described by Euclid. He conducted true demonstrations using lamps, tubes, and mirrors to show that both primary light and reflected light travel in straight lines. He placed the opaque cylinder over a lamp and made a small hole using Rania's long-lost pottery stylus to demonstrate the point-to-point propagation of light. He discussed the "small pain" in the eye caused by light, the after-image left on the retina, and how the optic nerve carried these signals to the brain. He briefly described how errors of vision and optical illusions occur in the brain, not in the eye, telling the story—which Sadeem had never heard—of how Mourad Al-Ghazi had used the sun's declining rays to fool a crowd of soldiers into thinking he had thrown a valuable dagger into the Nile. Alhasan pulled the jewel-encrusted dagger from his belt and held it up for all to see. The audience laughed and shouted its approval.

Alhasan discussed his discoveries and methods far into the evening. At a break for evening prayer, some philosophers and mathematicians went home, but most of those who studied the physical sciences remained.

"Isn't what you are describing just common sense?" asked one scholar. "Hasn't humankind advanced since time immemorial using trial and error? Isn't every bridge, building, fountain, and pool a 'true demonstration' of an architect's suppositions?"

"In a sense, yes, but not completely. For example, I was speaking with an apothecary the other night, my new friend Abdelilah—there he is. Abdelilah pointed out that if a medicine does not help a patient, and especially if it makes the patient worse, that medicine must be discarded. That is common sense. It does not matter who the authority is who recommends the medication nor how old and revered the treatise that describes it is: If the treatment fails, it is of no use. This is how progress is made in the medical arts.

"Similarly, astronomers have predicted the positions of the planets, conjunctions, eclipses, and so forth for centuries. Each time a celestial event is imminent, astronomers watch to see if the prediction is correct. If not, the tables and calculations must be revised. So, yes: Observation, trial, error, and revision are not new.

"But to my mind, it is one thing to observe nature and make predictions about it, but quite another to manipulate nature and force it to answer a single question. A true demonstration is designed to test a discrete hypothesis, and it is performed in such a way that anyone, anywhere, using the same apparatus in the same way will achieve the same result and arrive at the same answer. It is a new way to determine what is true."

Alhasan stayed until every question was answered. At the end of the discussion, a well-known medical scholar named Farzin Farzaneh stood.

"Abdelali," said Farzaneh, "I want to you thank you for arranging this remarkable presentation."

"It was my pleasure," said Abdelali.

"I have heard many lectures in my time," said Farzaneh, "but I believe this to be the most original and important one of all. As the senior member of the faculty of the House of Wisdom, I wish to make a recommendation."

"Of course," said Abdelali.

"I propose that the name Ibn Al-Haytham be inscribed on the pillar behind him, that we all might remember the day when he made this contribution to the furtherance of knowledge."

"Yes, yes," shouted members of the audience.

Abdelali bowed in the direction of the scholar. "I will ask Vizier Ali Farooqi for Caliph Al-Qadir's blessing on the matter, stating that you proposed it and this distinguished assembly supported it."

Farzin Farzaneh looked at Alhasan. "Young man," he said, "long after I and my colleagues are forgotten, and all of us gathered here are nothing but dust, your name will live on, not only in the House of Wisdom, but wherever men pursue the truth about nature."

Chapter Thirty-eight

Alhasan and Sadeem walked with Abdelali, Halima, and Essam toward Abdelali's house.

"Alhasan," said Abdelali, "I hope you will leave your *Book of Optics* with me so we can begin to make copies of it at the House of Wisdom."

"Well, I...." said Alhasan uncertainly.

"What is it, my boy?"

"What the grandson of The Lion is trying to say is that this is his only copy, and I promised to make another when we get to Basra," said Sadeem.

"I see," said Abdelali.

"Yes," said Alhasan. "I will be happy to send you the copy as soon as it is complete."

"Very well," said Abdelali.

"Besides," said Alhasan, "I would like to review the book and perhaps make some additions to it."

"What will you do once you return to Basra?" asked Abdelali. "I have not forgotten that I once promised to see if I could obtain a position for you at the House of Wisdom. After tonight's lecture, I am sure that proposal would meet with instant acceptance."

"Abdelali, that is a very generous offer," said Alhasan, "but I am afraid I prefer to work alone."

"So back to copying, is that it? Well, we gladly will pay your non-negotiable price for a copy of your *Book of Optics*."

"Alhasan will devote himself to further study," said Sadeem.

"And you will be the copyist?" asked Halima.

"I will make a copy of *The Book of Optics* for Abdelali, but that will not be our means of support."

"What will you do for income, if Alhasan devotes his time to study?" asked Abdelali.

"My father arranged for a stipend from the Fatimid Caliphate so that Alhasan can continue his research."

"He did?" asked Alhasan and Abdelali together.

"Yes, he did," said Sadeem. "It was in that letter he wrote in the desert. It appears that Sitt Al-Mulk decided to compensate you for your ten years of confinement."

"This is wonderful news," said Abdelali. "What will you work on next?"

"I'm not sure," said Alhasan, still stunned by the news. "I mean, I have always wanted to write a treatise analyzing the astronomical works of Ptolemy."

"Excellent," said Abdelali. "We will look forward to that."

Alone in the bedroom of Abdelali's house, Alhasan asked Sadeem about the arrangement her father had made on their behalf. "I take it his letter asks for the remittance for my return to be paid to us."

"Correct."

"That sly old soldier. Your father was determined to get those five thousand dinars for his family. But what makes you think Caliph Al-Qadir will go along with it? Surely he will want documentation of some kind. Perhaps an official visit. Proof."

"Surely he will," said Sadeem, lifting the top of a small wooden chest in the corner of the room, "and surely he did."

Even in the darkened room, the silver coins shone.

The next morning, Essam went to the central marketplace to find out if there were any caravans headed to Basra.

"One is leaving in three days," Essam reported. "I spoke with the guide. They want seven silver dinars for each of you."

"The price is high," said Sadeem.

"God willing, we will not have to do this again for a long time," said Alhasan. "We should join them."

For the next two days Alhasan and Sadeem visited the marketplace to purchase items available only in the capital—or at least that is what Alhasan remembered. Things might be different in Basra now; he had no way of knowing for sure. With their newfound funds, the newlyweds purchased carpets, fabric, cookware, spices, and toiletries. At the end of the second day, they bought a small cart to carry their goods and to bear the weight of their money chest.

The following day, Alhasan and Sadeem said goodbye to Abdelali, Halima, and Essam and met up with the caravan at the marketplace.

The trip to Basra took seventeen days. Along the way, Alhasan pointed out historic sites and told Sadeem stories about traveling the road with her father—how Al-Ghazi had taught him horsemanship, swordsmanship, and hand-to-hand combat. "His lessons saved my life," said Alhasan, remembering the time he lay in the death grip of a bandit.

"You saved his life, too," said Sadeem. "Father told us. I have always been grateful to you for that."

Basra had changed, but not as much as Baghdad had. Alhasan found his way through the city with ease.

"We should not impose on Nada and her family," said Sadeem. "We can afford an inn."

"I agree, but I would like to stop by an old friend's first," said Alhasan. "Unless he remarried, he has no wife or children. I am sure he would enjoy having visitors."

From the end of his old block, Alhasan saw the olive tree in the garden of his former home. As he and Sadeem passed the end of the street, he looked toward his former residence. Nothing, it seemed, had changed.

Alhasan pointed out the spot where he had bumped into Sadeem's father. Sadeem laughed as he told the story.

"I can see how out of place his clothing must have seemed," said Sadeem.

They crossed four more streets and then turned left. Halfway down the block, they stopped in front of the ornately carved door of Rashid Al-Bariqi, dismounted, and knocked.

The door opened silently on well-oiled hinges. "Peace be upon you," said a young man in his twenties.

"And upon you be peace. Khalid, is your master home?" asked Alhasan.

Al-Bariqi's servant smiled. "Ibn Al-Haytham? Is it you? Please come in."

Sadeem looked toward the cart and then toward Alhasan.

"It will be fine," said Alhasan. "We will only be here a moment. I just want to see the look on my friend's face before he hears that I have returned."

Alhasan and Sadeem removed their sandals and entered the home.

"This way," said Khalid, motioning toward the library. "I will get some water."

"Can you bring that hot beverage you make?" asked Alhasan.

Alhasan stood in the middle of the library, admiring the leather-bound manuscripts that filled shelf after shelf. "Wait," he said, spotting a book. He stepped to the shelf and took it down. "Yes, this is one of the copies I made. Look, Euclid's *Elements*." He held out the book to Sadeem.

"My favorite," said Sadeem, opening the book. She thumbed through the pages. "This is beautiful work, Madman."

"And here is Ptolemy's *Almagest*, Theodosius's *Spherics*—everything I copied, except for Autolycus's *Rising and Setting of Fixed Stars*."

"Is this it?" asked Sadeem, thumbing through a book that lay open on a table by the wall. She turned to the title page. "Yes, Alhasan, this is it."

Alhasan went over and took a look. "He must be reading it now. That's exciting."

Khalid entered with a tall porcelain pot in his left hand and two small cups in his right. "Please be seated," he said. As Alhasan and Sadeem sat on cushions near the wall, Khalid poured a small amount of the steaming, yellowish beverage into each cup.

"Taste it and tell me what is in it," said Alhasan.

"I haven't seen you this excited since, well, since I brought you *The Book of Optics* outside Cairo," said Sadeem.

"Taste it. It's delightful," said Alhasan.

Sadeem sniffed the beverage and took a sip. "Smooth, slightly bitter, with a hint of cardamom."

"Yes," said Alhasan. "You have an excellent palate."

"What is it?"

"What do you call it, Khalid?"

"*Khawa*, Sir."

"It's made from a bean that grows in al-Kabasha; is that correct?" asked Alhasan.

"Yes, Sir," said Khalid. "Every time a ship comes from al-Kabasha, I make sure I get some beans from the crew."

Khalid poured another small amount into each of their cups. Alhasan drank his and asked, "Where is Rashid Al-Bariqi?"

Khalid placed the pot on the carpet and sat on a cushion opposite the guests. "I am afraid I have bad news, Ibn Al-Haytham: Rashid Al-Bariqi died six summers ago."

Shocked, Alhasan said nothing. He bowed his head and stared at his lap.

"May God have mercy on his soul," said Sadeem.

"Yes," said Alhasan. "May he rest in peace until the day of judgment."

"We are extremely sorry for your loss," Sadeem said to Khalid.

"Thank you. He was very good to me," said Khalid. "He gave me a large sum of money and asked me to stay here and keep up the house."

"How generous, but how strange," said Sadeem.

"It is not that strange," said Khalid. "I need to tell you a story, and then you will understand."

Alhasan swirled the dregs at the bottom of the porcelain cup around and around.

"My master read your copy of the *Rising and Setting of Fixed Stars* every day, and he enjoyed it so much that he had a small observatory built on the roof. Every night he went up to his observatory and studied the stars and planets. One night, he came down with a strange look on his face. 'Ibn Al-Haytham is alive,' he said. We had heard rumors that you were dead, but that night he came down from the observatory and, standing right here in the library, he said, 'He is alive, Khalid. I was looking at the stars, and I felt it. I felt he was somewhere looking at the same stars.'"

"I know this night," said Alhasan, looking up from his cup.

Sadeem looked at her husband, searching his face for a clue as to what he meant.

"He was good man, Sadeem. He was like a father me."

"That night," Khalid continued, "my master told me that if anything were to happen to him, that I was to stay in this house and await your return."

"His return? For what?" asked Sadeem.

"I imagine he wanted me to have his library," said Alhasan, looking at the books and smiling at the generosity of his old friend.

"That is correct, Ibn Al-Haytham. He wanted you to have his entire library. He said it would be of more value to you than any person alive. But that is not all. He asked me to not look for employment if he died, because he wanted me to work for you. That is, if you need a manservant and would accept me."

"We do need one," said Sadeem, "and we would be happy to have you join us."

"Thank you," said Khalid. "I am most grateful to you."

"You can make *khawa* for us every afternoon," said Alhasan.

"It would be an honor, Sir."

"We will return tomorrow," said Sadeem, handing her cup to Khalid, "but we have to find an inn for the night."

"Yes," said Alhasan, handing his cup to Khalid. "We must go."

"Go?" said Khalid. "You must not go. You must stay in the master's bedroom. It is ready for you."

"Ready?" asked Alhasan.

"Yes. I have kept it ready for your return for six years."

"I don't understand," said Alhasan.

"Master Al-Bariqi wanted you to have it—the library, the observatory, the bedroom, the entire house. It is yours, Master. Welcome home."

That evening, still astonished by Rashid Al-Bariqi's generosity, Alhasan and Sadeem dined in their new home and prayed at the mosque, giving thanks for all they had received. Before they went to bed, Alhasan took Sadeem by the hand and led her up the stairs to the observatory. In the northeast, Auriga continued on his endless journey. High overhead, a faint band of light stretched cross the heavens.

"See that pale light?" asked Alhasan, pointing at the sky. "It looks like the vapor that that lies close to the ground in the morning."

"The Sadeem. I like that," said his wife. "You must call it that in your treatise on astronomy."

Alhasan put his arm around Sadeem's shoulders.

"I am so blessed," he said, hugging his wife to his side. He looked around at the heavens. "I never expected any of this. There was a time when my only companions were the stars. I had nothing but my robe, my Qur'an, and my prayer rug. Now I have more than I ever imagined."

"Don't worry, Madman," said Sadeem. "You have earned it. You have given the world far more than it could ever give to you."

"That is not true," said Alhasan, turning toward his wife and putting his arms around her waist. Her dark eyes sparkled with the light of a million stars. "Because it already has given me you."

THE END

Acknowledgments

Telling the story of a genius who lived one thousand years ago in a culture very different from mine was fraught with challenges and potential missteps. Knowing this, I reached out to many people for assistance, and they responded. This book would not have been possible without their help. I would like to acknowledge some by name:

First, my wife, Eva Steffens, for her unwavering belief in me and this tale, and for her endless patience and support;

Ruth Marvin Webster, who, after interviewing me in 2007 about my biography of Ibn al-Haytham, said, "That is an amazing story; it would make a great historical novel;" without your suggestion, I would never have even thought of writing this book;

Sadeem Jawhar, my confidant, my consultant, and ultimately, my muse; your enthusiasm for the story and its characters shaped the book in countless ways;

Simon Ponsford, who aided me with plot suggestions that kept the story moving forward;

Hend Al Qassemi, who inspired me with her own tales of the Middle East and was always there to lift my spirits and keep me going;

Ertan Salik, who not only corrected several errors but also championed the story at just the right time, in just the right way, to just the right people;

Mandy Ison, Bruce Robinson, Julie Blanks, Farzin Farzaneh, Robin Wright Young, Nada Al-Sharif, Tom Fox, Kareem Darwish, Lisa Gould Richardson, Petya Kirova, Cherryl Madrelejo, Barbara Rector Russell, and Hala Saadani, my first readers, whose comments, corrections, and suggestions improved the book in ways large and small;

And, finally, my beloved son Zeke, who died during the period I was writing this novel, but who knew of it, encouraged me to complete it, and inspired me with his own writing; his love, good humor, and inspirational spirit were always with me.

Many thanks to all of you.